P9-DNP-303

ANCIENT, STRANGE, <small>AND</small> LOVELY

ALSO BY
SUSAN FLETCHER

THE DRAGON CHRONICLES:
Dragon's Milk
Flight of the Dragon Kyn
Sign of the Dove
Ancient, Strange, and Lovely

Alphabet of Dreams
Shadow Spinner
Walk Across the Sea

THE

DRAGON

C H R O N I C L E S

ANCIENT, STRANGE, AND LOVELY

SUSAN FLETCHER

ATHENEUM BOOKS FOR YOUNG READERS
NEW YORK . LONDON . TORONTO . SYDNEY

ATHENEUM BOOKS FOR YOUNG READERS
An imprint of Simon & Schuster Children's Publishing Division
1230 Avenue of the Americas, New York, New York 10020
This book is a work of fiction. Any references to historical events, real people, or real
locales are used fictitiously. Other names, characters, places, and incidents are products
of the author's imagination, and any resemblance to actual events or locales or persons,
living or dead, is entirely coincidental.
Copyright © 2010 by Susan Fletcher
All rights reserved, including the right of reproduction
in whole or in part in any form.
ATHENEUM BOOKS FOR YOUNG READERS
is a registered trademark of Simon & Schuster, Inc.
For information about special discounts for bulk purchases, please contact Simon &
Schuster Special Sales at 1-866-506-1949 or business@simonandschuster.com.
The Simon & Schuster Speakers Bureau can bring authors to your live event.
For more information or to book an event, contact the Simon & Schuster Speakers
Bureau at 1-866-248-3049 or visit our website at www.simonspeakers.com.
The text for this book is set in Garamond 3 LT.
Manufactured in the United States of America
0811 MTN
First Atheneum Books for Young Readers paperback edition September 2011
2 4 6 8 10 9 7 5 3 1
The Library of Congress has cataloged the hardcover edition as follows:
Fletcher, Susan, 1951–
Ancient, strange, and lovely / Susan Fletcher. — 1st ed.
p. cm. — [The dragon chronicles]
Summary: Fourteen-year-old Bryn must try to find a way to save a baby dragon from a
dangerous modern world that seems to have no place for something so ancient.
ISBN 978-1-4169-5786-7 [hardcover : alk. paper]
[1. Dragons—Fiction. 2. Poaching—Fiction. 3. Fantasy.] I. Title.
PZ7.F6356An 2010
[Fic]—dc22
2009053797
ISBN 978-1-4169-5787-4 [pbk]
ISBN 978-1-4424-2002-1 [eBook]

for Kelly

CONTENTS

PART III: JOURNEY

PART IV: DRAGON

EPILOGUE

ANCIENT,
STRANGE,
<u>AND</u> LOVELY

PROLOGUE

The language of birds is ancient, strange, and lovely,
bearing equal parts heartbreak and joy.

—from *Lost Secrets of the Animal World* by Mungo Jones

 BIRD DAY

One rainy day, I climb up to the attic, unlock the trunk, lift out the falling-apart boxes of family pictures, and hunt for the kids with the birds. I sit cross-legged in the puddle of light on the floor and riff through all those retro analog prints—the colored ones, the black-and-white ones with the crinkly edges, the paleo-old ones with the brownish tints. I pick through the weddings and the picnics and the graduations and the vacations until I have a pile of them—just those birthday portraits, just those five-year-old kids with their birds.

Bird day, we call it. In our family, kids get birds when they turn five. One bird per kid, that's the deal. Nobody knows when it started, but it was back there a ways. I know that now. It had to be way, way back.

These kids with the birds, they're not smiling. They all look, like, dead serious, which you might think would be funny, actually, considering they're tricked out in their Sunday best with all seismic random kinds of birds—one each—on a shoulder or a wrist or a finger or even pecking at an ear or a strand of hair.

These green-eyed five-year-old kids with their birds. There's this one girl with a screech owl perched on her little straw hat, glassy-eyed and staring, like it's taxidermy or something.

You'd think you'd want to laugh. But you don't.

Someday I'm going to scan them. I'll amp up the encryption so no one can get in. Maybe I'll even scrapbook, pretty it up. Put in little quotes and emoticons and stuff.

You've got to wonder why they kept doing it. Setting up their little kids with birds. Encouraging it. It had to be rough when people outside the family found out what was going on, which they sometimes did. Some of them suspected witchcraft, and once I heard Mom say they maybe even burned one or two of our guys, a long time ago, at the stake.

You wonder what they thought it was all for, this weird little thing we can do. (Some of us. Not all of us. But enough to keep it going.) It must have seemed pretty pointless until now. Like being able to wiggle your ears, or curl your tongue lengthwise, or dislocate your shoulder on purpose and put it back again. Yeah, it's actually better than that. It's like satisfying. I want to say the word "delight."

But how was it worth the risk? How was it worth all those generations of being different, being strange? How was it worth the loneliness?

How did they know it would be so important?

How did they phaging know?

PART I
EGG

Something old,
Something new,
Something broken,
Someone blue.

What was whole
Has come undone.
Something's broken,
Someone's blue.
    from "Broken & Blue," by White Raven

Mercury and PCBs,
Nitrogen dioxide,
Arsenic and desert dust
Blotting out the sun.

Breathe in.
Breathe it all in:
Now you and the celumbra are one.
—from "Sky Shadow," by Mutant Tide

THINGS THAT GO THUMP

I woke in the middle of the night, came straight up out of sleep. Then sat there, heart pounding, in that numb, blind space where you can't quite kludge together exactly what's just happened or where or when you are.

It was that dream again. That dream of running, searching. Of stepping off the edge of something, of falling. The sickening lurch in the gut. The dropping down and down through black nothing and not quite landing. The full-body spasm when I *would* have landed, jolting me out of it, out of the dream, out of sleep.

From a dim corner, Stella stirred: a floofing of feathers, a dry *click, click* of talons across the perch. I kenned her, felt her in my head: edgy now, but not alarmed. Nearby, on the shelves, I could make out the shadowy outlines of other birds—ceramic and glass and stone.

Safe in bed, in Aunt Pen's guest room. No one searching. No one falling.

A wind gust shook the house. Against the far wall, the shadows of rhododendrons waved in the streetlight glow. They looked huge, out-of-scale, like from a monster vid: Jurassic rhododendron. Something thumped down there—a stray cat, maybe, or an unlatched gate, or somebody's tipped-over plastic trash can. Some ordinary, safe thing, probably jolted by the wind.

A chill shuddered at the edges of the air, seeped through my PJs, raised gooseflesh on my back. I slid down in bed and cocooned myself in blankets as the other nightmare came to squat in the heartspace of my chest. The nightmare that lived with me now, a Fender bass static hum that never went away, not even when I woke.

Mom.

Thump. Thump-thump.

I sat up. That sound again.

When I was little, I was one of those scaredy-cat kids; I heard weird noises all the time. In the closet. Under the bed. Down the hall. When I got panicky, Mom would tell me, "It's an adventure, Bryn. Just breathe." Dad would wrap my little-kid hand in his massive one. He'd talk me out of bed, take me on a tour. Night patrol, he called it. "Think it through, Bryn," he'd say. "Where's it coming from? What does it sound like? What do you see?"

Usually, the sounds hadn't come from where I'd thought. Nothing under the bed—not even once. Mostly, they were outside. Ordinary things, in the days before the swarms. A tree bough scritching against the house. Wind knocking a gate against a jamb. Later, it was the swarms. Voles or mice. Possums bumping around in the recycling bin. They would stare at us, mirror-eyed in the flashlight beam, then scuttle off into the night.

On night patrol, even though I could still feel my heart thumping in my throat, I could also feel this other thing happening—a leaning away from fear toward a puzzle to solve, a mystery to unspool. I would strain all of my senses against the night, hoping *I* would find the answer.

Thump-thump.

I felt that scaredy-cat kid inside me now, whining like she always used to: *I don't wanna.* You'd think, by the time you got to be fourteen, that kid would have disappeared with all the other ghosts of childhood past: the thumb sucker, the training-pants wetter, the sippy-cup drooler.

But, no. And I still couldn't sleep unless I *knew*.

I sighed. Kicked off my blankets. Pulled on my fleece. Opened Stella's cage and kenned her to my shoulder.

She sidestepped nearer, ducked under a clump of my hair. I stroked the soft feathers on her belly. She stretched up, softly nibbled at my ear.

I padded through the dark cave of the hall, past Aunt Pen's room. She would be mortified to know she snored. Snorted, actually. *So* uncouth. Outside the den, I hesitated. I cracked open the door, peered inside, found Piper's skinny little curled-up shape in the tangle of blankets on the air bed.

Softly, I shut the door. I crept downstairs into the dim moonlit glow of the kitchen and kenned Stella to the top of the cabinets. She pushed off my shoulder and lit there, rocking forward, her topknot flat against her head. I could sense her puzzlement, her unease. I synched with her a moment, tweaked her some comfort vibes. She settled down, fluffed her feathers, flicked her topknot back up to the "systems normal" position.

I opened the hall closet, slipped into my coat and boots, took Aunt Pen's flashlight from the shelf.

Don't wanna.

Too bad.

Outside, I breathed in the faint, burnt-rotten smell of the celumbra, the cloud of dust and crud that regularly blew across the planet from places where the droughts were bad. Wind churned high up in the branches of the fir trees and stirred in the rhododendrons as I scanned Aunt Pen's small front yard with the flashlight.

Nothing swarming, that I could see.

I moved along the side of the house and tugged at the wooden gate.

Latched.

It could be the other gate that had thumped—the one closer to where I'd been sleeping. Or maybe the wind had knocked over one of the empty plastic planters back there. Maybe smacked it against the fence.

I reached over the gate to unlatch it, groping with my fingers along the splintery wood. Then I set out along the stone path through the garden, where long, twitchy shadows shivered across the face of the moon. Bright copper tonight—seismic stunning in the haze of the celumbra.

Piper would need her inhaler tomorrow.

I moved past the back door to the garage—closed—past the

plaster statues of cranes and sparrows, past the little pond, across the deck. The wind picked up, lifted bits of old leaves and dirt and flung them in my face. Rounding the far corner of the house, I swept the light across the row of empty pots and planters. I could still hear the wind, but I didn't feel it now, sheltered in the narrow space between the fence and the house.

Nothing moved. Not in the planters. Not by the gate.

I stood, waited, strained my ears to hear.

Nothing. Only the *whoosh* of wind.

It could have been anything. Some squirrels on the fence. A raccoon out hunting. A cat on its nightly prowl.

I shone the light up into the high, dark branches of the fir trees, first the ones that loomed above me now, and then the ones in my own backyard, directly behind Aunt Pen's. The trees seemed alive—restless and sad. My hand moved, all on its own, to train the flashlight on Mom and Dad's bedroom window.

Empty.

Dark.

I stood staring at it, breathing in the smell of distant deserts, trying to hold it all together.

Sometimes you never do find out what's happened.

Sometimes, you just never know.

2  PLEATHER

EUGENE, OREGON

Back in the house, I put everything away—coat, boots, flashlight. I kenned Stella down to my shoulder and was heading upstairs when I jerked to a stop. Stella lurched forward on my shoulder, flapped her wings for balance, and about poked out my eye with a feather.

There was Piper on the landing—rumpled nightie, ducky slippers, round glasses too big for her five-year-old face. Sitting there. Watching.

"What are you doing up?" I kept my voice quiet. Aunt Pen was a sound sleeper. Once the hearing aid came out, she was gone; out for the night. Still, better not push it. Aunt Pen would seriously rupture if she saw Stella uncaged.

"Looking for you," Piper said.

"Well, I'm here now. Get back to bed. We'll both go back to bed."

"Will you catch Luna?"

"Luna! Did you let her out?"

Piper shrugged.

I groaned. Inside, though—not out loud. I'd look pretty dim getting on her about Luna, with Stella sitting right there on my shoulder.

"Where is she?" I asked.

"In the basement."

"The basement!" I remembered Aunt Pen and took it down a notch. "How did that happen?"

"I was looking for you. And I opened the basement door and she flew down."

"Did you try to ken her back?"

"She wouldn't come!"

"Shh!" I put my arm around her. She leaned against me, buried her face in my shirt. "Hey. It's okay." It actually takes years to get kenning worked out with your bird—no matter how talented you are. It's more complicated than you might think, and Piper'd had Luna for less than a year. Luna: as in *Stellaluna*, our favorite picture-book bat.

I might have been able to summon Luna myself, but it's not the thing to ken another person's bird. It's just not polite.

A thought struck me. The basement.

I held Piper's shoulders and pushed her away so I could see her face. "Why did you open the basement door? Did you hear something down there?"

"No."

"Sort of a thumping sound?"

"No! I was just looking."

Okay. I breathed. Okay. "Did you see where she went?"

"It was dark. And I couldn't reach the switch."

Don't wanna.

I *so* wished I could leave this till morning. But no way would Piper go to sleep without Luna.

"You wait here," I said.

I fumbled for the light switch just inside the basement door. Way down below, the ancient fixture clicked on—buzzing, flickery, and dim. I peered into the shadows. No sign of Luna. Ditzy bird. I started down the steps, breathing in eau de basement—metallic-smelling, sort of, mixed with chemicals and dust. Halfway to the bottom, Stella pushed off my shoulder and glided past the sputtery light, into the shadows.

"Hey," I said.

I tried summoning her, but she slipped away. I could feel her, faintly, farther back, but she was dissing me.

Bad bird. Bad, bad bird.

I heard a scratching sound as Stella lit down someplace I couldn't see, then a little greeting *peep* from Luna.

I hesitated on the bottom step and scanned the room. Hadn't been down here in years. There was the furnace. The lawn furniture, stacked and covered, waiting for spring. The banks of floor-to-ceiling shelves with their plastic bins, all neatly labeled and color-coded, Aunt Pen–style. HOLIDAY DECORATIONS. PAPER PRODUCTS. CLEANING SUPPLIES. LIGHTBULBS. STYROFOAM PACKING PEANUTS.

No Stella. No Luna. At least, not that I could see.

I moved past the first bank of shelves, then deeper back, past the next. PAINT. CARPET REMNANTS. EBAY. GOODWILL. There were a couple of plastic bins labeled DAMAGED FIGURINES—

a tidy little graveyard for those bloodless birds of hers. Birds that didn't shed feathers or strew seeds. Birds that didn't poop.

The furnace snicked on, grumbled to life. A draft stirred the cobwebs at the tops of the shelves. I wished I'd put on my flip-flops. The concrete was seismic frigid, and bits of grit clung to the bottoms of my feet.

Ahead, at the far, dim end of the room, six or seven beat-up cardboard boxes sat in a heap on the floor. They looked so different from Aunt Pen's pristine plastic bins, I knew what they must be.

The ones Dad had sent last week. The ones he'd found in that storage locker in Alaska. Full of Mom's research stuff, he said.

We'd never even known about the locker until the overdue notice came. They were going to "dispose of the contents" unless someone paid like pronto. So Dad went right back up to Anchorage, hoping to find some clues, and left Piper and me to stay with Aunt Pen.

There, at the top of the pile of boxes, were Stella and Luna. One each: cockatiel and canary. They seemed to be staring down into the narrow space between the boxes and the shelves. Ignoring me completely.

Could they smell Mom, maybe? Was that why they'd come down here?

I crept up behind Luna, pressed a finger against the backs of her twiggy legs. She lifted one foot and seemed about to fall for it—to step back onto my finger—but at the last second she tumbled to my nefarious plan and fluttered up to the top of the shelves.

"Twit," I muttered.

The box, I saw, was marked up and tattered, having spent its previous life shipping ink cartridges from Taiwan. I strained to decipher the tiny postmark in the stuttering light. *Anchorage, AK.*

I ran my fingers across Dad's handwriting—the careful, rounded letters, the hopeful upward dips at the ends of words. *Soon,* he'd said when he'd called earlier this evening. He would come home soon.

When is soon? I'd asked. It was nearly two weeks already. But he couldn't answer that. Had he found anything, any clues? *Too soon to tell,* he'd said.

I sighed, feeling the familiar ache hollowing out my insides.

"Bryn?"

I turned around. Piper was leaning into the doorway at the top of the stairs.

"Bryn, did you find her?" She sounded a little wheezy.

"Yes. I'll be there soon." I heard the echo: *Soon.*

"With Luna?"

"Yes. In a minute. Go get your inhaler, would you?"

I looked to where the birds were staring and saw that one of the boxes seemed to have tipped off the stack and landed on the floor on its side. The flaps had popped open; little clumps of wadded paper spilled out across the concrete, behind the other stacked boxes, beneath the lowest shelf.

A shiver brushed the back of my neck. Something had happened here. But what?

I synched with Stella and felt a weird, restless energy. Curiosity—on steroids. Something drawing her in.

18

I squatted beside the tipped box. It had been closed up with that brown paper sealing tape—not the stronger, plastic stuff you're supposed to use for mailing. It looked as if the glue had come ungummed, and then the tape had torn.

It was mostly dirt samples in the boxes, Dad had said. Dirt with microbes in it. Bugs, Mom called them. She was always looking for promising new bugs. Bugs that would eat toxic waste. Dad had sent half the samples to Taj at the lab and half here, just to be safe.

I righted the box, set it on the floor beside the other ones. I raked through the crumpled paper inside. Nothing. I peered beneath the shelf, following the trail of newsprint.

Something there. Roundish. Hard to see way back in the shadows.

A soccer ball? A volleyball?

From here, it looked kind of like leather, but it wouldn't have to be. It could be that plastic synth leather. Pleather. It seemed to have sections, sort of, like crocodile skin or tortoiseshell. And it wasn't quite round. More ovalish.

An egg? Some kind of megahuge egg?

Ostrich?

Emu?

Whatever it was, it definitely wasn't dirt.

"What are you into, Mom?" I murmured.

Luna fluttered down again, beside Stella. Both of them still fixated on that egg. "I hate to break it to you, ladies," I said, "but this is way out of your league."

Maybe, when the egg had rolled out of the box, it had bumped the wooden post that held up the shelves. Ergo, the mysterious thumps.

Maybe. But wouldn't that happen just once?

"Bryn?" Piper again. "Are you coming?"

"Soon! Wait there."

I got down on my hands and knees, reached way back beneath the shelf. I touched the egg. It gave a little, like a rubber ball. I scootched forward, stretched full-out on the floor, gently cupped my whole hand over it.

Weird. It felt maybe a teensy bit warmer against my palm than it should have. Not very warm, but it was chilly down here. You'd think the egg would be too.

And something else. It had a funny kind of vibe to it. So faint, I almost couldn't tell if I was imagining it. But I didn't think I was.

All at once, sprawled out there in the dark, with so many mysteries bumping around in my head . . . all at once, I knew one small thing for absolute certain.

Whatever was inside this egg . . . it was alive.

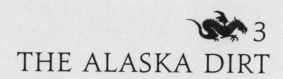

3

THE ALASKA DIRT

EUGENE, OREGON

When Taj rounded the corner, he saw with relief that the small scrap of graph paper was still wedged between the door and the jamb.

He had to laugh at himself, though. How many bad spy vids had he seen with that old cliché—the telltale scrap of paper to test whether the door had been opened while he was gone? Probably nobody really did the paper thing, even spies. Except for movie actors, Taj thought. And me. I'm paranoid, for sure.

He swiped his card in the keypad and opened the door, retrieving the paper scrap from the corridor floor. Inside, the lab was dim, but Taj knew it so well he hardly needed light at all to find his way to his bench. He drained the last of his Coke, tossed the can into the trash, then shrugged into his lab coat and clicked on the little gooseneck lamp. He pulled on a pair of latex gloves, perched on his stool, and wiped down his benchtop with ethanol. From the drawer, he pulled out four little stoppered glass bottles, each containing a slurry of media and dirt with broken shells. Alaskan dirt and shells, presumably. The last samples Robin had collected.

Taj had put other stuff in the bottles, too, just fifteen minutes ago, before he'd stepped out for the Coke. A suite of toxic compounds: endocrine disruptors. He'd soon find out what was left of them.

He lined up the bottles on the dark Formica countertop. He got out the syringes, the needles, the filters, the solvents, the pipettes and disposable pipette tips, the glass extraction and sample vials. He knew he had to hurry—it would be dawn in a couple of hours, and some of the other grad students came into the lab insanely early. Even Dr. Reynolds sometimes showed up at random times. And it wouldn't do for Reynolds to find out what Taj was up to. Not at all.

Still, Taj needed to sit there a moment. He needed to look at those bottles. He needed to breathe.

What if this was for real? What would he do? Who could he tell?

They looked so ordinary, the bottles did. Like a thousand other bottles in the lab.

And probably they were ordinary. Probably he'd made a mistake. The first time he'd tested the Alaska dirt, he'd been certain he'd messed up some way. Well, virtually certain. Ninety-nine point ninety-nine percent. The second time, he'd probably done something wrong again. Ninety-eight percent sure of that. He *had* to have screwed up. The microbes in the dirt—they couldn't have eaten the entire suite of nasty compounds. And they certainly couldn't have eaten them so fast. The endocrine disruptors

weren't gone in days or weeks or months, but at time zero—
fifteen minutes after he'd introduced them.

Which never happened.

Which never, ever happened.

So, if he hadn't messed up . . .

Those little bottles, lined up there on the bench? They weren't
even close to ordinary. This could be huge.

But with Robin gone and Jasmine pregnant, the timing
couldn't be worse.

A wind gust rattled at the windowpanes. Taj turned to look.
The orange, celumbral moon peered in at him, seemingly from
just across the quad.

Get it together, Taj told himself. Focus. He shook his head,
trying to clear out the muzziness. If he was going to solve this
puzzle, he'd better get moving right now.

He turned on the Bunsen burner, adjusted it, picked up the
needle and the syringe. Third try, with the Alaska dirt. He'd
been extra, extra careful setting up the experiment this time.
There was a control for everything. Most of them in triplicate.

Time zero, now. Let's go.

Half an hour later, he had collected, extracted, and filtered his
samples, then transferred them into four small sample vials.
He'd tested the control in the GC-MS, and it had come out
fine—just as he'd expected.

Now for the moment of truth.

He removed a drop of liquid from one of the sample vials.
Injected it into the GC-MS.

Pressed GO.

The GC-MS cycled through its familiar ditty of clicks and beeps. Taj watched the screen, waiting for the graph line to form. "Tell me what we've got," he murmured to the machine. Though he wasn't 100 percent sure he really wanted to know.

4
DROPPED OFF THE FACE
OF THE PLANET

EUGENE, OREGON

Somehow, I survived my morning classes the next day. I had an annoying, sleep-dep headache, and everything was processing slow. I'd texted Dad on the way to school, but he didn't get back.

Now I slogged through the lunch line. Nothing looked good. I settled for a bean burrito and a bottle of detox water. I would have killed for coffee, but they don't let us have caffeine at school.

It had been a monster long night. I'd put the egg back in its box and set it on the floor—no more falling off the stack for *you*. Then I'd had to snag Luna, who was totally ditzy and uncooperative. Piper came down to help with Luna and saw the egg; I made her promise not to touch it, and especially not to tell Aunt Pen. After that, Stella refused to be kenned. Flat-out dissed me. I settled Piper into bed, and then I couldn't sleep. Instead, I lay awake and worried. As in: What was I supposed to do with the egg? What if it hatched? Aunt Pen would go nova. She'd call the Authorities, go on the news, turn it all into a huge production, the Aunt Pen Show, just like last fall, when Mom . . .

Stop it, I'd told myself. Don't go there. Sleep.

But of course I did go there. I couldn't push it away. It all came crashing in again and I had to ride it out, keep my head above water, try not to drown.

Now I took my tray and scoped out the quad—kids on couches, on benches, on tables, on the floor. Last year's junior high crowds had broken up and reformed into new ones. The Goths and 'tants were easy to spot, but the rest all blurred together.

I didn't really have a crowd, myself.

Across the quad I spotted Lucy with her friends, the drama kids. Sometimes I ate with her. But they were into something now. Rehearsing, maybe.

I wavered, feeling seriously off, kind of brittle and teetery. The old loneliness leaked out of its cave and into my chest—the loneliness that came from being different, from being *outside*. From the secret part of me my school friends weren't allowed to know.

I watched Lucy a moment. She was laughing. Talking with her hands, the way she does. How would it feel to be like that? Like you could be totally yourself, yet still slip into a group and belong?

I took a couple of steps toward her, then stopped, uncertain. Someone plowed into me from behind, ramming a tray into my back. I heard her curse me out before I saw her—one of the varsity basketball players. A bright grape juice stain Rorschached her white sweater. Her sandwich sat in a purple puddle; juice dripped from her tray to the floor.

"Would you move!" she said. "Don't just stand there blocking traffic!"

"Sorry," I said.

"You are majorly in the way. Oh. My. God. Look at this! My brand-new cashmere!"

"I'm sorry."

"And what am I supposed to eat?" She pointed at her soggy sandwich.

Did she expect an answer? I couldn't give her one. Serious brain-freeze happening.

"Let's just go," one of her friends said. "We'll clean that up, and you can have half of my sandwich. C'mon."

Basketball girl made an exasperated sound, rolled her eyes, and left.

My back hurt from where the tray had jammed into it. The sleep-dep headache had morphed into a multitentacled creature of pain, leaning its weight against the back of my left eye. I peered into the quad, packed solid with kids, with no place for me to *be*.

I fought off that feeling, the one you sometimes see in the eyes of the slow-to-catch-on kids and the supertall ones, the kids who stutter and the ones who look way young for their age. Not just loneliness, but worse. Where you start to wonder if there's something deeply wrong with you; if you might be, like, defective.

I knew I should move, move right away, the sooner the better.

Blocking traffic.

Majorly in the way.

I'd been an outsider all my life; I could deal. But my defenses were low now; I somehow couldn't move my feet.

"Have some dignity!"

It was just above a whisper, right behind me. I whirled around to see a girl, one of the 'tants, passing by. Her name popped into my brain. Sasha. She jerked her head, signaling me to follow. I gaped at her.

"Oh, for godsake," she hissed. She shifted her lunch tray to one hand, gripped my elbow, and towed me to a bench on the far side of the quad.

"Sit," she said in a regular voice. "Eat." She plopped onto the bench, yanked me to sit beside her, and began to wolf down a huge chili dog.

I felt naked, as if I had no skin, as if all of my shameful rawness was exposed for everyone to see. I clamped my lips together, pressed hard against the trembling.

"Here," Sasha said, seeming annoyed. She thrust a wad of napkins at me. I swiped at my eyes, groping through my memory for everything I knew about her. She was a junior, maybe. In my pre-calc class. There were a bunch of 'tants at school, but not so many in accelerated math. And something else . . . The school newspaper? Yes, that was it. A picture blinked into my mind: the National Merit Semifinalists. All these Ivy-looking kids, and then Sasha. Smirking, as if the whole thing were a huge joke.

"You can't do that," she said now, between bites of chili dog. "You dropped your shell."

I blew my nose. "What?" I said. Shell? What was she talking about? What shell?

"Shell! You dropped your shell! You were completely out there, all like pasty-soft. Like a shucked oyster, or a slug. You—"

I got up to leave.

"No, wait," the girl said. "I don't mean that in a bad way. Sit down, would you? Sit!"

"You mean it in a good way?" I demanded. "That I'm a slug?"

"Hey, there you go," she said. "That's better. Anger looks good on you. No, seriously. That's what I'm talking about. Anger can be an excellent shell, when your usual one starts to slip. Now, c'mon, sit down. There's ten more minutes of lunch, so what are you going to do? Hide out in a bathroom stall? Pretend you're texting all your bazillions of friends?"

I had friends. I did. Nobody all that close, but . . . I talked to people. I ate with people. But I couldn't go hunting for them now, all raw and . . . shell-less.

I sat. I took a bite of burrito, glancing sideways at Sasha. *She* had quite the shell. Her hair, gelled stiff, sort of hovered around her face. She'd bleached it bone-white, except for a livid patch of purplish blue that resembled a giant bruise. She'd had herself skwebbed: a webbed flap of synth skin fanned out from one ear to her neck, and another flap of skwebbing stretched between the middle and ring fingers of one hand. Her arms had that patchy, acid-burn look the 'tants went for, which they achieved, I'd heard, with a combination of tanning gel and loofahs. There was a really big, uneven mole either painted or tattooed on one side of her neck. Melanoma chic.

"Thing is . . ." Sasha sucked up a strawful of Antiox Splash. "People who drop their shells, they scare the living crap out of other people. 'Cause everybody's like that inside—all pasty-soft and vulnerable—but nobody wants to be reminded of it."

I looked at her. Was she saying that *she* was soft like that inside? Hard to imagine.

"In a way, it's actually rude to go around without a shell," she went on. "'Cause it puts it right out there in everybody's face. That they're all so . . . squishable, really. Don't you think? That's why some kids, they see someone without a shell, they just have to go and stomp 'em."

Sasha shrugged and smiled at me. It was surprisingly sweet, that smile.

I took another bite. The burrito was going down okay. I blew my nose again. We sat there and chewed for a while. The headache had notched down a little.

And it was true, what she'd said about the shell. If you let it slip, people treated you different. Not out-and-out mean, necessarily, but it was the dignity thing. You lost standing, sort of. Like you suddenly got younger. I'd found out about that last fall.

"I get what you're saying," I said. "About shells. I've been through some stuff lately, though. My . . ." I didn't know if I could say it. "My mom . . ." I stopped, pinched my lips together against a new surge of trembling.

"Disappeared," Sasha said. "Dropped off the face of the planet. That would frag anybody's drive."

"You know about that?"

Sasha swiped at her face with a napkin, crumpled it up, tossed it into the wreckage of the chili dog. "It's not so usual, having your mom disappear like that. I mean, a divorce, who'd even notice? And cancer . . . one in four, baby. Happens all the time. But flat-out disappearing. That's the kind of thing . . ." She shrugged. "Well, people hear about it. People talk. It's not like they're evil or anything. It's just how they are."

The lunch bell rang. Sasha stood up. "It's brutal out there. 'Specially for kids like us. Not so much the joiner material, you and me, huh?"

She smiled that sweet smile again, brushed a hand across my shoulder, picked up her tray.

"Do yourself a favor, kid," she said. "Hang on to that shell."

5 TRIPLE SHOT

EUGENE, OREGON

My phone rang when I was halfway home from school. Dad, maybe? I stopped, turned my back into the sideways rain, and checked caller ID.

Taj. From Mom's lab.

Dad, Taj, and I had exchanged numbers after Mom disappeared. But he'd never called me before.

I picked up. "Taj?"

"Hey, Bryn. How're you doing?"

"Uh, okay," I said. Feeling suddenly awk. Not only because both of us knew I wasn't really okay—couldn't possibly be okay. But also—and this was dumb, I know—because Taj was kind of cute. Too-old-for-me cute. Married cute. But still. Sometimes the cute ones were harder to talk to than the not-cute ones. Proof of the randomness of the universe.

"Listen, I've been trying to reach your dad. He's still in Alaska, right?"

"Uh, yeah." All at once, I had this like massive urge to spill to Taj about the egg. Make it his problem, not mine. But no, better nor. There were so many secrets in our family. Mostly connected to kenning, but they seeped into other places. I'd better wait and check with Dad tonight.

"I thought I had his number, but I can't get through."

"Dad can be hard to get hold of. Mom . . ." I heard myself say it. Hardly hesitating at all. "Mom had the sat phone, so all he's got is a cell, and there are huge coverage gaps up there."

"Oh, jeez, Bryn." Silence on the line. A car swished by, splashing water on my shoes. I moved toward a bookstore window. Took cover under the awning. Pushed my hood off my head. "I forgot about the sat phone," Taj said. "God, I'm sorry."

"I know you are," I said. "I know you miss her too."

"Yeah, well." Rain thumped down on the awning. Breathe, I told myself. Just breathe.

"But he's in touch, then," Taj said. "Your dad." It was a question.

"Yeah, I talk to him every night."

"You know he sent me some samples at the lab."

"He told me about that."

"Do you know if there's any more? Of those dirt samples he sent? Or any notes or anything? About exactly where Robin got them?"

Something funny in Taj's voice. "He sent some boxes," I said. "Aunt Pen put them in her basement. Dad said it's mostly dirt samples. He sent some to you and the rest to Aunt Pen, just to be safe." Redundancy. Mom was big on redundancy. I hesitated. "What's going on, Taj?"

"Oh, probably nothing important. Just something odd I found."

"What? What did you find?"

"Oh, just . . . nothing really. Anyway, nothing I can talk about yet."

"'Cause I think I know what it is. And I found one too."

"One what?"

Uh-oh. If Taj had found one of those eggs, he wouldn't have had to ask.

"What did you find, Bryn?"

"What did *you* find?"

"Just a strange result. Not like a *thing*."

"Oh." I felt myself slump. A drop of water splashed on my forehead and dripped into one eye; the stupid awning leaked. I had so wanted to fork over the whole egg-thing to Taj. Or at least talk to him about it. Talk to somebody about it. But if Dad had wanted Taj to know about the egg, he would have sent it to him. Wouldn't he?

"Hey, Bryn. I'm on your side. I'm on Robin's side. You know that."

I did. Taj was devoted to Mom. After she had disappeared last fall, Dr. Reynolds had taken over her lab—just temporarily, he had said. Trying to save her research grants, he had said. The dean had gone along with it. Mom had megaquantities of grant money, and the department didn't want it all going away. So they told the granting foundations that her work would go on, under Dr. Reynolds's so-called capable supervision.

But Reynolds started steering things toward his own research. Some of Mom's equipment showed up in Reynolds's lab, and his grad students started invading Mom's lab, using her stuff. Plus,

Reynolds was making snarky comments about her work. Taj and a couple of Mom's other grad students had protested to the dean, but it hadn't done any good. After that, most of Mom's grad students had left. When Mom's lab manager finally quit in disgust, she'd called Dad and told him everything. It was an out-and-out power grab, she said. Usually Dad wouldn't talk about stuff like that to me, but this time he was seriously cheesed.

"Bryn?" Taj said.

"Yeah?" The canopy was bulging down on one end, sagging with the weight of the rain. I moved toward the door, away from the bulge, but right then a woman came out so I had to move back. The door slammed shut behind her, something went *pop*, and a truckload of water dumped down on my head.

Crap! I was soaking, soaking wet all over. And my sleep-dep headache was back again, and the only thing I'd done to deserve it was try to be responsible. It wasn't fair to put me in this position. Of having to keep a secret like this, not knowing who I could and couldn't tell. Running off like that—both of them, Mom and Dad—and leaving me here to deal.

Taj was talking in my ear. "Bryn? What's going on there? Bryn?"

"I found an *egg*," I said.

"A what?"

"An egg."

"Like what kind of egg?"

"I don't know. A big one."

"Goose egg big?"

"Volleyball big."

35

Silence on the line. Somebody came out of the shop; I gave up and just moved into the rain. "Listen, Bryn," Taj said at last. "You busy right now?"

I was so pathetically not-busy.

"'Cause I'd like to see this egg," he said.

I felt a little twinge. I shouldn't have told. I should have waited for Dad. "Aunt Pen's home this afternoon," I said. "And I don't think she should find out about it. She wouldn't want it in her house. No telling what she'd do. She might give it to the cops—or the Audubon Society."

"Oh." Taj sounded disappointed. "Well, can I at least buy you a bagel or something? Ice cream? Coffee? A beer?"

I laughed. Surprising myself. It would be good to go someplace that wasn't school or Aunt Pen's or the sad, haunted spaces of my own empty house. With a semi-cute guy, safely old and married, and not all that hard to talk to.

"I think I can work you in," I said.

It wasn't until I was sitting across the table from Taj—warming my hands on the ceramic cup, breathing in the steam from my triple-shot caramel macchiato, feeling the caffeine lighting up the circuits of my brain—that I noticed that he looked tired too. Dark, leathery circles rimmed his eyes, which were kind of pinkish at the edges, and his face seemed, I don't know, older. More serious. Worried.

He'd ordered a triple-shot too.

Now he asked me again how I was, really looking at me, like it mattered what I said. I didn't want to blow him off with a perky "fine," or even just "okay." But I couldn't think of a way to put it that was true, yet still something you could say in a coffee shop to someone you actually didn't know all that well. I shrugged.

He nodded. Like that was all he needed.

"Tell me about the egg," he said. "Everything."

I did. Starting with those thumps I'd heard. Then Piper and Luna and the boxes. I didn't tell about the kenning, of course—that was strictly verboten. But I described the egg itself as well as I could.

"Vibrating?" Taj asked. "More like a little trembling pulse kind of thing, or more like something actually moving around in there?"

"Like a pulse, I think. Or maybe humming, sort of."

Taj looked thoughtful. I took another sip of macchiato. There was a soft buzz of voices in the coffee shop, and a clattering of ceramic cups and plates on granite tabletops, and the sudden, harsh hiss of the espresso machine. It smelled damp in here—damp coats, damp boots, damp hair—blending with the dark, skunky musk of coffee.

"It's strange it should be alive," Taj said, "with nothing down there to keep it warm. How warm is your aunt's basement?"

"Not very," I said.

"Hmm. I don't know what to say. We raised chickens in India, when I was growing up. When the eggs are near to hatching, you can hear the baby chicks in there. You can feel them, moving around. It's not exactly a vibration, though. It's more like a wobble. Did you feel anything like that?"

I took another sip, trying to remember. But no. It hadn't wobbled. Not that I had felt. "But maybe it wobbled before," I said. "There were those thumps. And it fell out of the box."

Taj shrugged. "Many things can go bump in the night," he said. "And you don't know how that box was put there. It could have been off balance to begin with. Maybe it's decomposition you felt. Or the egg matter settling."

Maybe. It hadn't seemed like that, though. And there was something itching at me, way back in my mind. Making me edgy. Squirmy. "How long before they hatched?" I asked. "Those chicken eggs. I mean, once you felt them move."

"Oh, I don't know. A day or so?"

So if Taj was wrong and the egg was going to hatch, it could happen anytime. And I couldn't take care of it. Aunt Pen would find out. Besides, I didn't know how; I'd probably kill it. "I think maybe you'd better come get it," I said. "The egg. Like, tonight, if you can."

Taj looked at me. Seemed puzzled.

"Aunt Pen's going to be home all evening. But she takes out her hearing aid when she goes to bed. I can let you in, and—"

Taj held up a hand. "Whoa," he said. "I do want to see this egg. And I also need to take a look inside those boxes. But sneaking into your aunt's house in the middle of the night? I don't think that's such a good idea."

"Then I'll bring it to you," I said. "Park outside. I'll take it to your car."

"And what would I do with it then?" Taj asked. "I don't have anywhere to put it."

"You can take it to the lab!"

"There's no place I can hide something big like that. Reynolds won't want it there. He's made it clear that I'm not to bring any more of Robin's . . ." Taj sighed. Looked at me with those tired, older-than-I-remembered eyes. "I'm sorry to tell you this, Bryn. But he's shutting down all of Robin's experiments. Letting me wrap up some of what we've started but not begin anything new. I'm already taking a risk—" He broke off. "Well. Anyway. He wants me to finish my work quickly. Get my doctorate and get out."

Shutting down Mom's experiments? I gaped at him. "All of them?" I asked. "Nothing she's worked on will be left?"

"Not in . . . that lab, no."

I had a moment of vertigo, as if the planet had lurched, dropped away beneath me. *Dropping down and down through black nothing.*

"And I can't take the egg home," Taj was saying, "because I have a tiny apartment and a very pregnant wife who hates that I work with toxic chemicals and won't let me bring in *anything* from the lab."

"But—"

"Look," Taj said. "You said you didn't feel it wobble."

"Well, no, but—"

"So even if it is going to hatch—which I doubt—we probably have some time. Your dad will call tonight, and he'll have some ideas, and I'll ask around, too, to find a place for it. The zoo might be an option, I don't know. I have a friend there. I'll talk to him and call tomorrow. It'll be fine, Bryn. Don't worry."

He smiled and patted my hand. Like I was a little kid. I snatched my hand away.

Like a baby.

But it wasn't just about the egg. Not anymore. It was about Mom. About her work. Which was so much of who she was. And if that went away—everything she'd ever worked for . . .

I knew it didn't make sense, but this is what it felt like:

It would mean she was really dead.

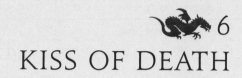

KISS OF DEATH

EUGENE, OREGON

Dad called at nine, like always. Piper got him first, like always. In the Brynworld, Piper always goes first. It was good to see her happy, though. Chatting away about her day. Gold stars and holo art and crayons. The yeti dance and monkey bars and swings. 'Cause it hadn't all been good, poor kid. She'd really been sucking on the inhaler. There'd been a break when the hard rain came and cleaned the celumbral junk out of the air, but now the cloud was back.

I listened in to make sure she didn't spill about the egg. Aunt Pen's ears were flapping. Seriously, you could practically see them twitch. When it was my turn, I took the phone upstairs.

Aunt Pen gave me a look.

"It's my *dad*," I said.

I closed the door, set Stella on my shoulder. "What's this about the egg?" Dad asked.

I told him.

"Vibrating?" he said. "I didn't feel that. It was cold when I found it. Not moving at all. I thought it was dead."

"I'm just telling you what I felt."

"I believe you. You feel things I can't." He hesitated.

Stella climbed up a strand of my hair and started nibbling at the top of my head.

"What is it?" I asked. "What kind of egg?"

"Not sure. Listen, I'll contact Taj. He'll take it off your hands."

"No he won't. I talked to him today. Didn't he get back to you?"

"He left a couple of odd messages. But I wanted to call you girls first."

I'd let Taj break the news about Reynolds. "Well, he won't take it. Unless you can talk him into it, I'm stuck. Can you picture Aunt Pen if she knew there was some monster bird egg in her basement? Alive?"

"Oh, God, please don't tell her."

"What's it worth to you?"

"No, I mean it. No telling what she'd do."

"Yeah, well, what am I supposed to do if it hatches?"

"I'll make some calls. Nothing's going to happen tonight."

"How do you know?"

"What are the chances, Brynster? It was in the storage locker for at least six months. It's been in the basement for the past two weeks. Nothing's been keeping it warm. What are the chances it'll hatch at all, much less pick this very night—out of however many nights it's been around—to hatch?"

Never, ever say stuff like that. Just don't. It's called tempting fate, and when you do, it's like the kiss of death.

‡   ‡   ‡

Three hours later, I still couldn't get to sleep. Which makes zero sense because I was in serious sleep-dep mode already. My whole body felt antsy, and a ragged, low-grade static crackled just below the surface of my so-called thoughts.

Triple shot: maybe not such a great plan.

Deep in the distance, I heard the stuttery growl of thunder. I watched the giant rhododendron shadows seethe across my wall, until lightning strobed the room.

Stella let out a whistle. The unhappy kind.

I groaned, turned onto my stomach, pulled my pillow over my head. Stella clicked back and forth on her perch, whistling like a maniac.

"Shut up," I said. "Go to sleep."

More thunder. Quiet. Then . . .

Clank. Clankity clank. Clank.

I raised up on an elbow, peered through the dark at Stella. She was pecking at something: the door latch of her cage. I stilled my mind, tried to synch with her.

Edgy, agitated. Borderline alarmed.

I could feel the buzzy storm energy now; I could smell the coppery tang of rain.

Stella didn't like thunderstorms. I knew that. But she was going at the latch so hard, I was afraid she might get hurt. Maybe crack her beak. I got up, wrapped my index finger in PJ cloth, and pressed it against the place where she was pecking. I kenned her to stop, calm down.

Not happening.

I eased the cage door open, thinking maybe I'd stroke her

tummy feathers, maybe coax her back onto her perch. But she slipped out through the cage door and took off flying.

I watched, totally plexed, as Stella circled the room, whistling hysterically.

A soft tap at the door. It opened. There was Piper. "Luna escaped," she said. "She went downstairs."

Thunder, again. Louder. Stella veered toward the opening in the doorway and sailed right through.

"Piper, look what you've done!" I snapped—and instantly regretted it. Piper's lower lip began to quiver. She put the inhaler to her mouth and dragged in a long, rattley breath.

Oh, jeez. I held out my arms. "Sorry. Come here?"

She leaned in toward me; I folded my arms around her. She was bony and bird-light. I could feel her quivering. I reached for a Kleenex, wiped her nose. "C'mon," I said. "Let's go find those birds."

But we both knew where they'd be.

We sat together on the bottom step, watching the birds peck at the basement door. I could feel Stella's impatience. I sent her a calming kenning; she flicked me off.

Piper took another drag off her inhaler. "I think the egg is hatching," she said.

I turned to stare at her. "Why do you say that?"

She shrugged.

"Piper?"

"I peeked," she said. "After school. When Aunt Pen was on the phone."

"Did Aunt Pen find out about the egg?"

"No."

That was a relief. "You didn't tell anyone else, did you?"

Piper shook her head, then seemed to reconsider. "Maybe I told McKenzie."

Piper's kindergarten buddy. Both girls were known for their "lively imaginations," so probably no one would believe them. But I wondered how long before McKenzie's mom sensed something strange about Piper and cooled the friendship. Which happened to everyone in our family, eventually.

"It had a crack in it," Piper said. "The egg. Just a little one."

That couldn't be good.

I ought to just snag the birds right now, stuff them back inside their cages. Let them squawk all night if they wanted. Tuck in Piper on the air bed, and then go back to bed myself. Talk Taj into coming over tomorrow night when Aunt Pen was at her book group. Let him deal with whatever was happening downstairs.

I looked down at Piper. Her face was eager, alive.

And I could feel it too, thrumming through my blood, cutting crosswise against my fear: That eagerness. That wanting to know.

Whatever hatched out of that egg . . . whenever it did hatch . . . it would need food.

Wouldn't it?

"Listen, Piper," I said. "If I let you come down with me, will you promise to do what I say?"

Piper nodded.

"Then stick close behind me. And be careful on the stairs."

I opened the basement door; Stella and Luna swooped down into the dark. I switched on the light and followed.

Thunder again—closer than before. At the bottom of the stairs I stopped, waited for Piper, took her hand. We walked past the furnace, the lawn furniture, the plastic bins. Just ahead lay the stack of tattered cardboard boxes. Stella and Luna were perched on the rim of the box with the egg. Watching.

We squatted beside the box. In the dim light I could see a gash in the egg, some kind of fissure between the sections.

"It's bigger now," Piper said.

"What is?"

"The crack."

It was thin at the ends, the crack, but it gaped open in the middle. Wide enough that I could see inside.

Something dark in there. I could smell something, something dampish but not unpleasant.

The egg lurched, and I heard a soft ripping sound. The crack grew longer, wider. Something poked out of it, something small and hard to see.

Thunder boomed.

The birds flapped their wings. I jerked backward, lost my balance, and sat down hard on the cold, concrete floor. I leaned forward, knelt, fixed my gaze on the thing in the slit, unable to look away.

It was a claw.

The tiny, needle-sharp tip of a curving claw.

7

THANK YOU, MR. FRANZEN

EUGENE, OREGON

Your ostrich has a single claw.

It was a ridiculous thought, I knew it was ridiculous the moment it occurred to me, gaping down at whatever was trying to get out of that egg.

The claw wiggled, disappeared.

Your ostrich has a single claw and only two toes, to aid it in running more swiftly.

Mr. Franzen, sixth grade, Highland Drive Elementary. He was always going for what teachers call "enrichment," which was actually great. I knew all sorts of random factoids, thanks to Mr. Franzen.

"Brynnie?" Piper reached for my hand. I closed my hand around hers, small and warm. "What is it?" she asked.

"I don't know. I'm thinking maybe some kind of really big bird."

Your emu, by contrast, has three toes in a tridactyl arrangement.

Weird how some of this stuff sticks. But how many toes, I wondered, does your dodo bird have? Or something equally strange?

'Cause it could be something like that. It actually could. Not a tropical bird, of course—not in Alaska. But maybe something new, unknown to science. Your basic cryptid species. Which would be seismic cool. Only not right now, with both Mom and Dad gone.

Thunder rumbled. Piper squeezed my hand. Stella and Luna stretched up and flapped their wings. I could feel a charge in the air, an electric buzz that tingled at the roots of my hair.

The claw reappeared, raked against the seam in the egg, lengthening the crack.

Okay, so what was I supposed to do now? If some kind of strange cryptid thing was hatching in the basement, how was I supposed to keep it alive?

Stella leaned toward the egg, her topknot flared. I copped a quick ken.

Not worried. Curious.

The egg rolled a little. The claw strained. A bit of pleathery eggshell gave way with a soft *pop*. The gap widened; it was now a wedge of darkness sliced out of the surface of the egg.

Inside, I could see something gray and glistening and wet.

Didn't look all that birdy. What other kinds of things hatched from eggs? Lizards? Turtles?

Light flashed in the window; thunder boomed. The birds, startled, took off. They circled the room, landed on another box, higher up the stack. The gray thing pressed against the fissure in the egg. Then, suddenly, the head was out.

Eyes tightly squinched shut beneath sticking-out bony brow ridges. No beak, but wide nostrils at the end of a long, narrow snout. No feathers, but a bony crest on its head, covered with some kind of loose, wrinkly, skinlike stuff with a fuzzy microfiber nap.

Piper let out a gasp. I scrambled backward, pulling her with me, heart pounding in my throat.

Okay, so we could definitely scratch *ostrich* off the list.

More like a lizard, maybe. Some megaweird kind of lizard.

With fur.

The head swiveled around, nostrils dilating, like it was sussing out its new world by smell. It made a sound—a hoarse, grating, pathetic, rusty-hinges squeak. Made me borderline cringe, but still it somehow had that pull on me—that feed-me, take-care-of-me pull, like kittens at the pet store or Stella when she was little. Except this thing was totally creep-out strange and, like, damp.

It struggled pitifully to break out of its shell, still squeaking. I halfway wanted to pry the egg apart to help it and halfway wished it would duck back inside and disappear forever.

The thing gave a massive lurch, ripped the shell wide open. It slithered out—all of it—and lay panting on the crumpled papers.

Thunder again. Far away. Rain pinged against the metal window wells and gurgled in the downspouts.

I pulled Piper into my lap. She looked up at me. "Brynnie?" she said.

"Yeah?"

"I don't think it's a bird."

Right.

I leaned forward, studied the thing. Still heaving for breath. Heartbeat pulsing in its throat.

Yeah, it must be some kind of lizard. About the size of Asteroid, the neighbor's little cat, and covered with that grayish, dampish, microfiber skin/fur stuff. Its head seemed far too big for its body, far too heavy for its spindly neck to support. It was allover skinny, with lots of hard little bumps and nodules. Four legs. Long, ridged tail. Mostly bones and skin and claws.

Ugly.

Seismic ugly.

The claws, I saw, weren't bidactyl, like your ostrich claws. Or even tridactyl, like your emu claws, but . . . I counted. What was the Latin prefix for "five"? Pent? As in pentagon? Pentdactyl? Pendactyl?

Suddenly, I remembered a time when Mom had told me about another lizard. Super-rare. Someone had done some work with the microbes in its mouth and found, in the early experiments, that they seemed to degrade PCBs. Like, made them go away.

But hadn't that been some kind of tropical thing? It wouldn't have come from Alaska.

Would it?

So maybe this was something else?

The thing lifted its head, sniffing. It had that prehistoric look, like crocodiles and possums. Like it had been around since way before we got here. *We* as in humanoids. Eons and eons before.

A shiver jolted through me, an under-the-skin tremor: a premonition that I'd stumbled onto something way beyond me, something huge and primordial and . . .

What was that word Mr. Franzen had used when he was talking about raw power in nature? Things like volcanoes and hurricanes, things like black holes and nebulae and quasars?

Oh, yeah. *Sublime.*

It cranked up with the annoying squeaking thing. Pathetic-sounding, but bossy too. It must be hungry. Had to be. It flicked out its tongue. Skinny. Pink. Forked.

Your snake has a forked tongue. It tastes particles on the air, and that's how it learns what's in its environment.

Thank you, Mr. Franzen.

By the way, Mr. Franzen:

What the hell is this?

8

MR. LIZARD

EUGENE, OREGON

"Piper," I said, "would you go upstairs and get my laptop?"

"Why?" Piper asked.

"I need to figure out what this thing is. So we know what to feed it."

"Okay," Piper said.

"Unplug it first. The laptop."

"I know."

"Don't drop it."

"I won't."

"And don't wake Aunt Pen."

"I won't!" Piper scowled. "I'm not a baby."

I watched as she shuffled her ducky slippers toward the stairs. I could have snagged the laptop way faster by myself. But it didn't seem like a good plan to leave Piper or the birds down here alone with the baby lizard-thing. It looked helpless, but you never knew. Some lizards were really quick. They could grab a bird, say, and stun it or kill it in a fraction of a second. Some lizards had poisonous spit.

Thunder in the distance. I could still hear rain tapping against the window well, but the worst of the storm seemed to have passed. Stella and Luna leaned down from their perch. I synched with Stella and felt a sort of friendly curiosity.

I bent to study the lizard, careful to stay out of spitting distance. Whatever that might be.

Long, lizardy body. Long, lizardy tail. Raised crest all down its spine. Kind of alligatory/crocodilian—except for that nappy skin/fur. Bulbous eyes, squeezed shut. Darkish almost everywhere but in the little patches where it was starting to dry, where it looked pinky-tan. I could smell it now—a warm, animal-baby smell, and something else, something that seemed familiar.

The thing was still squeaking. And shivering.

Did lizards shiver when they were cold? I seemed to remember they just shut their bodies down. Went dormant. But definitely it looked like a lizard. A huge one. Maybe some random, cryptid lizard that nobody even knew about.

Now it started making another kind of sound—little sucking, smacking sounds.

Hungry sounds.

It stumbled around in the box, searching blindly. Then, with a hopeless squeak, it sighed and flopped down onto the wadded-up newspaper.

Honestly? I didn't think it could spit or stun or kill anything at the moment. I collected the pieces of its shell and moved them into a corner of the box.

Stella lit on the edge of its box, cocked a curious eye, and whistled. Luna sailed down beside her, skootched right up against her. Stella nibbled at Luna's feet.

"I hate to break it to you, ladies," I said, "but this is not a bird. I don't think it's going to be your friend."

Piper didn't take long. I pulled up a patio chair and fired up the laptop.

"It's shivering," Piper said.

"I know."

"I think it's cold."

"Yeah, listen," I said. "Does Aunt Pen have a heating pad? Have you ever seen one? Like what Dad puts on his back when it's sore?"

"Aunt Pen put a hot water bottle in my bed."

"Really?"

"She put it by my feet."

"Could you get it?"

"Okay."

She shuffled off again. I searched "large lizards." There were several: the Australian water dragon, the Chinese water dragon, the bearded dragon, the Gila monster, the Komodo dragon.

Dragons and monsters. Perfect.

I couldn't tell what kind of lizard this guy was because of the weird skin/fur, which hid its markings and ridges so I couldn't compare them to the pictures online. I was guessing it was a baby thing, the skin. Probably it would molt. But so far I found no pictures of baby lizards.

Still, all the big lizards had five toes. So did our guy. Ours looked more birdy than lizardy, but maybe that was a baby thing too. Maybe the toes would change.

Food! What about food?

Turns out, lizards can be herbivores, carnivores, or omnivores. Which didn't help at all.

"I got it!"

I looked up. Piper was clutching the hot water bottle to her chest. "Hey, good job, Piper. Let's set this up."

I filled the bottle with hot water from the sink near the washing machine. I tucked it into the lizard's box, right next to its belly. I made sure not to actually touch the damp skin/fur. Eesh. I knew the bottle wouldn't stay warm for very long. And hopefully the thing wouldn't pop it with its claws.

I pulled up a chair for Piper. She settled in, took a long, phlegmy hit off her inhaler.

"You okay?" I asked.

She nodded.

Poor kid.

Well, what do baby lizards eat?

The water dragons seemed to be omnivorous, so far as I could tell. Bugs and leaves. You were supposed to feed them greens with plenty of calcium, like dandelion greens and kale.

No problem there. Since Mom disappeared, our backyard was practically a dandelion farm.

The Gila monsters were straight carnivores. Small mammals, lizards, birds, and eggs.

Yikes. I checked out Stella and Luna, close enough that the lizard could maybe reach out and zap them with its tongue. Not likely, though. It was too scrawny, too weak. But still. I kenned Stella, asked her to move back to that higher box. This time, she obeyed, and Luna followed.

Fabulous.

The Komodo dragons, as it turned out, were carnivorous too. But worse. Much worse. Deer, goats, pigs, dogs . . . children.

Children?

I scrolled down. They weren't exactly poisonous, apparently, but they had horrible, festering bacteria in their mouths. They'd killed adult humans too. They were known to dig up human cadavers in cemeteries and eat them.

"Omigod."

"What?" Piper asked.

"Uh, never mind." No need to give her nightmares. For now, this was just a helpless baby. I clicked on another link. "Hey, I think I found something."

"What?" Piper asked.

The two most popular foods for baby lizards: crickets and mealworms.

"We're fresh out," I muttered.

"Out of what?"

"Crickets and mealworms."

"When did we have crickets and mealworms?"

Excellent question.

The lizard raised its head and started squeaking again. Such a needy little critter. But the noise triggered my old sleep-dep headache, made it hard to think. Piper slid off her chair and leaned toward the thing, fingers outstretched.

"Don't!" I said. "You don't know where it's—"

Been, I almost said. *You don't know where it's been.* I was starting to channel Aunt Pen. "Seriously, Piper. It might have poisonous—"

The forked tongue darted out and struck Piper's hand. Piper squealed and jerked backward.

Spit. Poisonous spit.

I dropped the laptop. Grabbed Piper's hand. Held it up to the light and inspected it.

It looked okay. So far. "Does it hurt?" I asked.

"I don't think so."

"Well *feel* it. What does it feel like? Is it, like, burning, or . . ."

Piper shook her head.

I let out a breath. "Look, we don't know very much about, uh, Mr. Lizard. So let's not touch him. For now. And let me know if that starts to hurt."

Piper nodded. She looked a little scared.

I folded in the flaps of the lizard's box. Interlocking them, just in case.

Web surfing again. On a site called The Cold-Blooded Gazette, I found an article about feeding sick lizards.

Baby lizards would be like sick lizards, right? They'd both have tender stomachs, right?

I scrolled through the article. The Cold-Blooded Gazette liked a liquid diet for sick lizards. Especially strawberry ReliaVite.

Aunt Pen sometimes drank something thick and pink for lunch. Strawberry ReliaVite, perhaps?

I took Piper's hand, examined it again. Still fine. "Come upstairs with me," I said. "I need your help with something."

I headed for the stairs, with a warning ken to Stella, who, with Luna close behind, had hopped onto the closed box and was pecking away at the cardboard. If Mr. Lizard weren't so feeble, he might be able to bust right through those flaps. The ladies would be snacks.

But they were probably safe for now.

I searched the pantry. No ReliaVite. But I did find something else. Slendah. Strawberry Slendah.

Close enough.

Hopefully, Aunt Pen wouldn't miss just one can. I handed it to Piper, then got a small bowl from the cupboard.

Downstairs, the lizard was squeaking again, but softer, maybe getting hoarse. I shooed the birds off the box, pried open the flaps. I took the Slendah from Piper, popped the tab, poured a little into the bowl, and set down the bowl inside the box. The thing suddenly stopped squeaking. It beelined for the bowl, scrabbling its little toenails against cardboard, shoving the newspaper aside, making those smacking sounds again. It flicked out its tongue. Not actually into the bowl but just above it.

I picked up the bowl, hoping the thing's tongue would touch the Slendah, maybe clue it in that the pink stuff was food. But now it backed away, stopped flicking its tongue, and started squeaking again.

"Lap it up!" I said. "Do I have to do everything for you?"

Faint, gray light was beginning to seep through the basement window. It wouldn't be long before Aunt Pen woke up, and then . . .

More than anything, I wanted to gather up Piper and the ladies and take everybody upstairs. Shut the door on the stupid thing. Let it live or die, whatever.

But I couldn't. It was Mom's. She'd found it, collected it, put it somewhere to keep it safe. It must be important to her.

Back to the laptop. The Cold-Blooded Gazette. *Force feeding*, it said. *With a syringe.*

Hmm. I had a thought. "You stay here," I said to Piper. "Don't go near Mr. Lizard, and shoo the birds away if they get near. Don't touch it, whatever you do."

I hurtled up the stairs, hunted through the kitchen, through every single drawer.

Not there. Where did Mom keep hers?

I found the roasting pan way back in a corner of the pantry. When I lifted the lid, there it was:

The turkey baster.

I grabbed it, ran halfway to the basement door, reversed back to the kitchen, snagged a drinking glass, then booked it down the stairs.

Everybody okay. The ladies still watching. Mr. Lizard still squeaking. Piper serenading them all with a song from Pixel Slippers, her favorite kinder-rock band.

I poured the rest of the Slendah into the glass. I squeezed the air out of the bulb at the end of the baster, then sucked up some pink liquid. The thing's mouth, wide open when it squeaked, was lined with rows of tiny, needle-sharp teeth.

Teeth already? Don't you guys, like, gum things for a while before you teethe?

I positioned the tip of the baster just outside the teeth. I squeezed.

The Slendah dribbled straight down into the box.

Not enough suction.

I sucked up more Slendah, angled the baster so the pink liquid rested in the bulb. I squeezed the bulb, really hard this time.

Splooge! A jet of Slendah hit the thing in one eye and splattered all over the box.

"You missed," Piper said.

"Yeah," I said. "Thanks."

I filled the baster again. The thing wasn't holding its head still. It was squeaking, stumbling around in circles. In full-out meltdown mode.

I was going to have to touch it.

I steeled myself, got a grip on the back of its flailing head and neck. I was stronger than it was; I forced it to stay still. Its skin/fur felt damp, but not exactly slimy.

I rested the tip of the baster on the thing's teeth, squeezed the bulb again. This time, most of the Slendah jetted straight into its mouth.

Bull's-eye.

The mouth shut. I could see a swallowing movement in the skinny throat. Then the tongue came out and licked all around, hunting for more.

Do it again: Suck up more Slendah. Tip back the baster. Nudge it between the teeth. Squirt.

The critter made blissful little moaning sounds. Its throat began to work again. Swallowing. I missed a few more times—

got pink stuff on its head and chest and decorated its box with pink splotches and squiggles. But the critter downed maybe half the can. At last, it settled back into newspaper, leaned against the hot water bottle, curled up, and shut its eyes.

"I think Mr. Lizard was hungry," Piper said.

Check.

Rain streaked down the windows, doing strange things to the early light, making it seem trembly and uncertain. The thing lay there with its sides bulging out, with its Slendah-spattered body rising and falling in the rhythms of sleep. In the wavery light, it seemed to alternate between bandwidths: between something from now, and something very, very old.

I blinked. Rubbed my eyes. Massaged my temples.

Stella fluffed her feathers, seeming to sigh. I could hear the faint sounds of cars on the boulevard—the early risers. I could hear the furnace's hum.

"Piper," I said. "You can't tell anyone about this."

She nodded.

"Seriously: no one. Not even McKenzie. Not unless I say it's okay."

"I won't!"

But I knew she would. The kenning secret—that was drilled into her, practically from birth. But *this* was going to come out someday.

The lizard stirred, curled more tightly into itself, tucked its head under its birdy claws. I hesitated, then touched it, ran my fingers down its sides and back, avoiding the pink goo. I could feel the sharp little bumps along its spine, and assorted other nodes and lumps and knobs beneath the dampish layer of fuzz.

My fingers felt creamy, like they had hand lotion on them. I brought them to my nose.

Sort of like . . . licorice, maybe?

What are you into, Mom?

The critter began to knead the newspapers with its claws. I touched it again and could feel a vibration under its skin. A funny thrumming, like the purring of a cat.

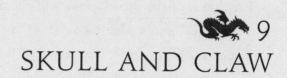

9
SKULL AND CLAW

RESURRECTION PEAKS, ALASKA

Josh stepped into the cave and waited for his father to catch up. He breathed in the damp, mineral smell as his eyes adjusted to the dark. The cave roof rose higher than he would have guessed, and a long, sandy track snaked down into the gloom among heaps of scree and fallen boulders. Josh wondered how old the track was. Hundreds of years? Thousands? He wondered what kinds of animals had sheltered here over the eons, and if any of them were remotely like the things they'd come looking for.

It had been a long, hard climb to get here. Drifts of snow still covered parts of the trail, and Josh's father—Cap, everyone called him—had been difficult the whole time. Withdrawn, and quick to criticize. Like always, when his knee slowed him down. Josh had stayed back with him, let the others go on ahead. Which seemed to annoy Cap even more.

Now, waiting, Josh felt the familiar dragging sensation in his gut. His brother Zack seemed to love these expeditions, but they bothered Josh. True, he always felt the tiny flare of excitement at the possibility of finding something amazing. But after the excitement came the dread.

Far ahead, in the darker regions of the cave, Josh could see two flashlight beams. One raked across the sand and boulders on either side of the track, heading steadily deeper. That would be Zack. Needing to be first, like always. He'd been born first, eleven months before Josh, and ever since, he'd had to be first in everything. When, last year, Josh had made varsity soccer as a freshman, Zack had gotten more competitive than ever.

If that was even possible.

The second light jittered from Zack to the cave mouth and back again to Zack. That would be the college guy, Quinn, who had found the things last fall. At least, that was the story he'd told.

Josh didn't know Quinn well, but he could pretty much guess what was happening now. Quinn didn't want some high school kid getting ahead of him; he wanted to point out his find himself. On the other hand, he wanted Cap to be there when he did it.

Everybody wanted to impress the Captain.

The lights disappeared around a bend.

"Did you get the coordinates?"

Josh jumped. Cap always managed to do that to him. Josh had missed something, something he should have been doing, something Cap had to point out to him. Again.

Josh pulled out the GPS and captured the coordinates. Quinn had claimed he didn't have coordinates, but that was probably because he didn't want people coming up here without him. You couldn't trust Quinn, couldn't tell what he was really thinking. He reminded Josh of a fox: sharp-faced, ruddy-haired, and sly.

Now Cap edged past Josh and into the cave. His limp, Josh saw, was more noticeable than before. He was tired, but he'd never admit it.

Josh followed. Roof and walls closed around him, muting the sounds of seabirds and wind, dimming the brightness of the day. Josh clicked on his flashlight and headed down into the dark. The crunch of his boots on sand sounded loud. The dread came crawling in again.

Josh knew it was impossible for Cap to make a living as a hunting guide anymore. Too little wildlife. Too much regulation. And the knee. Cap had had to find another way, and there were worse ways than this.

But what they'd come for now was illegal. They were poaching. Not live animals, which would have been worse. Cap wouldn't do that. Yeah, he got testy about all the permits and tags. But he'd spent hours in the field patiently teaching Zack and Josh how to tell a legal kill from an illegal one. Josh knew by heart the difference between cow and bull caribou; he could recite in his sleep the exact antler spread and bow tine count of a legal moose. Josh had never, ever seen Cap hunt out of season or go over limit.

But still. This was taking things they had no right to. And if they were caught, there'd be a fine for Cap. Maybe even jail time. Cap had told Josh that he had it handled. Told him he shouldn't come if he was scared.

He was scared. A little. And admitting he was scared was not an option. So Josh had to go.

But everyone could tell he wasn't happy.

Rounding the first curve, Josh saw Zack's and Quinn's light beams crisscrossing, probing the surface of a field of rock debris ahead.

"They're here, Cap." Zack's voice echoed in the dark.

"Wait," Cap said.

They're here.

Josh shivered—wanting to rush forward, wanting to hold back.

By the time he and Cap caught up, Zack had unpacked his tools and turned on the lantern.

"Spawn, eh?" Quinn said. He spread his arms wide, taking in the expanse of rocky floor, casting a cartoon-monster shadow in the blue light of the lantern.

"Spawn?" Cap muttered.

Josh translated: "Cool." He looked, but he couldn't see what Quinn was talking about.

Cap grunted, shrugged off his backpack. He took out the hammer, the whisk broom, the chisels, the picks, the trowels. He brushed aside a top layer of fragments and debris. Now Josh could see that some of the rocks were different, lighter colored. They humped out of the surrounding stone, about the size and shape of half-buried soccer balls. Rough and jagged soccer balls. And not quite round, exactly. Ovoid? Was that a word? And flattish. Sort of dark gray, flattened ovals.

Josh drew in a sharp breath. Couldn't help himself. In all the time they'd gone hunting for fossils, he'd never seen anything like this.

Yeah, it could just be the way the rocks had formed. Some kind of crystallization pattern.

But they sure looked like eggs to him.

So maybe Quinn's story was true.

On his first trip to the cave, Quinn had told them, he'd found a different kind of egg, an egg that seemed newer than these. Bigger. Rounder. Leathery—not made of stone. Shattered pieces of other newer eggs lay nearby. Quinn had carried the whole egg down the mountain and shown it to one of his professors, who had talked Quinn into turning it over to him.

A couple of weeks later, the professor had asked Quinn to lead a woman, another professor, to the cave. For pay. She'd found these things. Petrified eggs, Quinn claimed. Fossils. She'd chipped out one and had taken it for herself, but had refused to chip one out for Quinn.

Quinn had come back up alone with a hammer and chisel, but he'd wrecked everything he'd tried to pry out. Then winter had set in, and snow blocked the trail to the cave. In the meantime, Quinn heard about Cap and his skill with fossils.

"Think you can get them out whole?" Quinn asked now.

Cap bent down, eyed the eggs. If they really were eggs. "Think so," he said. "You saw the one she extracted. Was it the same as the new one? Except older, turned to stone?"

Quinn shrugged. "These are smaller. Kind of squashed. But the woman seemed to think they were the same. Said she could tell by the ridge patterns."

Cap shook his head. "You'd think there'd be some intermediate stages, between the fossilized eggs and the new ones. You sure you didn't see anything like that?"

"No, nothing."

"Did you *look?*" Zack asked.

"Yeah, I looked! I—"

"We should check it out," Zack said. "In case he missed something." He turned to Quinn. "Where are those fragments you told us about?"

Quinn looked torqued, like he didn't want to answer. His eyes flicked to Cap. "I found a way out, at the other end," Quinn said. "Hard to get to from outside. They're inside the edge of the opening."

"Well, they aren't going anywhere," Cap said. "We'll open up one egg to see what we've got, but we'll keep the others whole. Worth more that way."

"How will people know what they're buying?" Quinn asked.

"We'll get them X-rayed and certified." Cap knelt, examined the ground around one of the flattened spheres. He brushed away the broken rocks and gravel, then took off his gloves and probed with bare fingers at the places where the sphere intersected with the ground. "Ah," he said. "A nice fracture." He set the chisel into the crack and tapped it with the rock hammer. Bent down for a closer look. Tapped again. Moved to another place and tapped some more.

The dry *chink* of steel on steel echoed through the cavern. Josh's breath came out in frozen puffs, stained blue by the lantern's light. He stamped his feet, trying to thaw his toes.

He missed the actual moment when the chunk of rock broke loose because Zack had gradually shouldered in between Josh and Cap, until Josh couldn't see what Cap was doing. Wasn't it enough that Zack was with Cap every day? Since Mom and

Cap's divorce, Josh had lived with Mom, in Haines. "Would you move?" Josh said.

"*You* move."

Josh sighed. I always move, he thought. He moved.

The thing rested in Cap's hands now. It hadn't come out completely clean, but, where the lantern light was strongest, Josh could make out a pattern of bumps and ridges on the surface, a pattern that didn't look like any rock he'd ever seen.

"Josh," Cap said. "Want to hold?"

"Yeah!"

Cap set the thing in Josh's cupped hands, then tapped it lightly with the blunt end of the rock hammer. He tapped it again, a little harder. On the third try, with an echoing *chink*, the rock split into two clean halves.

"Ah," Cap said. As if everything was now perfectly clear. Josh looked down at the shallow ridges, pits, and folds in the rock. In one of the halves, he thought he saw something that looked like a curled-up claw, but he couldn't make out anything like a skull. Cap glanced at him. "Here," he said. He took both halves from Josh and set them on the ground, placing one right beside the lantern. Josh squatted to look. Cap moved a finger along the surface of the rock. "Here are the jaw and the teeth. Here's the top of the skull, and the back. Here's the base of the spine. Legs here. Tail here. Do you see?"

Josh nodded. Yes. He did.

Quinn was looking too, but Zack eyed Josh in that annoying way he had—*he* didn't need anyone to point that stuff out to him. Josh didn't care. He sat there, letting his gaze move across the shadowed hollows and lighted crests in the rock, memorizing the shape of the little animal. He pulled off a glove. Touched it with a bare finger. It was cold and smooth. Ancient. Who knew how old? He felt the grooves of the tiny, curled claw, then traced the bumpy curve of spine and neck back up and over the skull.

Some kind of dinosaur. Had to be.

This felt different from the fossils from the other expeditions. It wasn't just that Josh had never seen a dinosaur egg before—he hadn't—but he'd also never found anything *whole*. Before, it was just fragments, bits of tooth and bone and claw. Like pieces from different puzzles, all jumbled in together. But this one, its every vertebra finely etched in stone, felt somehow real in a way the others hadn't.

Josh's finger pricked on something sharp, high on the fossil's back. He looked at Cap, questioning.

Cap nodded. "Good eye, son. I caught that, too. Could be a lot of things, but maybe . . . it could be a wing bud."

"A wing bud?"

"Maybe the wings hadn't formed yet on the embryo. Or it could be a vestigial wing from an animal that used to fly but evolved out of it."

Josh drew his finger across the little spur again. Wings! "Have you ever found anything like this before?" he asked. "Or parts of one, this kind of animal? Do you know what it is?"

"Hard to tell," Cap said. "We have plenty of unidentified fragments. And I've heard stories about flying lizards for years. Some people trace the rumors to those rock carvings they found up there in the Klondike. As to fossils, though . . . no. Nothing like this."

"Hey," Quinn said. "My professor has a bunch of old sketches of flying lizards framed in his office."

Cap looked up, interested. "Really?" he said. "The professor with the egg?"

"He has all kinds of stuff like that."

"So," Josh said, "this could be a new find? Some kind of winged dinosaur nobody knows about yet?"

Cap smiled. "Yeah. Just might."

Josh felt something expanding inside him, growing huge and calm, forcing little cracks and fissures in the brittle crust of his everyday self. He'd felt this way sometimes, lying on his back and watching the stars at night. Suddenly knowing for absolute certain that the universe was vaster and stranger and more amazing than anyone could ever imagine.

"It should be in a museum," he said.

"What?" A dangerous note in Cap's voice.

Josh blinked. He hadn't quite meant to say it aloud. But now that he had, he didn't want to take it back. "It should be in a museum. People should be able to see it. It doesn't belong on some rich guy's coffee table. And the scientists . . . they should be here, not us. They can figure out stuff from how it's positioned. They should study it, find out what it is."

Cap stood. "I've about had it with you, Josh. You've never been with the program, always dragging your feet."

"But—"

"I can *feel* your moral indignation, and I'm up to here with it.

We're not hurting anything. Whatever these things are, they're already dead. And I don't know where you get off feeling so damn superior when this is paying for the clothes on your back. So just . . . go off somewhere. I don't care where. Zack, come here and help."

Josh's face burned. He got up, turned around, and stumbled toward the path.

It was wrong. Cap wouldn't admit it, but it was. Not just illegal. Wrong.

Behind him, Josh heard Cap and Zack murmuring, and then the *chink* of a hammer. *Go off somewhere.* Okay. He would. Josh clicked on his flashlight and headed back, deeper into the cave. He pushed down hard on his anger, tried to keep it in control.

When he was little, he'd pretty much thought Cap walked on water. But now . . . well, things had changed. Even Cap's nickname sometimes set Josh's teeth on edge. Most people assumed he'd been a captain in the navy, and Cap was happy to have them think it. Josh himself had thought so until a couple of years ago, when it slipped out that Cap had been a chief petty officer.

Which was fine. Nothing wrong with it. Just don't pretend to be something you aren't.

Josh kept going. He swept his flashlight beam over the ground, keeping an eye out for those intermediate-stage eggs.

After a while, the cave grew lighter. Quinn had said something about an opening back here. And egg fragments. When Josh caught a glint of something in the rocks at the side of the path, he stooped to look.

Not an egg fragment. That was for sure. Josh set down his

flashlight, dug down among the loose rocks, and pried the thing out. He brushed it off, held it to the light.

A phone.

What the hell?

How did *this* get here?

PART II
LIZARD

Twitch your feelers,
Flap your gills,
Give those flippers a clap.
Shake your antlers, and
All together now:
Do the Chromosome Snap.
—from "Chromosome Snap," by Osmotic Creep

You think you're all that virtuous
But you're a pirate like the rest of us.
Pirate,
Biopirate,
Plundering the Earth.
—from "Biopirate," by Radioactive Fish

10
WAY FUSED OUT

EUGENE, OREGON

"I think I'm sick," I said.

Aunt Pen looked down at me. I couldn't grok her expression. She'd just shaken me awake. The clock said 6:30. Only an hour since I'd tucked in Piper and Stella and Luna.

"Do you want to stay home?" Aunt Pen asked. She was wearing a blue linen pantsuit, one of about a thousand matching pantsuits she owned.

I nodded. Made no move to get out of bed.

She frowned. She'd never had kids herself, and I could practically see her processors blipping away, calling up images of things she'd heard about teenagers left alone in houses: of beer, of drugs, of sex, of wild parties trashing everything. Of little broken bird figurines scattered all over the floor.

Sometimes it got me how different Aunt Pen was from Mom—wiry, quick-moving, frizzy-haired Mom, who never missed a chance to ken with a wild bird or dig in the dirt to unearth something strange. Though apparently, when they were little, Aunt Pen had had some serious kenning cred. She'd once called down a flock of herons from the sky—by accident. They'd scratched her up pretty bad, and a bunch of people had seen it, and she was the butt of some mean kids' jokes for years after. The whole thing had messed her up. Her own bird had died young, and after that, she'd stopped kenning completely. Cold turkey. *Denial of the gift,* Mom called it.

Mom says it means "to know," the word "kenning" does. It's not about power—calling your bird, sending her places. It's about companionship. About knowing and being known. But, because it has to be secret, it winds up cutting you off from *people.*

Ironically.

"I'm going to take your temperature," Aunt Pen said now.

Oh, no. "Look, I don't have pneumonia or anything. I just don't feel so good. I didn't sleep well. And I have a headache, and my throat feels kind of scratchy, and I just can't face school today. I just need to sleep some more, okay?"

All true. But I could feel the lie sitting there behind it.

"Bryn," she said, and her voice was softer now. She perched on the edge of the bed. Her hair was perfectly combed, like freeze-framed into position. But a speck of mascara had fallen on her cheek, and her lipstick wasn't quite even. "Do you want me to stay with you?" she asked. "You'll need to eat something. And if you're sick, you'll need me to take you to the doctor."

God, please no. But I swallowed, thinking, She'd do that? She'd actually miss a day at Bountiful for me? She loved her job doing paralegal stuff for the foundation. Of everyone in our family, Aunt Pen and Dad were the ones with the most friends. The ones most *comfortable* around other people.

"Anyway," Aunt Pen went on, "Piper looks kind of tired, too, this morning, and—"

"Is Piper staying home?" I cringed. Even I could hear an unmistakable Note of Alarm in my voice. I'd blown it. I'm a terrible liar.

Aunt Pen narrowed her eyes. Processors churning. "Piper actually wants to go to school," she said.

"I'll be fine," I said. Unable to look Aunt Pen in the eye. "I can scrounge some food. I just need rest."

Aunt Pen studied me, then came to a decision. "Okay," she said. "Call me at work if you need anything."

Not sure she believed me, but she was letting it go.

She headed for the door. Looked back. "Anything at all, do you hear?"

A case of strawberry ReliaVite, I thought. But I didn't say it.

Taj showed up around one. He hadn't liked the idea of sneaking over. Not at all. But when I'd called and told him the egg had hatched out something strange and lizardy, he'd changed his tune. Also, though I'd done my best to sound chill, possibly he could tell from something in my voice that I was right out there on the edge.

I'd told him about the turkey baster, and that I needed some strawberry ReliaVite. I'd told him about the hot water bottle. I was going to ask him how the zoo deal was coming, but he hung up before I got a chance.

"I come bearing gifts," he said, when I opened the door. He set two bulging sacks full of stuff on the kitchen counter. "Now let me see this lizard of yours."

Ours, I corrected him silently. Don't leave me all alone here, Taj.

"What about the zoo?" I asked.

"I'll tell you in a minute. But I'm dying to see this *thing.*"

In the basement, we knelt beside the box. The lizard was still dozing. "Whoa," Taj said. Then again: "Whoa." He reached out, ran a finger along the critter's snout, then rubbed its side. "It's like skin," he said. "And it's warm. Is that from the hot water bottle?"

I shrugged. "I'm trying to keep it warm."

We watched the critter together, its eyes still shut, its sides rising and falling. Finally, Taj rocked back on his heels. "That is without a doubt the weirdest animal I've ever seen," he said.

"Can you tell what it is?"

He shook his head. "I'm no herpetologist, but I'm pretty sure there's nothing out there quite like it. Nothing known to the scientific community, anyway. I looked at some sites this morning. Unless . . ."

Taj squinted at the critter.

"Unless what?"

"Well, I didn't check fossils. It could be a Lazarus."

"A what?"

"A Lazarus species. Disappears from the fossil record and shows up much later. After the guy in the Bible who was raised from the dead. Not to be confused with an Elvis species."

"You're kidding, right?"

"No. For real. An Elvis species: an impersonator. Looks like the other guy but isn't. Anyway, I'd say Robin's found herself an animal unknown to science: a cryptid. And it's a dooze."

He pointed at the pink splotches on the lizard. I'd had to feed it again at about eleven. After I'd had a three-hour nap and two cups of instant coffee. "I thought you said you didn't have any ReliaVite," Taj said.

"It's Slendah."

"You fed it Slendah? Have you read the ingredients in that stuff? It's not even food, it's just chemicals in suspension."

"Like ReliaVite is any better! Anyway, it's lucky I found anything to feed it. I can't drive, you know. I can't just go out and buy stuff. And I have no clue how to keep it alive. I'd kill it." Taj didn't get it. How hard it was. Like, impossible.

"Yeah, well," Taj said. "You don't seem to have hurt it any. Whatever it is." He picked up a piece of shell and studied it. "Can I have this?"

I shrugged. "I don't care. So what about those options you were looking into? The zoo? Can they take it?"

Taj pulled a couple of plastic baggies out of his backpack. He put the shell in one, poked around in the newspaper for a lizard stool and dropped that, along with the damp paper, in another. "I'm not sure the zoo's a good idea," he said.

"Why not?"

"Well . . ." Taj stood, stretched his back, eyed the stack of boxes. "Mind if I rummage around in there?"

"Go ahead. The zoo?"

Taj pulled out a pocket knife, cut through the tape, opened a box. Rummaged. I watched. It was a bunch of paper, mostly.

Folders, notebooks, books. "So, I did some research this morning," Taj said. "I found out there's a huge surge in the trade of rare and endangered animals. Huge. People are speculating in them as if they were real estate or stocks. Black-market animal-part shops are springing up all over the planet. Then there's the Internet trade. Exponential."

"It's illegal, though, right?" I said.

"Oh yeah. But that doesn't stop it." He pulled out a stack of lab notebooks. "Mind if I take some of these? I'll scan them and get them back."

He opened one. There were Mom's little bird scratchings. So familiar. You had to strain to read when she left you a note. I stared at the page, swallowing against a sudden thickness in my throat.

"Okay." I trusted Taj—because Mom did. She'd want him to have whatever he needed. Anyway, the cat was already out of the bag, lizardwise.

Taj cut into the second box. Supplies: cotton swabs, rags, latex gloves, baggies, sterile wipes. Spade, flashlight, pH paper, scale. "So," he said, "you've got your poachers, most of them trying to get by, some of them trying to get rich. You've got your rich people, collecting rare animal artifacts the way they collect art. You've got your tribal medicine men, using exotic-animal body parts for so-called medicinal purposes. You've got your high-end restauranteurs, if you can believe it, serving up exotic animals for the cachet. You've got your cryptid hunters, because they want their name on a new species. You've got your speculators, stockpiling rare stuff of any kind whatsoever to sell later when it's even rarer. You've got your biopirates, collecting for the genetic resource. . . ."

"But . . ." I said.

Taj looked up. He seemed uncomfortable. "Your mom gets clearance," he said. "There's a difference."

"Does she have clearance for . . ." I nodded toward the lizard.

"Uh, I'm looking into it."

"Like the zoo."

"Already did that. Not sure it'll work." He cut open another box. Rummaged. It was full of crumpled advertising flyers and paper-wrapped jars full of dirt. "Mind if I borrow a couple of these?"

"No. What's wrong with the zoo?"

Taj slit open the fourth box. More dirt. "Turns out," he said, "rare animals are disappearing from zoos right now. They think there might be a black-market syndicate, with some people in zoos getting paid off. The FBI is working on it, but just last week another blue-tongued lizard went missing from the Oregon Zoo."

"Then what am I supposed to do? How can I feed it all the time? I have to go to school. I have to sleep. And it squeaks. If Aunt Pen hears it—just once—she's gonna go full-out seismic orbital; you have no idea what she's like. She exterminates *squirrels*." I took a breath. I could hear myself—over-the-edge, way fused out—but I didn't care. "There were squirrels in her attic last spring—squirrels *raising their babies*—and she called in the exterminator and had them all murdered. All of them, Taj. Every single one."

"Whoa there," he said. "There might be a zoo somewhere that's okay. I'll find out—"

"What about you? Why can't you take it? Why is it all *my* responsibility?"

"Bryn," Taj said. "I can't. I live in married student housing—"

"But it's Mom's, Taj. It's Mom's. It's her work. Am I the only one who cares?"

"—in a tiny apartment with my very pregnant wife. Who is having trouble with the pregnancy, thank you very much, and has been sent to bed on doctor's orders. The last thing she needs is some needy cryptid baby to take care of, when she ought to be taking care of herself."

Oh, God. I'd had no idea.

"Look," Taj said. He closed up the box, set it back on the stack. "Seems to me there's a short-term problem and a long-term problem. I can do some quiet calling to people I trust. But it's going to take a while. Meantime, there's your Aunt Pen to deal with. You're going to have to do that."

I'd wanted Taj to take care of it. Just take it off my hands. If not today, tomorrow. But I could see that wasn't going to happen. Taj's idea of short-term was way too long for me. Hopefully, Dad would come up with something.

"Can you think of a place where you could keep the lizard for a little while?" Taj asked. "Like maybe at your house? The garage? Some kind of outbuilding? Someplace you could get to easily, and where nobody could hear?"

Dad's ceramics studio. It was far enough from Aunt Pen's that you probably wouldn't hear the lizard squeaking from there.

It might work for a few days.

I told Taj. "Perfect!" he said. "You take the lizard, I'll get everything else."

"But what about the feedings? I can't stay home from school every day."

"It's a short-term problem," he said. "Maybe I can help."

11 CRYPTID, DORMANT

EUGENE, OREGON

We made our way across Aunt Pen's back deck, along her tidy stone path, and through the gate that led to my backyard. Whole different ecosystem, this side of the fence. I led Taj through tall, wet grass dotted with clumps of weeds and scattered with birdhouses and bird feeders mounted on poles. Mom and Dad called our yard "natural"; Aunt Pen called it "the jungle." She was always complaining about the dandelion fluff that supposedly wafted over the fence and took root in her lawn. Though I'd never seen a dandelion in Aunt Pen's yard. Not once.

The shed stood a little way off from our house, behind the garage. I balanced the lizard box on one hip, then, on tiptoe, reached up and felt along the top of the doorjamb. Found the key. Let us in.

Daylight leaked in through the smudgy windows; ancient spiderwebs sagged from the ceiling. I wiped my shoes on the mat, then set down the lizard box on the marble-topped work-table, beside the tools for cutting and shaping clay. The studio smelled of clay dust, like Dad. I breathed it in, absurdly hoping to find him sitting at the wheel, where darkness thickened at the far side of the room.

I flipped the light switch. The lone compact flo on the ceiling pushed the shadows back into the corners and deep into the shelves, behind the rows of pots, glazed and unglazed, waiting for the kiln. The potter's wheel stood empty in the light.

Taj set the shopping bags on the floor. "This is your Dad's place? Where he works?"

I nodded. "He left Intel, when Mom——"

I stopped. So many sentences did that to me—ambushed me in the middle and headed straight for Mom. Dad had taken an indefinite leave of absence to look for Mom. He'd grown a beard, which made him look like a big, old gentle bear.

"Yeah," Taj said. Sounding uncomfortable. "Yeah, well, look. Your dad wouldn't mind if we cleared off a shelf, would he? Doesn't feel right to have the lizard out in the open, unprotected. We could find another place for some of the pots and fit the box here."

We moved the pieces carefully, shifting some to the shelf with the glazes and others to the top of the kiln. Clay dust silted the air and twinkled in the sideways shafts of sunlight that cut through the window grime.

It was kind of spooky, looking over Dad's work. Like scanning some deep, secret part of him. When he'd first taken up pottery, he'd turned out plain, geometric vases, urns, and bowls. Form follows function. Like that.

But after Mom disappeared, his work had gotten darker, even bizarre. Goblets with huge, prickly thistles winding up their stems. A set of mugs shaped like a family of gargoyles. An urn with a crocodile growing out of its side. And here on the unglazed shelf were mostly things that had no function at all. A seated harpy. A yawning troll. A prancing dragon. Three griffins—one rearing up on its hind legs, one sleeping, one laughing. Dad had penciled in titles on slips of paper tucked underneath each of the griffins. Heraldry terms. Rearing: *Griffin Rampant*. Sleeping: *Griffin Dormant*. Laughing: *Griffin Riant*.

"Is that a refrigerator?" Taj asked.

I nodded. Dad liked to have cold drinks while he was working. He was a fiend for Dr Pepper.

"So if it doesn't drink a whole can of ReliaVite at a single sitting, you can save what's left over in the can," Taj said. "It'll last longer that way."

That *you* again. "If it'll drink it cold," I said.

"Ah, yeah. You're going to have to try that."

What's with the *you*, Taj? I thought you said you were going to help.

Taj pulled a bunch of stuff out of the shopping bags. He ripped the cellophane wrapping off a litter box, lined it with plastic, and poured in a bunch of sawdust pellets. "This is what they do in pet stores," he said. "Put pellets on the bottoms of the lizards' cages. They keep their lizards in aquariums, but the litter box'll be fine for now. Your guy's not going anywhere for a while." He brandished a blue pooper scooper. "Pretty soon you'll be a pro with this."

Superb. I'd been blocking out that part.

"Look what else I got." He pulled out a little bag with an

REI logo. "I'm brilliant," he said. "They're not going to call me 'doctor' for nothing."

"Uh-huh." I'd known a lot of people called "doctor" who didn't seem all that brilliant to me. "What is it?"

Taj opened the bag and pulled out two pairs of socks.

"Socks?" I said. "This is brilliant?"

"SolarSox. Charge one pair while you're using the other. No cords required. Say good-bye to the hot water bottle."

Okay. Good call.

It occurred to me that Taj must have spent a significant amount of money on this. His own money, since old Reynolds sure wasn't going to pay for it. And grad students are notoriously poor.

"Do you think it's okay?" I asked him, suddenly insecure. "The Slendah? The ReliaVite and the socks? I mean, we don't know what it is. What if we're, like, killing it?"

"I checked around too, Bryn. I think it's okay. You did good."

We looked down at the lizard, still sleeping. Still pinkish tan. It wasn't just the Slendah drips. The pink was all over.

"You want to do the honors," Taj asked, "or shall I?"

Strangely, I did. I slid my hand under the lizard's belly, picked it up. It was limp, and actually kind of warm. It moaned and melted in against me. Like a friendly old cat, but lighter. Its little birdy claws hooked themselves into my sweater. I unsnagged them, one at a time. The critter swiveled its head around, snuffled blindly at my neck, and revved up with the vibrating.

Taj opened the REI bag, started fiddling with the socks. I

pulled the critter close and nestled its head against one shoulder, like Mom taught me to hold Piper when she was a baby. Its microfiberish skin had dried. It felt velvety and soft. I could feel it breathing against me, easy and slow.

Cryptid, dormant.

Taj clicked the solar collectors into the socks and set them on the windowsill. He turned to me and bowed.

"Bravo!" I said.

He smiled. Still cute. "You'll have to do the water bottle until they charge. And, hey," he said, "do you think it would bite me if I took a mouth swab?"

"I don't know," I said. "I don't think so." The critter seemed pretty mellow at the moment.

From his backpack, Taj produced a glass jar and a cotton swab. He nudged the swab tip into the corner of the critter's mouth and swabbed around in there. The critter yawned.

Taj dropped the swab in the jar. "Have you told anyone else about this guy?" he asked. "Any of your friends?"

"No. Only, well, Piper knows."

"You told *Piper*?"

"I couldn't help it. She was with me when it was hatching. I thought it was going to be like an ostrich or something."

"I hope you told her not to tell anyone."

"Of course I did. But she's five. She's going to tell, eventually."

Taj swore under his breath. "So there's probably not much time."

The critter nuzzled one bony cheek ridge against my shoulder. I reached up, scratched above its eye ridges. It moved its head so that I was scratching just beneath its chin. Taj frowned.

"What?" I asked.

He dove into another bag, pulled out the six-packs of Relia-Vite. "How much did it drink last night?"

"Maybe half a can."

"And you fed it again this morning?"

"Yeah. Another half can. It doesn't all get inside him, though. The feeding's kind of tricky."

"Problems with the delivery system? Or is it your technique?"

Like to see you try, I thought. But no. Be nice. He's helping.

"I think we're going to have to feed it three or four times a day, at least," he said. "For a while."

We. I liked the sound of that. "Okay," I said.

"Seems like you could maybe get up early and feed it before school. And then again in the afternoon. I could do a late-night feeding. I work till eleven most nights. And you're practically on my way home."

"But the critter'll be alone most of the day. Probably scared. Probably squeaking."

"It'll be fine, Bryn. And no one will hear it out here. I'll need a key, though. Can I take this and get one made? I'll leave the old one on the doorsill tonight."

"Stellar," I said.

The critter's thrumming ramped up. I looked down at him, scratched along the edge of his jaw. He started to knead my shoulder, knead me with his claws. Good thing I had on a thick sweater.

Silly Mr. Lizard.

"What?" Taj asked.

I turned to him, plexed.

"You're smiling," he said.

"He, like, purrs."

"With you, it does." Taj was frowning again.

"What?" I asked.

"You called it *he*."

I shrugged. It just felt like a *he*.

"Aren't you going to put it in the new box?"

"I will in a minute."

Taj narrowed his eyes. "You know what imprinting is?"

"No, Taj, I've never taken a bio class in my life. I don't know any biologists, and I've never heard anybody even mention the word 'imprinting.'"

Taj sighed. "No need to get pissy. I'm just saying. It acts as if it thinks you're its mother or something. And if it is imprinted . . . well, the zoo is going to be tough."

I stroked the critter's head. He pressed against my fingers, tilting so that I was rubbing a place just between his squinched-shut eyes.

"I'm going now," Taj said. "I'll return the key."

He was halfway out the door when I called to him. "Hey, Taj."

He turned back.

"Thanks. I mean it. Thank you."

He nodded, let himself out.

I moved my hand to rub against the critter's eye ridges. He butted against my palm, and the purring thing amped up until there was a river of vibration flowing across my body.

I think you're in trouble, I told myself.

Seriously in trouble.

12

SOMEPLACE REALLY REMOTE

EUGENE, OREGON

Dad called that night, but the connection was bad. He was someplace really remote, he said. He was "onto something," he said. Onto what, I never quite got. I told him about the lizard, but I wasn't sure he understood. He said something like "Does Pen know?" Or maybe it was something about a window. There was a bunch of static right then. I couldn't hear a thing.

But if he had really understood me, wouldn't he have done something? I didn't know exactly what, but something. Instead, he said he might not be able to call for the next several days, maybe even a week, but that I shouldn't worry. As if I could keep from worrying. "Why can't you call?" I asked. He was onto something, he said again. Then came another blast of static, and the phone went dead. "Love you," I said into the empty air.

I set down the phone, slumped back against my pillow. Stella nipped down from my shoulder and meandered around on my chest. She stretched up, nibbled at my ear.

Onto something. What could that mean? Onto something about Mom?

I knew I shouldn't hope for too much. That's what everybody said. Even the ones who told me not to give up hope when Mom first disappeared last fall. But now it was: Don't get your hopes up too high.

But hope, it just does whatever it's going to do. Sometimes it flakes out on you when you really need it. Other times it hangs around way too long, after everybody's left the party and the lights have all been turned out. You can bust out trying to squish hope down, but you're wasting your time. If hope wants to lift you up out of the wreckage so you can get creamed again, you just have to take it.

One good thing: The feedings were going okay. Mr. Lizard was really glugging down the ReliaVite. Even cold. Not that it didn't take me a while to get the hang of it. Over the next week, I managed to squirt pink goo on the critter's neck, on his back, on his chest, and on his tail. Plus all over the new box and the pellets and the floor. Once, I accidentally squirted ReliaVite up one of the critter's nostrils. He started shaking his head and doing a funny whuffing thing, kind of like sneezing. He kept it up for a monster long time. I've killed him, I thought. I've murdered the last of a super-endangered species. But he calmed down after a while.

My only consolation was that Taj was having trouble, too. Every morning I found new pink splatters in assorted inappropriate locations.

Trouble with the technique, there, eh, Taj?

The business with the pee and the poop turned out not to be so bad, but I went through a megaton of sawdust pellets. At first, I scooped the dirty ones into plastic baggies and threw them in Aunt Pen's garbage can. But the bags started mounting up, looking kind of obvious in there, looking like something Aunt Pen might notice. So I tried strewing the stuff over the parts of Aunt Pen's backyard where there was bark dust under the trees, and that seemed to work pretty well. Sometimes I raked it, to mix it with the bark. Make it, like, match. I didn't think it would hurt the trees. It was organic, right? Fertilizer.

Piper was a problem. Not so much with the early-morning feedings but in the afternoons. My first plan had been to tell her that the critter had gone to a secret lizard farm out in the desert of eastern Oregon, a farm with special sun-warmed rocks to bask on and buckets of yummy crickets and mealworms to eat. That way, if Piper spilled it, people would think she was making it up. Crazy kid. What an imagination!

But Piper went to the after-school program only three afternoons a week, and when she was home she pretty much barnacled herself to me, and Mr. Lizard had to be fed. I had no choice. Had to take her with me. Every time, though, I swore her to secrecy. Literally. I made her raise her right hand and swear.

One night at dinner, Aunt Pen kind of casually said to me, "Unless I'm mistaken, your dad hasn't called for five days."

I looked up from my enchiladas. Piper did too. Aunt Pen didn't expect to talk to Dad every time he called. "I'm not *his* sister, after all," she had said. She had said this more than once. But apparently, she was keeping track.

"Yeah," I said. "I told you. He's someplace really remote. He warned me he might not be able to call for a while."

Aunt Pen said, "Hmm." It was quick and light, that *Hmm*, but there was a whole world in it. Mom's disappearing. The chance that lightning could strike twice.

By the time a week had passed with no word from Dad, I was pretty much a train wreck. *Maybe even a week,* he had said. I hadn't let myself think about longer. Now the scenarios started scrolling through my head, just like last fall. The good ones, where Dad had found Mom somewhere or other, and she was fine, and they were out of phone range, or they couldn't use one for some reason, or Dad had lost the charger, or maybe they were planning to show up on Aunt Pen's doorstep: Surprise!

Then came the web-of-doom scenarios, crowding out the good ones: the car wrecks, the airplane crashes, the botulism beans. The heart attacks, the rabid dogs, the chemical spills. The drownings, the freezings, the falls.

It got harder and harder to sleep. It's true that I was totally wiped, but I had this weird, restless energy; I couldn't stand to be inside my own skin. I wanted to squirt right out of it and fly off to a different time, a time in the near future when I knew that Dad was okay. Or maybe to some alternate universe where Mom was safe at home, where that professor, that Dr. Jones, had never called her and invited her up to Alaska.

I floated through classes in a strange kind of bubble, seeing but not seeing, hearing but not hearing. I crashed at random times. Zoned out in pre-calc. Nodded off in pan-global. Almost fell off my chair in Chinese.

Once, in the hallway, I almost walked smack into an open locker door. "Whoa there, zombie girl!" I turned toward the voice.

There was Sasha, just behind me. "Wake up!" she said. "You just about got *doored*." She put a hand between my shoulder blades and eased me away from the lockers and into the flow of moving kids.

The one thing in my life that—bizarrely—seemed to calm me down and center me was the critter. By the second week, we'd settled into a routine. He started squeaking when I stepped in the door, but stopped the moment I spoke to him. He swiveled his head around, eyes still squeezed shut. Sniffing—seeming to track my movements by smell.

I took to feeding him on my lap. I sat cross-legged on the floor, supporting him with one hand and squeezing the turkey baster bulb with the other. He leaned back into me as he drank. Thrumming in his throat. Kneading my legs with his claws. When I stroked his skin/fur, a fine powder came off on my fingers. If I blew on them, the powder lifted off, hung in the air, shimmered in the light. It felt like we were in the center of a hurricane—a little hollowed-out space of peace.

Things were changing in the critterworld. For one thing, he was growing. Kind of mediumish cat-size now—way bigger than petite little Asteroid.

One day, I noticed that his skin/fur stuff had started to pull away near the tops of his feet. Underneath, I could see tiny, pinkish scales. The next day, a row of pointy spines poked Mohawk-style through the skin/fur on his backbone. I fingered two hard nodules on either side of his spine. He was a bumpy guy, but these seemed bigger than before.

Another day I brought Stella with me, buttoned inside my

jacket. In the shed, I kenned her to my shoulder. We leaned over the critter, still sleeping in his plastic box. I tickled him under his chin. He yawned, lifted his head . . . and, for the first time, opened his eyes.

Whoa.

He stared straight at us, eyes wide. Acid green. Almond-shaped. Weird, vertical pupils.

Stella chirruped low in her throat. The critter chirruped back, sounding eerily similar. Stella jumped onto his back and pecked at bits of loose skin/fur, grooming him. "Hey," I said. "I don't think that's safe." I tried to ken with her, but something was happening with her—happening with *them*—some private exchange I couldn't port into.

Talking to each other?

And then I felt it, a kind of seeking, a tingle in my mind.

Kenning?

It felt clueless and glumfy, like my first kennings with Stella when she was a baby bird. But there was a deeper freq too, almost subliminal—a hum beneath the surface.

Then it was gone.

Kenning.

This guy kens.

I shivered. In all the family stories, no one had ever kenned with anything other than birds. Never.

Stella fluffed her feathers. She made that sound again, that throaty, chirruping thing. She cocked her head and fizzed me a proud little ken.

"How long have *you* known about this?" I asked her.

Late that night, I heard voices. I stepped into the hallway to listen.

Only Aunt Pen, talking on the phone. "What in heaven's name is he thinking, stringing the girls along this way!"

I froze. There was a pause.

"Well," she said, "they need their father at home. Especially now. They seem to be holding up—God only knows how. They're tough little gals. But it's not fair to them. Not fair at all."

Must be one of Aunt Pen's friends from Bountiful. Her door stood partway open. I tiptoed near to hear better.

"He *was* calling," she said. "He promised to call every night. But now it's been well over a week. Nearly two weeks. Stubborn, selfish man!"

I ducked back into my room, shut the door behind me. How dared she! Dad wasn't selfish—he was trying to find out about Mom.

But still . . . I felt a sting behind my eyes. *Tough little gals.* I never knew she thought of us that way.

I sat on the bed and mentally scrolled through that last conversation with Dad. He'd sounded sorry, and stressed, but there'd been something else too. *Onto something.*

Was it Mom he was onto?

Last fall, the police had checked her e-mail for clues. Maybe there were some clues in Dad's inbox. But to snoop his mail . . .

No. That was just wrong.

For sure he'd call any day now. Maybe tomorrow.

I skootched under the covers, flipped over into fetal, tried to get some sleep.

Onto something.

What? What was Dad onto?

13
JUST WRONG

EUGENE, OREGON

In the end, I had to snoop.

The next day, I did the after-school feeding, then headed over to the house. My house. Hadn't been there for a while.

I let myself in the front door, and something crunched under my shoe.

I lifted my foot. Three squished bugs on the floor. Ladybugs. Little globules of yellowish liquid bled out of their shells. Another ladybug dropped with a soft *click* onto the tiles.

I looked up.

Clouds of ladybugs trembled on the ceiling. They pixilated the windows, the table, the couch, the walls; they crusted over the skylights. Another *click*: A ladybug fell from the ceiling and landed on a lampshade. *Click* on the woodstove. *Click* on the coffee table. *Click. Click. Click.*

A drift of ladybugs lifted off the skylight and floated across the room. Their wings caught the sunlight, morphed watery images of color and shadow and light across the walls. It felt like a visitation of something spooky-sacred, like when people see unexplained lights in the sky, maybe, or one of those deals where the Virgin Mary shows up in the glass wall of a hospital or a bank.

But there was something *wrong* about it too. Broken. Out of whack. Like the swarms of possums and voles and raccoons. Like the whales beaching themselves and dying. Like the deformed crocodiles in Florida swamps. Like the spate of mutant human babies in Texas and Iowa, born with webbed fingers and flippery toes. Like the plumes of toxic chemicals on Mom's maps— stretching their poisonous tentacles into water tables and rivers and lakes and oceans.

Another bug cloud spun off from the ceiling. It fluttered down, passed through me, and now I was full of them: my face, my hair, my sweater, my hands.

Terrible. Wonderful. Terrible.

I shook out my hair, brushed at my sweater, aching so fiercely for Dad to be here, or Mom. They would know what to do, what powers to invoke. No poison would pass the threshold. But there would be smoke, or there would be noise, or there would be cardboard traps that snagged their prey live, or there would be *something*, something that shooed the little critters out of our space and encouraged them to find new homes.

I tiptoed around the ladybug clusters on the floor, made my way to the home office. Way fewer bugs in here. Still, I brushed a couple off Dad's chair and blew one off the keyboard. Sat down. Powered up Dad's CPU. Logged on to his e-mail.

Which also felt wrong.

I scrolled past messages from the Potters' Guild, the American

Ceramic Society, the Association of Retired Public Relations Professionals. Word-a-day. Amazon new book alert. Sporting Cosmos loved Dad, apparently. So did Hardware Arsenal. There was an e-mail from his friend David Larkins, asking if he could go hiking next week. There was one from his clay supplier, telling him about a great new offer if he reordered now. A few were from his old Intel friends. *How are you, Buddy? Any news?* One guy, Cliff Moray, seemed worried. *Pardon my saying, but maybe you should see someone. You've been through a lot.*

Seismic creepy, spying on your very own dad.

One e-mail had a red "urgent" marker. From mjones@alaskastate.edu.

mjones: Dr. Mungo Jones. The professor who had called Mom to come up last fall. And then she'd disappeared.

Call me, the e-mail said. *With all due haste.* No signature block. No phone number. Nothing.

It was dated two days ago.

With all due haste? Who even talks like that?

Alaska State was in Anchorage. I knew that from before. And the storage locker, the one with Mom's boxes . . . also in Anchorage.

I clicked on Dad's database, checked for Dr. Jones. Nothing there.

Back to the e-mail. I hit reply. *What is it?* I wrote. But I couldn't send it. Just wrong.

I exited Dad's e-mail program, googled "Mungo Jones." Found him on the Alaska State College website. Biology Department, specializing in wildlife biology, zoology, and cryptozoology.

He'd written a bunch of books. I scrolled down to a picture of him in what must be his office. Black man. Salt-and-pepper hair. Deep-set greenish eyes that looked kindly and amused.

I zoomed in on the picture, clicked around, checking out the office. Lots of books in cases. Framed documents and sketches of animals on the wall.

Strange-looking animals.

Wait a minute. Something there among the books. I zoomed in closer. A bird, perched on a shelf. Some kind of falcon.

Might be taxidermy, but it looked real.

Green eyes and a bird.

Could it be?

No.

I'd never heard of a kenner outside of our family.

Who was this guy? Why had he called Mom up to Alaska? Why did he want to talk to Dad now?

My phone rang. I blinked.

Dad?

I checked caller ID.

Blocked.

"Hello?" I said. No answer. "Hello?"

Hope pushed up inside me. "Dad?" I asked. "Are you there? Dad?"

The phone went dead. I stared at it. Beeped off.

Probably some phaging telemarketer.

Click. A ladybug landed on the desk. I stared at it a moment, then logged onto Satellite Earth. I zoomed in on Alaska, then Cook Inlet, then Anchorage.

Where are you, Dad?

Zooming out, now, panning east. Mountains. Narrow, winding roads. Clicking randomly across the maps. South, to islands. North and east, to mountains. Trying to peer down into the spaces between the pixels.

Is anybody there, anybody lost, anybody stranded, anybody hurt? Anybody wearing a Pendleton shirt and a navy blue jacket, anybody with a thick, brown-bear beard? Some stubborn, selfish man who doesn't care enough about his daughters, left them with all that hope hanging out there with nowhere to go.

What was he thinking?

Where are you, Dad?

Where are you?

Aunt Pen found me facedown on Dad's desk, drooling on the keyboard. "Bryn!" she said. *"Bryn!"*

Even half asleep, I could tell she was seriously annoyed.

I lifted my head. Dad's screen saver was running, the one he'd downloaded from Mom: tiny microbes munching away at the sludgy brownish desktop until it was all clear, all clear blue water. Then it crudded over and the microbes went at it again.

I couldn't have been out long, or the computer would have gone to sleep. Still, it was darkish in here now. The screen bled blue onto the empty desk, and red and green LEDs glowed in the shadows.

"Bryn. There are *bugs* all over the house."

I rubbed my eyes. "I know."

"It's positively infested!"

I shrugged. The bugs didn't seem like such a huge deal, considering. Dad hadn't called for nearly two weeks. That was a problem. The bugs were just bugs.

"I'm speechless, Bryn. You should have told me right away. I can't—" Aunt Pen stopped, took a deep breath, seemed to reboot. "You'd better come home, Bryn. Dinner's ready and—"

I *am* home, I thought.

"—and your dad might call—"

On the phone I carry with me everywhere, I thought.

"—and you shouldn't be alone now, honey. You just shouldn't. Bryn—"

Aunt Pen drew near, her perfume too sweet—annoying—and I knew she wanted to hug me. I felt my body stiffen.

Aunt Pen sighed, moved away. "Bryn, I'm worried too," she said. "I miss him. I miss both of them. I was missing you. Come home, please?"

When Dad didn't call that night, Aunt Pen began to Take Things in Hand. She put Piper to bed early, then set up a control center at the dining room table and mobilized forces like an army general—calling people, texting them, IMing them, paging them. Dragging them away from their evening activities, summoning them to her at half-hour intervals throughout the next day. The cops would send a detective tomorrow morning. A lawyer, an accountant, and yard and housekeeping services would all show up.

Plus an exterminator, for the ladybugs.

Mom and Dad would never have let an exterminator in the

house. Never. But Aunt Pen insisted they'd use only *safe* pesticides. As if there were such a thing. She said our bugs weren't ladybugs at all, but Asian lady beetles. Invasive. Like kudzu. She had a wild look in her eye—neat fiend on overdrive—kind of desperate and fried.

The list stretched out on the pad in front of her. Forward Dad's mail to this house. Cancel the magazine subscriptions. Leave phone and e-service for a month, then re-evaluate.

"He's not gone," I said. "He's just a few days late."

"I'm not saying he's gone!" Aunt Pen snapped. She lowered her face into her hands. Stayed like that for a couple of seconds. Looked up at me again. "Preparing for eventualities is not saying they're going to happen. It's just preparing."

But she *was* saying it. Everything she did was screaming it. *He's lost too. He's not coming back, not ever.*

I felt a tight, airless box closing around me, a box that sealed out my old life, a box where I couldn't be Bryn anymore, a box that didn't admit the possibility that Dad could turn up tomorrow or the next day, apologizing like crazy but otherwise fine. And maybe—miraculously—with Mom beside him.

And what about the critter? There'd be random people wandering all over our house and yard. And the police—they'd investigate Dad. Download his database, like they did with Mom. Root through his stuff. Confiscate "evidence" and not give it back.

And sooner or later, somebody was bound to come sniffing around Dad's studio.

I ran upstairs and called Taj. "We've got trouble," I said.

"Tell me about it."

Very un-Taj sounding. Ironic. Like he knew all about trouble, had plenty of it himself. But I didn't want to hear about his trouble. Just plowed on through with my own. Told him what Aunt Pen was doing. "She's gone stratospheric—treating a bunch of ladybugs like they're carrying hantavirus or something. And the critter's not safe anymore. They could fumigate the shed. Anyway, someone's gonna go in there, an exterminator or the cops, or . . . someone. They won't care that the critter's super-endangered. They . . ."

Funny background noises coming over the phone. Lots of voices. Some clattery sounds.

"Taj?" I asked. "Where are you?"

He sighed. "I'm in the hospital. Jasmine has gone into labor early and they're trying to stop it."

All the words flew out of me.

"It's not as bad as it sounds," Taj said. "I don't think. It happened once before and it was fine."

"I . . . I'm sorry," I said. "I mean, not that it was fine, but—"

"I know what you mean. Look, I still have some ideas. Although . . ."

"Although what?"

"I'm having a hard time imagining where this thing belongs. Where's its ecological niche? Does it even have one? And what happens if we introduce it someplace it doesn't belong? And if it's this big now, think how big it's going to get. It's going to be dangerous, Bryn."

"But—"

"Okay, I'm looking, though. Long term. But about the short term . . ." More voices in the background. "You've got enough food and everything for a couple of days, don't you?" he said.

"Yeah, but—"

"If you had a friend with a car, you could just pack everything up for a few hours if it looks like someone's going in there."

"I'm a freshman. None of my friends have cars."

Background noises. A siren.

"I still think the lizard's safer in the shed than anywhere else I can think of," Taj said. "Maybe nobody'll go in there. I'm working on it; I'll come up with something. And if . . . if they find it, well, you can't blame yourself. You did the best you could."

"That can't happen."

"Yeah, but if it does . . ."

"It's Mom's. It's *her* thing, Taj. Nothing can happen to it."

Voices. Someone talking to Taj.

"I have to go, Bryn. Hang in there. I'll call you when I can."

14  RATTLED

NEAR HAINES, ALASKA

Josh heard a crunch of gravel and looked up to see Wayne Hazleton's pickup heading up the drive. He lifted the axe overhead and brought it down once more, relaxing his grip a second before the blade bit into the wood. The wood split clean and easy, all the way to the block. Josh set the pieces in the pile, inhaling the sweet smell of fresh-cut hemlock. He'd been hoping to finish the stack before dinner, but Wayne was going to want to talk. Going to want to hear about the eggs.

"Joshua," Wayne said, sliding out of the truck. He shut the door and ambled over to the woodpile, hitching up his belt beneath his belly overhang. Wayne was a big man, big all over. But he moved with a gliding kind of grace, like a walrus in the water.

Josh nodded. "Wayne."

"How goes the battle?"

"Can't complain."

"Hear you found yourselves some eggs."

There you go. Wayne was in on the fossil poaching. Tight little unit, led by Cap and sworn to secrecy. Wayne was also

Josh's boss in the summers. Owner of the gillnetter he worked on

Josh nodded. "Yeah. On the Kenai. Petrified. Some kind of lizard or dinosaur."

"Think you got 'em all?" Wayne asked.

Josh shrugged. "A couple broke. And there were supposed to be some others, some newer ones. You hear about those?"

"Yup."

They never had come across those fragments Quinn had talked about. But Quinn had stuck to his story. Claimed his prof had threatened to turn him in for poaching unless he surrendered the newer egg to him.

"I hear some of our guys went poking around for it," Wayne said.

"Poking around for what?"

"That other egg. The one Quinn gave the professor."

"Where?" Josh asked.

"Prof's office. And his home."

"He let them in?"

Wayne pushed back the bill of his cap. Squinted at him.

"They *broke in*?"

Wayne shrugged. "This is serious business, Joshua. It's not just the money. You know what would happen if a fresh one ever surfaced. A TV reporter behind every bush. Tree huggers and G-men swarming in here like a plague of locusts. Poachers popping off anything that twitched. And lawyers! You couldn't take a crap without an affidavit."

But Josh was still with the break-in. They actually broke in? "Did *Cap* know about it?" he asked.

Wayne didn't answer. He spotted a beetle on his jacket and flicked it off.

Cap couldn't have known. Could he? He'd have put an end to it. Taking fossils was one thing, but this was something else.

"Didn't find anything, anyway," Wayne said. "That Quinn guy probably made it up."

Right. Quinn liked to talk, make himself look important. But Cap . . .

Wayne cocked his head, studying Josh. "You're still with us, right, Joshua?"

"Yeah," Josh said. He looked down at the dirt, scuffed his toe. Was he with them? He wasn't sure anymore. He didn't like the poaching—not at all. And Cap had changed, since the divorce. Times had gotten tough for him, and he seemed . . . harder than he used to be.

"Cap said you were kind of rattled about those eggs."

Rattled. Josh felt the blood rush into his face. Was that what Cap had said?

He hadn't been rattled. He'd been ticked. Annoyed at Zack. Bothered about the poaching. Humiliated by Cap.

Which was why he hadn't told about the sat phone right away. The phone he'd found near the far opening of the cave.

He'd planned to tell Cap. Eventually. After he'd charged the phone and found out whose it was.

But he'd held on to it way too long, deciding what to do, and now it was too late. If he told now, Cap would know he'd kept something from him. Wasn't with the program.

Had Cap sent Wayne to check up on him?

"I'm fine with it," Josh said. "I'm fine." He set up a piece of hemlock, lifted the axe, brought it down hard, all the way to the block. The shock of the striking blade jarred the tense muscles in his arms and shoulders and back.

"Whoa, easy there, son," Wayne said. "Keep that up, you're gonna tear yourself apart." He hitched his belt. "A word to the wise, Joshua: Don't mess with us. We need total commitment. If you can't give us that . . ." He shrugged. "Well, I know Cap. He won't say much, but he will cut you out."

Josh watched him as he left. The sun, sinking toward the western mountains, struck glittering sparks off Lynn Canal. Overhead, an eagle caught a thermal and drifted slowly higher. When Wayne's pickup had disappeared around the bend, Josh sat down on the chopping block. Pulled the sat phone out of his pocket. Turned it on.

It hadn't been hard finding a charger; eBay'd had a bunch. Josh had played around with the phone long enough to figure out whose it was. That other professor, the woman from Oregon. The one who'd disappeared.

Josh scrolled through the options, brought up the family pictures. Or at least, he guessed they must be family pictures. There was a studio group shot of the professor herself and a husband and two daughters. Vacation shots of the same people at a mountain, a beach, a lake. Close-ups of each daughter alone. A girl who looked five or six, with a canary sitting on top of her head. An older girl with a cockatiel on her shoulder. Eighth grade, maybe? Ninth?

Something about the older one got him. Not that she was hot or anything. But something about her . . .

Her eyes were green. So were her sister's. He'd never seen eyes that green. The older girl's eyes turned down a little at the corners, making her look serious, even when she smiled. He wondered if she was the one he'd called. On the speed-dial line called "B." After he'd blocked caller ID.

He could still hear her voice, the saddest voice he'd ever heard: *Dad? Are you there? Dad?*

Josh could relate. He knew what it was like to miss your father. Sometimes even when you were with him.

He turned off the phone, stuffed it back in his pocket.

He'd better get rid of this thing. Dump it. Next time he was in town, he'd throw it off the end of a dock.

15
A FRIEND WITH A CAR

EUGENE, OREGON

The thing that got wedged in my brain and wouldn't come unstuck was what Taj had said about a friend with a car.

I did have a friend with a car.

Sort of.

Sort of a friend.

Sort of a car.

I'd seen Sasha in her car in the school parking lot. It was a little VW, paleo-old. Doors: rusted out. Paint: all patchy. Engine: rough and loud.

The possibility of a car changed everything.

I went up to my room at Aunt Pen's, found Sasha's number, and then sat there on the bed looking at it. Texting would be easier, but maybe not as safe. I put Stella on my shoulder for moral support. "Sasha's kind of scary," I explained to her. "Not bad-scary, but still. Plus she's a junior. Plus she doesn't know me all that well." Stella stretched up and nibbled my ear.

Just punch the buttons already.

I punched the buttons. Sasha picked right up. "Hey."

"Sasha?"

"Yeah, Bryn."

"Um, how're you doing?"

"Pretty good. You?" There was a *tone* to it, like, *We'll just do this pointless dance until you're ready to tell me why you called.*

I swallowed. "I have kind of a strange problem. Can I ask you a favor? But you can't tell anybody. It's important to keep it, you know, secret."

"Shoot."

"You won't tell anybody?"

"Cross my heart and hope to die."

Right. I explained, trying not to sound nervous. When I finished, Stella cocked her head and clacked her beak, like she had a comment to make. But from Sasha, nothing.

"Sasha?" I said. "Are you there?" I'd feel monster dim if the connection had broken and I'd just spilled the whole egg story to my bird. Not that I didn't talk to her. But still.

"Wow," Sasha said at last. "That's impressive. Nobody's got problems like you."

Well, at least I was impressive at something.

"I'm sorry about your dad," Sasha went on. "I'm sure he'll be back, though. Things always take longer than people think— that's a rule. But the cryptid lizard. That's exponentially cool."

"Cool" was not the word I personally would have chosen. But if Sasha thought it was cool, that could be good. "Then, you can help?"

"I am so all over it."

‡   ‡   ‡

At midnight, I pulled on a hoodie and jeans and tiptoed into the hall. I stopped by Aunt Pen's room, listened at the door. Snoring. Good. I crept downstairs, snagged a flashlight, whisked a steak knife from the block, and headed down into the basement.

Sasha was supposed to meet me at one, over at my house. But the cops might want to go through the boxes. They might confiscate stuff, like when Mom first disappeared.

I unstacked the boxes, opened the flaps, and set them in a circle around me. One box of supplies. One with folders, note-books, and books. Two with paper-wrapped jars of dirt. Plus the egg box, still full of crumpled paper, which I'd brought back from the shed.

Mom's things.

I imagined her with the boxes, maybe sometime in the future. Opening them up, sorting things out, putting them away. Cheerful and intent, the way she always was in the lab. As comfortable with beakers and pH paper and dirt as with saucepans and olive oil and garlic.

Wait. Something odd in one of the dirt-jar boxes. Wrapped in paper, like everything else, but a different shape.

I pulled it out. Unwrapped it.

It was a roundish, heavyish lump of rock. Almost volleyball size, but way flatter. I held it up to the light. It seemed sculpted, sort of, into mostly hexagonal plates with grooves between them, like the scoring on a chocolate bar. All textured, with little bumps and pits.

Familiar, somehow.

Turtle eggy.

Lizard eggy.

The markings were the same as I remembered, the same as the critter's egg. Except this egg was made out of stone.

Petrified. A petrified egg.

I took it in both hands, let it sit there. It felt heavy. Not just weight heavy but also heavy with—I don't know—some kind of presence. Something terrible and old. I shivered. All of a sudden, I felt cold. All of a sudden, the basement seemed monster dark.

What was I supposed to do?

Why didn't they *tell* me?

Do as your Aunt Pen says. Wait for me, I'll call. Don't worry. Chins up.

Well, I was tired of keeping my chin up. People disappeared. They let you down. Not on purpose, maybe, but they didn't tell you things, and then they left you alone to deal. How were you supposed to know what to do?

Outside, an owl hooted. Lonely sounding. Spooky. I checked my watch: quarter to one. Time to get moving. I had to do the best I could, that was all. Even though I could be messing up supremely. But last time, none of Mom's stuff had helped the cops find her, and we'd never seen most of it again. So the notebooks and the dirt and the weird rock were going out with me.

If the cops had a problem with that, they could just arrest me.

16

A SECURE, UNDISCLOSED LOCATION

EUGENE, OREGON

Sasha showed up at one fifteen. By that time, I'd hauled the boxes out of the basement, across the two backyards, and out to the curb near my house. Which pretty much wiped me out. Then I'd checked Dad's e-mail again and confiscated his backup drive.

I found her leaning against her car. "Hey," she said, her voice soft.

"Hey."

We each picked up a box and hauled it to her trunk. "This your mom's work stuff?" Sasha asked.

"Yeah."

"Biology, right?" She popped the trunk; we set the boxes inside.

"It's actually microbiology," I said.

"Meaning . . ."

"Tries to get microbes to eat environmental toxins. Like, you know, endocrine disruptors."

"Those things in plastics and pesticides? Making us sick?"

"Yeah."

"Wow," Sasha said. We headed back for more boxes. "They do that? Microbes eat that crap?"

"Only certain ones. But Mom knows how to find them." *Knows,* I said. Not *knew.*

"So this stuff is, like, important."

"Yeah." I picked up another box. Yeah, it was important. She had no idea.

When we'd loaded all the boxes, I led Sasha around the side of the house to the studio. It was quiet, except for the faint rattlings of some small animal in the bushes and the swish of our pant legs through the long, wet grass. The moon hung low in the sky—yellow now. No celumbra. I reached for the key on the sill, unlocked the door, pushed it open.

A thin wash of moonlight seeped in through the windows and leaked across the floor, the shelves, the clay-shaping tools.

"Phew," Sasha said. "Does that Taj guy smoke in here?"

It did smell funny, like smoke.

"He used to. I thought he quit." You wouldn't think a guy with a baby on the way would smoke. I beamed the flashlight on the critter. He was fast asleep, curled up with his tail around his nose, sides rising and falling.

"Whoa," Sasha said. She walked to his box, bent down, and stared. *"Whoa!"*

Pretty much the standard response.

"He's huge," Sasha said. "Like, freaky huge. Does he bite?"

"He's a big baby."

She reached out to touch him, then hesitated. "You sure?"

I shrugged. "No guarantees, but I think you're fine."

She moved her hand across his back. "He's got, like, skin or something."

"Yeah, but I think he's molting. Look." I pointed to where the skin/fur was pulling away near his feet, and where his backbone spines had poked through. But now other places were peeling, too. The top of his head. His neck. His belly.

Sasha's hand stopped partway down his back. "What's that?" she asked.

"What?"

"It's all spongy and lumpy in there."

There was a lump, slightly smaller than the palm of my hand. Actually two lumps, one on either side of the critter's spine.

Hadn't they been hard little knots before?

"He's just a lumpy guy," I said.

"What's his name?"

His name. "I don't know," I said. "Piper calls him Mr. Lizard."

"Mr. Lizard. Excellent. The amazing Mr. L. Well, better snag his peripherals and get out of here, huh?"

I bagged the turkey baster, the plastic cup, a couple of cans of ReliaVite, a baggie full of sawdust pellets, and the plastic pooper scooper. "Listen," I said. "The feeding's kind of tricky. You're probably going to make a mess the first time or two. Maybe you want to put down some plastic in your car. Garbage bags or something." It seemed like there was more I ought to tell her. Like maybe I should demonstrate a feeding. What if she couldn't do it? Those skwebs had to affect her dexterity.

"Are we ready?" she asked.

Strangely, no. I wasn't. I leaned over the critter, scratched beneath his jaw. He curled himself tighter, folded his long, curved claws across his eyes. I could feel a faint, thrumming vibration.

"Where will you take him?" I asked.

"To a secure, undisclosed location. So they can't torture it out of you."

Deadpan. She slugged me in the arm.

"Ow!"

"I'm actually not sure," she said. "I think I'll head out to this place where I go hiking. My phone'll be on, so you can give me the all clear."

"You're sure you don't mind cutting school?"

She looked at me. Dumb question. She probably did it all the time. I wondered about her family. Did they know? Did they care?

"I'll call you right after school," I said.

She hefted the grocery bag. I picked up the critter in the litter box. He was twitching his claws, the way I'd seen dogs and cats do when they were dreaming. Dreaming of running, maybe?

What could a brand-new critter have to dream about?

A strange, achy, bruised feeling spread out around my heart. I couldn't seem to move my feet.

Sasha headed for the door. "Let's jet," she said. "We don't have all night."

17
FLY AWAY HOME

EUGENE, OREGON

The moment school let out I powered up my phone and called Sasha. In the background, I could hear the critter squeaking. I felt myself go tense.

"Where are you?" Sasha demanded. "Are you home yet?"

"No, I'm in the parking lot."

Sasha swore. "Can you get home like pronto and find out if the coast is clear? Mr. Lizard doesn't like me. He hisses at me, and snaps. He won't eat and he won't shut up. My head's going nova."

"Sorry."

"Don't apologize. I hate that. Hurry."

The critter's squeaking tugged at me, made me antsy. I picked up the pace, jogged across the street. "Is he okay?" I asked.

"What do you mean, 'okay'? Can't you hear him? I'm going out of my pluperfect mind."

"He wouldn't eat?"

"Are you listening to anything I'm telling you? I couldn't get the pink stuff inside him. And he's swelling up, sort of, like he's got intestinal gas. He's scratching himself against the edge of his box and rubbing off his skin."

"What?"

"Skin! He's scratching off his skin. It's all gone from his head and his legs and his tail. So now what you mostly see is, like, scales. Pink scales."

I'd never seen the critter actually scratching its skin/fur off. Birds did that kind of thing, I knew, when they were stressed-out or sick. Plucked out their feathers. I walked a little faster. "It's probably just the molting thing," I said. "Lizards do that. They molt."

"*Pink* lizards?"

It was more like pinkish brown, but I wasn't going to argue the point.

"Hey, kids," Sasha said, "it's the Barbie lizard. Eats pink food. Craps pink poop. Lives in the Barbie mansion."

Jeez, she was coming unspooled. You wouldn't think a pink reptile would throw her.

"Does he look, like, sick?" I asked.

"Did you hear what you just said? It's a phaging pink lizard! How would I know if it looked sick?"

I sighed.

"Listen, Bryn. There's some other stuff I have to tell you, but not on the phone. Something wicked sketchy's going on. So would you find out—please!—if it's safe to off-load this thing from my car? ASAP! I mean it."

"Okay," I said. I beeped off. Then stuffed my phone in a pocket and ran the rest of the way home.

‡ ‡ ‡

The studio seemed fine. The dust looked undisturbed, so probably no one had been inside.

I picked up my phone to call Sasha, but then thought of something else. What if somebody was still in the house? No cars in the driveway, but I'd better make sure.

I hadn't noticed the yard on the way in. I'd been running. But now I could see what the landscapers had done: pulled out the brownish ground cover against the garage. Blown in bark dust. Hacked all the personality out of the bushes and clipped them into neat, rounded shapes—a row of giant jujubes. Ugly black plastic trays hung from the bottoms of the bird feeders, to catch those nasty seeds before they fell to the ground and sprouted.

There wasn't a dandelion in sight.

I unlocked the front door, stepped inside, and stopped.

Ladybugs. Speckling the floor, the couch, the tabletops, the chairs. Upside up and upside down, but all unmoving, all dead.

I'd known this was going to happen. I had. But seeing them here, all dead, every single one . . .

Ladybug, ladybug, fly away home. Your house is afire, your children are gone.

They're just bugs, I told myself. Not even ladybugs but Asian lady beetles. Invasive.

But they were beautiful, and they didn't bite people or suck their blood or pass along diseases. They only made you feel good, watching them, and they ate the bugs that ate trees and plants.

And it meant our house was full of poison. Microscopic

particles of toxic dust. No matter what those exterminator people tried to tell you, the poison was here, it would be here for a long time, and it did stuff, Mom said, that nobody understood.

The house was quiet. Totally.

Nobody home.

I covered my face with my hands. Breathed. Looked up. Pulled out my cell. Dialed Sasha.

"What!" she said.

"All clear."

"Right." She beeped off.

I crunched across the carpet of ladybug corpses to the study, extruding sad little drops of yellow bug blood. The monitor stood blank-eyed on Dad's desk. But the CPU under the desk was missing. I had the backup, and he'd probably saved everything to the cloud. But the cops had definitely been here.

I opened the study window, breathed in the scent of moist, green, growing things. Things that were alive. I sagged down onto Dad's chair, sprang up. Squished ladybugs on the chair. Yellow bug blood on my butt. I scraped off the corpses with Kleenex and sat down again. Dad's magnifying globe spilled an arc of refracted light across the desk. I cradled the globe, heavy and cool, in my hands. I gazed into it, moved it back and forth, watched the things on the desk stretch and bulge, mutating into weird shapes, familiar yet grotesque. Like my life.

Something wicked sketchy's going on.

I sighed, set down the globe. I got up and moved through the whole house, opening all of the windows, opening them wide. Ventilate. Let the poison out.

Just as I heard Sasha pulling into the driveway, I noticed something flickering in one of the lampshades. I crossed the living room. Looked inside.

A lady beetle. Miraculously, still alive.

I coaxed it onto a finger and walked to the front door. Opened it, held the bug up high.

Fly away home.

It stood there a moment, as if sniffing the air. Then it lifted its tiny wings and fluttered unsteadily away.

18 RAGING GEOTOX

EUGENE, OREGON

Sasha rolled down her window. I could hear the critter squeaking. "Can you make it stop?" she demanded.

"I think so."

"Then get in."

"Why don't we just take him to the shed and—"

"Make it stop *now*, or I'll bash in its demented little brains!"

No room in the backseat with the critter. Too much junk in there. I went around and pulled hard at the passenger door. It moaned, a deep, metal-grinding sound, a sound that said there were not so very many openings and shuttings left until it dropped clean off its hinges. The front seat was full of stuff. Sasha tossed a couple of books into the back and shoveled some papers to the floor, where they joined a pile of other junk— plastic grocery bags, empty Starbucks cups, a flattened Girl Scout cookie box, and wads of crumpled Kleenex. I slid in and hauled the door shut.

I reached between the seats and stroked the critter's head, now completely bare of skin. Some of the scales looked rough and raw and wounded, like when you pick off a scab too soon. Sasha had set aside the strips of discarded skin/fur in a soft, tattered lump at the edge of the box.

I felt a tingle in my mind. Still squeaking, the critter raised his head, then hooked a set of claws into my jacket sleeve. I tried to untangle them, so I could pick him up, but he hooked in his other front claws, and then his two back sets, and clambered up my arm until his head rested on my shoulder. I nestled him against my chest, kenned him comforting vibes.

The squeaking stopped.

"Kudos," Sasha said. "Clearly you're the fave."

The sharp crest on his head scraped against my neck, which hurt, but not all that much. It was pointy but soft, like a little kid's flexible toy knife. A few wrinkly patches of skin/fur still clung to those puffy, swollen-seeming places, but you could see the whole of his spine ridge—not just the tips—from the top of his head all down his long neck to the end of his whippy tail. His face looked different, less puppy-kitten cute. Bony shelves shadowed his eyes, like eyebrows. If he weren't such a baby, I would have said he looked fierce.

He relaxed against me now, grew heavier and limp, and started up with the vibrating thing.

"That's annoying," Sasha said. "He hates my guts." She reached to touch him. The critter stiffened, hissed at her. She stuck out her tongue at him. "See what I'm saying?" She tossed me a sweatshirt. "Cover him with this. Just in case. You take him, I'll take his stuff. Let's go."

In Dad's studio, Sasha set down the bag and slid the critter's box onto its shelf. I started to put him in it, but he latched onto my jacket and wouldn't let go. The sweatshirt slipped off. I handed it to Sasha.

"I'm getting weirded out," she said.

"What happened?"

"Well, for one thing, there's the smoke."

"You mean Taj? Smoking in here?"

"No, I don't mean Taj. I mean, I'm sitting there in the car, and pretty soon I realize I'm smelling smoke. And I don't smoke anymore."

"You used to smoke?"

"In eighth grade. But that's not the point. The point is, I'm sitting there and I smell it. I'm thinking maybe the car's on fire. So I pop the hood and scope out the engine. Then I get down on my hands and knees and look underneath. Nothing. But when I get back inside, there it is again, stronger than before. Just then, the critter yawns. So I lean down, put my nose right next to those vicious baby incisors. And I swear, it smells like smoke."

"But the whole car was smelling like smoke, right?"

"It was way, way stronger on the critter's breath."

I leaned in and sniffed. He didn't smell like licorice anymore. He smelled like something burnt. Burnt toast.

I admitted it: "Okay, that's strange."

The critter sighed against me. I looked down at him. His belly was bulging.

"You sure you didn't get any food in him?"

"Hardly any. He wouldn't sit still. Let's see *you* do it." She hunted through the bag for the feeding things. "So I'm in the car, before the squeaking starts? I'm starting to get bored, so I look in those boxes you gave me. I figured you wouldn't mind."

"I don't," I said quickly. Though I sort of did. That was Mom's stuff. It was personal. But I hadn't said not to look, and she was doing me a seismic favor.

Sasha poured the ReliaVite into the glass, sucked up a basterful, and handed it to me. The critter lifted his head, started sniffing. I sat on the floor and let the critter slip into my lap. I nudged open his jaws, and squirted.

Bull's-eye.

"You have skills," Sasha said. A little resentfully. She sighed, sat down beside us.

"You should have seen my first time."

"Yeah, well." She sucked up another basterful and gave it to me; I went on feeding. "Did you read those articles?" she asked. "Did you see the books? And the sketchbooks?"

I shook my head. "I didn't have time."

"You really should check them out. And that rock thing? Do you know what it is?"

I shrugged. "I can guess."

"Petrified, right? Some kind of egg?"

I nodded.

"What kind?"

Shrugged again. "I'm pretty sure it's the same as the lizard's, only older. The egg markings were almost identical."

"Right. And what kind of lizard, exactly, is it?"

"Taj and I web-searched lots of lizards, and it doesn't match any of them. 'Course, we don't know anything about lizards. It could be out there. But like I told you before, I'm thinking it's a cryptid."

"A cryptid. Meaning, you have no clue."

"Well, yeah, but—"

"Bryn. I have an idea. If your mom found an egg, other people might have found some, too. Maybe somebody knows what they are, but they might not want to put it out there in the open. It could be illegal."

Right. The black market. Like Taj was talking about.

"But I've got a full-out yen to know what this thing is," Sasha said. "It's creeping me out. I mean, does *anybody* know these things exist? Or is your guy, like, flagrantly from Mars? I want to know. Don't you?"

A tingling in my mind. The critter had tipped up his head, was studying me. Kenning. I looked down into those bright green eyes, searching for something, some clue to what bound us together.

Heck yeah, I wanted to know. I nodded.

"Okay, then," Sasha said. "'Cause I think I know someone who can help."

We drove past the main part of town until we came to a street of buildings tagged with graffiti. Sasha pulled up in front of a dingy storefront. TATTOOS it said on the window. MUTANT, TRIBAL, TRADITIONAL.

This wasn't one of those upscale salons like you saw near the university, boutiques with names like Body Electric and Ink

Dreams. This place didn't even have a name, unless you counted Tattoos.

Two 'tants came out as I watched. Eyes clouded with whitish 'tant contacts—cataract chic. Skwebbing like gills on their necks.

Radioactive Fish was blaring so loud it rattled my teeth, but I heard a buzzer go off as we stepped inside. From way back behind a beaded curtain door, someone yelled, "Just hold on a freaking minute!"

I smelled incense and, beneath it, a faint chemical odor. We wandered past a couple of wooden benches bolted to the floor, to a far wall papered with pictures of tattoos and skwebbing. Skwebbed fingers and skwebbed toes. Skwebbing from earlobes to neck. Neck skwebbing that looked like gills. Even underarm skwebbing, like flying squirrel wings.

It was ersatz, some kind of polymer. But you couldn't just whip it in and out again, like earrings. It was stuck there, anchored to your real skin, until somebody cut it out.

How would you even put on a shirt if you had those wing-looking deals? I wondered. But I didn't ask.

The whole 'tant phenom started with that spate of web-fingered, flipper-toed babies in Texas and Iowa a few years back. That, plus the cancer spike and the swarms. Basically, it's an in-your-face protest at the raging geotox our parents and grandparents have stuck us with.

The music ramped down.

"Hey, Sasha."

I turned to see him coming through the beaded curtain. Early to midtwenties, maybe. Skinny. Close-set eyes. Thin, stringy beard. He was kind of hard to look at because of the tattoos on his neck and arms—the 'tant kind, all crusty and skin cancery. He'd skwebbed his earlobes to his neck in long, pleated folds that ended in gill-like flaps.

"Hey, Gandalf. This is my friend Bryn I told you about."

Who would name their kid Gandalf?

He put out a skwebbed hand. I shook it gingerly. We followed him down a hallway, past a row of curtained doorways, to a small, cluttered office. He scooted some cardboard boxes across the floor and stacked them, teetering, in a corner; he jammed a heap of papers and books onto a shelf next to boxes of packaged needles, bright plastic bottles of ink, and tubes of skwebbing polymer. Now at least there was room for us to stand.

Also on the shelves I saw something that looked like a dried-up toad, something that looked like part of an armadillo, and something I'd have sworn was a monkey skull.

Gandalf sat, woke up his computer, and swiveled around to face Sasha. "So where's this *thing*?"

She looked pointedly at me. She'd asked me beforehand if I'd be willing to show him the egg. She'd told me he'd talked his way onto an encrypted black-market site. He surfed it out of curiosity but claimed he sometimes dropped clues to the police, if there was cruelty or something. She said he had environmental cred—a degree in environmental studies and a history of protesting with EcoFury.

But now I stalled. Could I trust him? "No one can know," I said.

"I won't tell a soul," Gandalf said. "Scout's honor." He held up three fingers in a mock salute, then wiggled them around, showing off the skwebs.

Sasha slapped at his hand. "Cut it out, Gandalf. She means it."

"Ouch! Jeez, Sasha, that hurt!" Gandalf cradled his hand.

"Promise," Sasha said. "Hope to die."

"Okay, I promise." Sasha glared at him. "Hope to die," he said. He made a face at her, then turned and smiled at me.

"Listen, he's my cousin," Sasha said. "I wasn't going to tell you because it's . . . well, whatever. I just wasn't."

Gandalf hung his head. "She's ashamed of me," he said. Messing with her. "She's too smart for the rest of us. National Merit whatever."

Sasha didn't bite. "So I've known him forever. I even know his real name, don't I, R—"

"Shut up!" Gandalf warned.

"—alph," Sasha finished.

Ralph. That explained a lot.

Sasha grinned. "He won't break his promise 'cause he knows I'd tell his big sister, and she'd frag his drive."

"Yeah, yeah," Gandalf/Ralph said. "So, the thing?"

I slipped off my backpack. Pulled out the egg. Unwrapped it.

Gandalf's face went still, but I heard his intake of breath. He reached out his hands; I gave him the egg. He rotated it one way and another under the gooseneck lamp on his desk. Fingered its fissures and bumps.

"Do you know what it is?" Sasha asked.

"I might," he said.

"Well, what? A petrified egg of some kind, yes?"

135

He turned to me. "Where did you get it, can I ask?"

I hesitated, then shook my head. I didn't want to tell him. Not yet.

"Need-to-know basis," Sasha said.

Gandalf shrugged. "Okay, I can respect that." He turned it once more in his hands before he gave it back to me, then spun around to his computer and started tapping at the keys.

"What kind of egg?" Sasha asked.

He didn't answer. Kept tapping.

"Damn it, Ralph! I hate when you do this—when you know something I don't and you have to milk your little drama to the bitter end."

Gandalf grinned at me and rolled his eyes. He typed a password in a rectangular box and waited as the screen went black. Another box popped up. He typed a second password, longer this time. Waiting. Finally, a complicated graphic came up on the screen—of animals, spaceships, da Vinci–looking sketches. He clicked on the eye of an echidna or something, which opened up a page with numbers swimming across it. He clicked on a number. The site opened up on an auction-like format.

Wow. That was some serious encryption. I bent down to see better. Yeah, it was an auction, all right, but this wasn't toaster ovens and minivacs.

Strange Rock with Embedded Manmade-Like Part: Of Alien Origin?

Lizard Skeleton Reptile Skull Bone Taxidermy.

Griffin Claw 3 ⅛ Inches, Real Taxidermy.

"Yeah, right," Sasha said. "I'll just bet it's real."

"Wait," Gandalf said. Scrolled on down the site.

Fossil Baltic Amber Wasp Inclusion.

Walking Cane Pure Unicorn Ivory, Authentic.

"Right, uh-huh," Sasha said.

Powdered Black Rhino Horn, Aphrodisiac Properties.

"Whoa, is that ever illegal," Sasha said.

Gandalf shrugged. "Interesting, though, huh?"

More like scary, I thought.

Scrolling, again. *Fossil Dinosaur Finger Bone Hell Creek.*

Real Human Shrunken Head Papua New Guinea.

Shrunken head? Sasha and I looked at each other. Jeez.

Scrolling. *Jurassic Archaeopteryx Skeleton Authentic.*

Coprolite Sauropod Dinosaur.

"What's coprolite?" Sasha asked.

"Fossilized crap. Oh, here we go." Gandalf pointed at the screen.

Fossilized Hadrosaurus Egg.

Fossilized Raptor Dinosaur Egg.

He clicked on the pictures of each one. The Hadrosaurus egg had a lot of tiny cracks in a random, crinkly pattern. The raptor egg was capsule-shaped, with a bumpy texture.

"I don't think that's it, either one," I said.

"Wait a minute, what about . . ." Gandalf clicked through more screens. Pulled up a picture of another egg.

And there it was. Exactly.

"What's it say?" I asked.

He scrolled down. "Nine inches across and six inches deep. Ovoid. Alaskan provenance. Kenai."

Okay, that would fit.

"But what *kind* is it?" Sasha asked.

Gandalf scrolled up. Sasha and I leaned in closer: *Petrified Dragon Egg.*

"What the—" Sasha said.

"Like, Komodo dragon?" I asked. "Chinese water dragon? Or . . ."

"Doesn't say," Gandalf said. "Just 'dragon.' Wait a minute, though. Let's try something." He clicked a few times and the screen morphed to display five things: the griffin claw, the unicorn cane, and the three fossilized eggs.

Bidding on the griffin claw was up to $24.95. The unicorn cane, $75. The Hadrosaurus egg was up to $2,500; the raptor, $3,800. On the so-called dragon egg, though, bidding stood at $200,000.

Two hundred grand?

For a couple of heartbeats, no one said anything. Then Gandalf quirked his eyebrows, turned to me. "What does that tell you?"

I thought about it. "The griffin and the unicorn are fake."

"Right," he said.

"The Hadrosaurus and the raptor are probably real."

"Uh-huh. What about the dragon egg?"

"Somebody *thinks* it's real," I said.

Gandalf nodded. "Yup. And they also think it's a *dragon.*"

19

AS IN *DRAGON* DRAGON

EUGENE, OREGON

Gandalf walked us to the car. "Hey," he asked me, "how many of those things do you have?"

"Just the one."

"Anything else of that nature? Fossils of any kind?"

"No, nothing," I said.

"Can I ask where you got it?"

"Already asked and answered," Sasha said. "You're not thinking of narcing us out, are you, Ralph? Her mom's a professor. They're going through legal channels."

"Then why didn't her mom come today?"

"Would you choke? We've got it handled."

Gandalf ignored her. "'Cause, Bryn, if you ever want to sell it . . . I know some people."

"What!" Sasha stopped, stared at him. "What are you saying? You're not involved with those puss-maggots, are you?"

He shrugged. "I've made a deal or two."

"Are you serious? You're an *environmentalist*. That's poaching. It's illegal."

"It's not hurting anything. These things are dead already."

"Wait a minute," Sasha said. "You're off the parental dole, aren't you? Aunt Alma's cut you off."

He hunched there on the sidewalk, like a scrawny baby buzzard. "I have a job," he said. "But I have plans. So anyway," he said, turning to me, "if you ever—"

"I can't believe you, Ralph. I can't—" She turned to me. "We're getting out of here. Now."

We climbed into the car. Sasha cranked up the engine, pulled into the street, and slammed her fist into the steering wheel. "Rat piss!" she said. "Toad suck! Phaging bastard whore!"

I turned back, but Gandalf wasn't there anymore, not where he'd been. He was crossing the street behind us. Moving fast.

"I don't believe it! We grew up together. I thought he'd be okay." Sasha took in a deep breath, blew it out. "This whole little outing was a mistake. I hate to say it, but I don't trust my own dear cousin. He is way too excited about that egg."

We didn't talk for a while. I stared out the window, watched the shops go by, watched the neighborhood segue from full-out seedy to college-town hippie-funk. There was a funny vibe in the car. Like one of those virtual fences for dogs where their collars zap them if they cross a certain line. There was something we weren't saying. Not going there. Not crossing that fence line, either one of us.

Thing is, you wouldn't pay two hundred grand for an egg from a Komodo dragon or a Chinese water dragon. At least, I didn't think you would.

You'd have to be thinking dragon, as in *dragon* dragon. You'd have to be thinking wings. You'd have to be thinking fire.

Wouldn't you?

There's a lot of delusion out there, online. People who like scamming other people, and people who want to believe. *Walking Cane Pure Unicorn Ivory. Griffin Claw.* People were actually paying for that junk.

But Sasha and I, we'd seen some stuff other people hadn't. We'd seen the critter himself, not just the petrified egg. And honestly? He was seismic weird. His feet, for one thing. They looked more like bird feet than reptile feet, with long, sharp, curving claws. I wanted to call them "talons." I'd web-searched lots of lizards lately, and not a single one had feet like that. Then there were those patches on the critter's back, where the skin/fur hadn't come off. Right where wings would be, if he had them. And the burning smell. How would you explain that? Logically, I mean.

I wished I could shrug it off. Just lock it in a box called "impossible." But I knew firsthand that some so-called impossible things are real.

"Hey," Sasha said. "Isn't that near your house?"

I looked where she was pointing. We'd come into my neighborhood now, houses with driveways and lawns. Up ahead, a thin column of blue-gray smoke twisted up into the sky.

It was very near our house. Maybe a little way behind it, or . . . Dad's studio.

Sasha pulled into the driveway. We jumped out and set off running. And there it was—billowing now—rising up from the shed roof.

Smoke.

I got there first, found the key on the ledge, threw open the door.

Inside, the air swirled with sooty smoke and ash. I could see the fire now, a patch of bright blue flame on the ceiling.

I felt my way along the shelves toward the critter's box. He wasn't there. Could he have climbed out, maybe, or fallen? I got down on my knees, groped under the shelves, behind the wheel, in the space between the refrigerator and the kiln.

Nothing.

I reached for him in the kenning way and felt a panicky little tingle.

Here. Someplace. But where?

I sat back on my heels. My eyes burned. "Do you see him?" I asked.

"No."

A sudden flare of bluish light, directly overhead.

"Holy crap," Sasha said.

It was the critter. Floating. Just floating in the air above us.

Breathing fire.

20
PULSE WORK

AN ISLAND IN THE KODIAK ARCHIPELAGO

Anna Eluska stood in the doorway of her cabin, gazing across the sea in the direction of the Kenai. Now it begins, she thought. She could make out the dark, indistinct shape of the boat that lurched toward the island through the heaving waves. So long between boats, this year. The storms had been bad, the sea white with churning froth all winter.

It wasn't until Easter that her grandson Peter had been able to cross. To find the man whose name she had found on a card in the woman's coat pocket. The man who was a professor at that university in Anchorage.

Would it be this man coming back to the island with Peter? This professor, Dr. Jones? Or would it be someone else? Some kinsman of the woman? Some friend?

Anna glanced back at the woman who lay sleeping on the bed. She had been here since autumn, broken in so many places after her fall. The woman's breath came loud and slow and ragged. By the light of the oil lamp, Anna could see the chiseled gauntness of the woman's cheekbones, the blue veins under translucent skin at her temples, the dark circles ringing her closed eyes. When Peter and his friends had brought her here, the woman's pulse had been fainter than the wing beat of a moth. Anna had feared that she would die.

But she hadn't. Not yet.

The woman's bones had knitted, but her pulse still wasn't beating true. After the healing teas and poultices Anna had made for her. After the hours of holding her in the warm steam of the *banya*. After the pulse work with Anna's hands, practiced in the healing ways—feeling here, and then there, just feeling and feeling.

Still not quite balanced. Still not quite right.

Outside, the boat disappeared behind a wave that danced and smoked with sea froth. The boat reappeared, a little closer. And now the faint buzz of a motor threaded in among the other sounds—the cries of the cormorants, the whuff of the wind, the slow rasp of the woman's breath.

What new energies would be entering the village? Anna wondered. Forces for harmony? Or for discord?

Anna gazed out to the west, toward the dim mountains across Shelikof Strait. Another storm, boiling in across the sky. Whoever came here on that boat, they wouldn't be leaving soon.

A sudden wind gust shook the little cabin and ruffled Anna's hair. She went inside, shut the door behind her. She moved to the table by the wall, moistened a cloth in the basin of water, then sat down on the bed beside the woman and stroked the cloth across her face. The room was cool, but beads of sweat stood out on the woman's upper lip. Her odd, frizzy hair clung damply to her scalp.

Anna hadn't asked for this, this woman. This woman and whoever was coming after her. Those foolish boys should have left her at a hospital, not carried her all the way here. Anna didn't like bringing strangers into the fragile balance of the village. Not at all.

But what is given to you to care for, you must take.

21 STEP AWAY FROM THE LIZARD

EUGENE, OREGON

A quick burst of blue flame, and then it was over—leaving me gaping, half-blind, with black spots floating in front of my eyes. I blinked until my eyes started working again, and the critter reappeared.

A little lower now. Just a foot or two above me.

"What the hell," Sasha said. "What the phaging hell."

I felt for him with my mind. Sleeping. Somehow, I knew. He was floating in his sleep.

I stretched up on tiptoe. Couldn't reach him. I jumped, trying to snag his tail or maybe a claw. Missed.

"Watch out," Sasha said. "That guy is lethal!"

It wasn't just the roof burning now, I saw. A bright bloom of flame had appeared on the back wall.

"Better get the fire extinguisher," I said. "It's by the door."

The critter was rising now, drifting slowly into the air. I climbed up onto the potter's wheel seat.

Tippy. Seismic tippy. And way smokier up here. My throat burned; my eyes were tearing up. I reached toward the critter.

My fingers brushed a talon. He twitched, drew his foot up tight against his belly, out of reach.

The sudden hiss of the extinguisher startled me; a stream of foam arced up toward the ceiling; I nearly slipped off the seat. The critter spewed out a bluish gout of fire and plummeted into my arms. I clasped him tight, squatted down, and stepped carefully to the floor.

One entire side of the shed had burst into flames. A loud *crack*, and the shelves did a slo-mo crumble—wood, pottery, glazes, tumbling to the floor. A scorching wall of dust and ash and sparks billowed into the room. I ducked, bolted for the door, and reached the outside air just as a section of roof gave way and collapsed, flaming, behind me.

Somewhere in the distance, a siren wailed.

I coughed, hacked up a blackish gob of phlegm and smoke.

"Are you okay?" Sasha asked.

"Yeah. You?"

She nodded. Frowned at the critter. "Just point that thing away from me, would you?"

He was awake but sleepy, fuddled. *What's going on?* he seemed to ask. As if he personally had nothing to do with any of this. The last bits of skin/fur had come loose from his back, and I could see now what he'd been hiding. Wings. Little papery wings, so fragile, they looked like a stiff breeze could tear them to shreds.

The siren wailed—louder.

"We better get out of here," Sasha said. "Unless you want to turn him over to somebody. Which might not be such a bad idea, considering. Think about it, Bryn. We could have been, like, flambé."

The fire roared, spewing sheets of flames and clouds of dense black smoke. All that pottery—Dad's hard work—gone.

"Let's go," I said.

I stumbled after Sasha. But wait. Two cars now, side by side in the driveway. Someone was climbing out of Sasha's car. Gandalf: clutching the box with the egg.

He turned to run, then stopped. Stared at us.

"Give it back!" Sasha said. She tucked the fire extinguisher under one arm and wrested the box from him. He let it go.

"What is *that*?" he said, pointing at the critter.

"Scram. I mean it, Ralph."

"No—what is it? Is it . . . ?"

The critter stiffened in my arms. I backed away, but Gandalf followed.

"I'm warning you," Sasha said. "Leave us alone."

He ignored her. "I only want to look at it."

The critter snorted out a cloud of sparks and blue smoke.

Gandalf yelled. Ducked. Looked up.

Sasha held out the fire extinguisher, threatening. "Step away from the lizard."

He came nearer. "I just want to see it, I prom—"

Sasha got him in the eye with a jet of spray. He cried out, covered his face. I dodged past him, yanked open the door, and flung myself into the car.

Sasha jumped in. Slammed her door. Gunned the motor. We lurched backward down the driveway.

People were running toward the shed with buckets and hoses. Sasha ground the gears; the car jolted forward, swerving to miss the fire truck, which blared and honked, barreling down the street.

I looked back. The fire truck stopped at the end of the driveway, blocking Gandalf's car. Smoke still churned up from the shed. A crowd had gathered in the street. I watched my house as it shrank behind us. Something pressed down on my heart. What would Piper do? How could she bear it, with all three of us gone?

And Stella—who would take care of her? Who would ken with her?

"Where to?" Sasha asked. "Any bright ideas?"

I looked down at the critter, curled against my chest. Trembling. Kenning me in terrified little fizzy bursts.

How could I possibly choose?

"Bryn! Get with the program," Sasha said. "Where to?"

"Anchorage," I said. "I've got to get to Anchorage."

PART III
JOURNEY

Cap of bottle, tooth of comb,
Packing peanut, dead cell phone,
Grocery bag, used battery,
Tire of truck, old CRT.

Double, double toil and trouble,
Toss in ocean, gyre and bubble.
Up the food chain it doth go.
In human blood it soon will flow.
—from "Witches' Brew," by Mutant Tide

I salute you
With my phalangeal mutation—
Genetic alienation
From your contamination—
I salute you
And all your phaging generation.
—from "Phalange Web Salute," by Radioactive Fish

FUGITIVE, ON THE LAM

EUGENE, OREGON
I-5 CORRIDOR, OREGON AND WASHINGTON

Sasha turned left on Harris, then zigged into an alley, rumbling way too fast along the rutted pavement. She gunned it straight across Potter to University, cutting off a herd of cars. She shrugged off the angry horn blasts and the one guy who gave her the finger. "Aw, get over it," she said. She flashed him the Vulcan live-long-and-prosper salute. With the skweb between her fingers, it looked seriously weird.

I glanced back to see if anyone was following—Gandalf, maybe. Or the cops.

Nope. So far, so good.

She turned onto 18th, then zoomed across two lanes of oncoming traffic, bearing left on Agate. All the loose debris on the floor migrated to the right. I set the critter on my lap, clutched him around the middle with one hand and hung on to the grab bar with the other. Tires: screeching. Other drivers: honking. Sasha: totally unfazed.

Right on Franklin, and it was almost a straight shot now to the freeway. The critter crouched, all tensed up on my lap. I was afraid he was going to do the thing again. The fire-breathing thing. I put my hand on his back between his wings, tried to ken him calming vibes.

And he did calm down a little. Surprisingly. I felt him ease down into my lap, tucking in his feet and tail. I scratched beneath his jawbone, and he began to thrum, kneading my legs with his talons.

Once we hit the freeway, Sasha put it to the metal. She zipped into the fast lane, cutting off a red Beemer.

The finger again.

Live-long-and-prosper.

Her little car was shaking, rattling so loud, it felt like it might fly apart. I kept my eye on the rearview mirror, scanning for flashing lights. We'd whipped right past that fire truck. Failing to pull over and stop. Leaving the scene.

Pretty soon, though, Sasha let up. "Speed trap," she said. Sure enough, I saw lights on the side of the freeway a little way ahead. "That sweatshirt's on the floor behind you," Sasha said. I reached back, felt sweatshirt cloth, and draped it over the critter. Still relaxed. Still thrumming. As we passed the cops, I turned my head away, in case they had like an APB out on me. *Five foot six, dark hair, one hundred fifteen pounds. Fugitive, on the lam.*

By the time we got to Albany, I'd started to breathe normally again. But a dark, sour dread weighed down in the pit of my stomach. I'd abandoned Piper and Stella. I couldn't bear to think of them waiting for me.

Waiting and hoping.

What had I done?

Sasha had grown more and more quiet. The adrenaline rush had peaked. She glanced at me. "We need to talk," she said.

I sighed. Yeah, we really did.

She cut off at the North Albany exit and turned into a Thrift Mart parking lot. The back of the lot was nearly empty, screened off from the road by a row of shrubs and trees. She pulled into a slot. Cut the engine.

"Okay, so what are we doing?" she asked. "What's your plan?"

I didn't have an actual plan—just a destination. Anchorage. That's where that professor was, that Dr. Jones. He'd wanted Mom to go up there in the first place, and he'd e-mailed Dad just a few days ago. *Call me. With all due haste.* He might know what to do. Maybe he'd take care of the critter himself. Maybe he'd help me find Dad.

I told Sasha my idea. She looked doubtful. "Kind of a stretch, don't you think?"

"I'm open to ideas."

She blew out through her lips. "Well, not so many options, unless you want to turn over Mr. Lizard to the cops or like the SPCA."

I shook my head. Beneath my hand, I could feel the critter thrumming. Asleep.

Sasha made a face. "Didn't think so. Hmm. It might be good if you could text this professor right now. But I'm not sure you want to use your phone. Or even mine, at this point. Your aunt might be looking for you and our phones are traceable. I think the cops could maybe actually track us by GPS.

Better not chance it. Sooner or later, though, they're going to get involved. We should power down our phones and pop out the batteries."

"Okay." We did.

"And also," Sasha went on, "that professor might side with your aunt. Adults tend to do that. Close ranks. Or he might just string you along, or try to off-load your issues to someone else unless you were standing right there on his doorstep."

I nodded.

"With your baby dragon."

The word hung there. *Dragon.* Because that's what the critter really was, wasn't he? Whatever scientific name for him they eventually came up with, whatever DNA connections they made, whatever evolutionary pathways they constructed for him.

Looks like a reptile. Has wings. Breathes fire. Whatever else you want to say about it, that's a dragon.

Sasha was shaking her head. She heaved out a sigh. "*Nobody* has problems like you, Bryn. You are the queen."

Sasha ran into the Thrift Mart and came back with two six-packs of ReliaVite, a plastic cup, a turkey baster, a box of plastic trash bags, some leather shoelaces ("to tie up its snout"), a package of disposable diapers ("in case it pees"), and two silicone oven mitts ("in case it flames"). She also bought two hoagie sandwiches, two Cokes, and a package of Oreos.

The critter woke up, started sniffing at the food bag. Sasha shook her finger at him. "Not for you, Mr. Lizard," she said.

"For us." The critter hissed at her, looking fierce. Sasha ducked. "Yikes! Muzzle him with the laces, would you!"

"I don't think he's going to do it. I think we're good for now."

"How do you know?" Sasha demanded.

I could feel it when I kenned him. A happyish fizzy tingle. I shrugged.

She cocked an eyebrow at me. "You're doing a thing with him, aren't you?"

"No," I said. Lying.

She looked at me. Didn't believe me, I could tell. I waited, dreading. If she really knew me, if she knew about my family . . . would she be creeped out? Would she leave?

"Whatever," she said. "I just have this thing about barbecue. I'd rather eat it than be it."

Next we hit the ATMs. Which we so should have thought of in Eugene. Now we'd leave an electronic trail; they could find out we'd headed north. We went to different banks, though, so we wouldn't both show up on the same security-camera feed. I had twelve hundred in babysitting and birthday money that I'd been saving forever, maybe for a car. I pulled most of it out, stuffed the thick wad in my purse. If I didn't use it, I could always put it back.

We fueled up, then took off north on I-5.

By the time we passed Salem, it was just after five. On a normal Friday, Aunt Pen would be picking up Piper from the after-school program. But today, Aunt Pen would be home. Someone would have called about the fire. Right around now was when she'd know for sure that I'd gone missing.

And Piper would know it too.

If only I'd had time to leave a message. I knew how she must be feeling. Raw. Lonely. Ripped-away.

Full-out seismic mad at me.

And Stella . . .

I was everything to her. I was her world.

Even after I fed him, the critter was way too interested in my food. He kept poking his snout into my sandwich, sniffing at it, trying to nip it. I tore off a tiny piece of turkey and let him taste. He gulped it down, then licked his snout with his tongue—his seriously weird, forky tongue. Then he burrowed into my sandwich again.

"Watch out," Sasha said. "He could get diarrhea or something. Constipation. He could barf."

I checked the diaper, unfolded on my lap underneath the critter. "We'll try just a little," I said. I pulled off another bit of turkey. If he could eat solid food, it would be way easier than the whole messy production with the ReliaVite.

What he really liked, it turned out, was cheese. I let him try a piece, and that was the end of my sandwich. He lunged for it, snapping those pointy teeth of his. I held the sandwich over my head, but he stretched up, put his claws on my shoulders, and nipped at it until it fell completely apart. Then he rooted around in my lap and on the floor until he'd gobbled up all the cheese.

So much for dinner.

We hit Portland in a massive clog of rush-hour traffic, which maybe was a good thing because it would be hard to search for Sasha's car in that mess. If anybody was searching for her car. She didn't think they would be, not yet. "Not that many people know we know each other," she said.

"What about Gandalf?"

She shrugged. "He won't call Mom. She's not exactly a fan of his. And he sure won't call the cops."

"What about the people who saw us leaving my house?"

"How would they know who I am?"

You're kind of distinctive-looking, I thought. Though I didn't say it. "What happens when you don't come home tonight?"

"Confession: I left a message when you were at the ATM. I told Mom I was going to spend the weekend with Jen. I do it all the time. She'll be fine with it for now."

For now. I wondered how far she'd go with me. I felt a sudden stab of loneliness at the thought of going on without her.

Was this what it was like to have a friend? A real friend—not just a Net friend or someone to hang out with at lunch.

We crossed the bridge into Washington. I tried to keep the critter on my lap, but he got wigglier and wigglier. He tried to clamber up onto the dashboard. He lunged at passing cars, climbing halfway up the window. When Sasha told him to chill, he hissed at her and snorted out sparks. Finally I dumped him into the backseat, let him explore.

He snuffled around a bit, then dived headfirst into the sack of supplies and started poking around in there, doing I don't know what-all, making the bag bulge and twist and scoot across the seat. He emerged with one of the oven mitts, shaking it between his teeth, looking proud of himself, like he'd heroically killed a rat.

"Hey, give me that," I said. He bounced away from me, to the floor behind Sasha's seat. I reached for the mitt, tried to pull it away from him. But he wouldn't let go.

Sasha glanced back, then laid on the horn. The critter jumped, startled, dropping the mitt. I grabbed it and stuffed it into the glove compartment.

But now the critter was shoulder-deep in Sasha's purse. "Hey!" I said. "Bad boy!" I undid my seat belt, twisted around between the seats, and pulled him out of there. He was chewing on a pink plastic hairbrush.

"Uh, Sasha?" I said. "How attached are you to your hairbrush?"

"Why?" she asked. "No, don't tell me. I don't want to know."

Tooth marks pitted the handle. The bristles were all mashed down and slimy.

"I'll buy you a new one," I offered.

"Whatever. That's the least of our problems."

Gradually, it grew dark. The critter climbed into my lap with his hairbrush and sleepily chewed. Traffic thinned; soon we were out of the city, passing through rolling farmland, dark groves of trees, wind farms, and photovoltaic arrays.

Sasha's car had zero audiotech, unless you counted the ancient AM/FM radio. Fiddling with it, we occasionally managed to tap into some faint, staticky eco-rock frequencies: White Raven, Mutant Tide, Ghost Meridian.

The stars came glimmering out. The critter thrummed

against me—asleep, I knew—and somehow, I didn't feel quite so lonely. I touched one of his wings, unfolded it. It reminded me of an umbrella, with thin, flexible ribs and a membrane between them—tissue papery, translucent, with tiny, branching veins.

He sighed, snorted out a puff of warm breath.

Burnt toast.

We pulled in at a rest stop about halfway to Seattle. When it was my turn to go to the bathroom, Sasha stayed in the car with the critter, not looking too happy about it.

Not so much the lovefest with those two.

A sweet old couple in a rusted-out Airstream trailer were giving out free coffee and cookies. I ate a peanut butter one and took another for later. When I got back, I noticed that the diaper under the critter was damp. I folded it, threw it in a trash can, and replaced it. The critter yawned, gazed up at me. I had a feeling he might have to go. I set him on the grass to one side of the car, out of sight of the coffee people. Right away, he produced a hill of those small, round, hard stools. Like goat poop.

Sasha came up beside us, stared down at the pile. "Is that normal?" she asked.

I looked at her. "Normal?"

"Point taken," she said. "All right, then. Vamoose."

I didn't mean to sleep. Sasha was driving, doing me a colossal favor, and it seemed like the least I could do was keep her company. But the rumbling of the car began to percolate into my bones, making them feel heavy—and then the heaviness seeped into the rest of me. I tried to fight it off, but my eyelids wanted to slam, and my brain kept gapping, and a couple of times I woke with a start, my chin resting on my chest.

I was way down deep when I heard the scream.

"Mitts! Get the mitts!"

I whiffed a stench of burning—a thick, acrid, petrochemical smell. Light flared against the windshield.

"Hurry!" Sasha said. "It's on fire!"

I twisted around. Flames, on the ceiling behind me. And smoke. Lots of smoke. I undid my seat belt. Where was the critter? I groped through the sack on the backseat for the mitt, got the other one out of the glove box. Started slapping at the fire, trying to smother it.

The flames died down, all but a few sparks. I clapped them between the mitts. Killed them.

Where was the critter?

I reached for him in my mind. Behind me, somewhere. Asleep.

"He was floating," Sasha said. "Like in the shed. He's a menace!"

I felt around on the backseat floor and found him there, right behind me. I scooped him up, set him in my lap. He blinked at me sleepily, then tucked his nose under his front talons and curled up tight.

Smoke hung in the air. It stank. I rolled down my window. On the ceiling, where the fire had been, strips of charred cloth hung down. Behind them, burnt foam rubber.

Oh, jeez!

"Sasha, I am so sorry," I said.

She shrugged. But I could tell she was upset.

I copped another ken. It was getting stronger now, the

kenning, with a more complicated vibe than Stella's. This had a surface level plus a deeper, low-frequency thing happening underneath. The critter seemed peaceful, though. I couldn't imagine he would flame right now.

But who knew what he would do, really?

"I'll pay to fix it," I said. "They've got to be able to fix stuff like that."

Sasha shrugged again. "Yeah, well. Forget it. You're going to need all the funds you've got."

23 MOTHER SHIP

It was midnight by the time we got to Bellingham. We chipped in cash for a cheap motel room and registered with made-up names. It was a gloomy, claustrophobic space with two saggy beds, two fake-wood nightstands, a fake-wood dresser, an ancient TV, and a funny smell I couldn't place.

Funny in a not-good way.

We didn't have much to take in. Sasha had stopped at a discount mall in Centralia and picked up some T-shirts, several packages of underwear, a replacement hairbrush, a couple of toothbrushes, and some toothpaste. She'd crammed them into a duffel, which she'd also found at the mall. She bought me a coat, too, since I'd left mine in Eugene. Not to be ungrateful, but the new coat was ugly. Kind of a yellowy-orangey quilty thing with grommets and little zippered pockets all over. It was warm, though. I'd give it that.

She'd picked up a litter box and some kitty litter somewhere too. But the coolest stuff she'd bought, she'd found in a sporting goods store. A fire extinguisher. A fireproof blanket. A fishing net with a retractable handle. And she'd replaced the SolarSox.

We'd been talking on the way up. And now we had a Plan. Foolproof, not so much. But better than no plan at all.

The door to the motel room opened straight onto the parking lot, so we smuggled the critter in without a hitch. I set him down on the carpet, which was thin and splotched with ancient stains—origin unknown. I wasn't going to work up a massive load of guilt if he had an accident. Though he actually seemed to be catching on. The last few times I'd taken him to the grass at rest stops, he got right with the program, and the diapers were staying dry in my lap.

Superb.

Now the critter looked around. He sniffed at the carpet stains. Which were apparently pretty interesting. Didn't want to think too much about that. He pranced on over to the dresser, like he had springs on the bottoms of his feet. He stretched up and sniffed in the direction of the bags of food Sasha had set on top. Egg McSomethings. Yum. His tongue flicked out. He couldn't quite reach the bags.

You'd think, being a dragon, he'd just fly on up. But the thought didn't seem to occur to him. Come to think of it, I'd never actually seen him fly on purpose—only when he was asleep. And those flimsy little wings of his, sort of twitching around? They looked, like, decorative. Not quite functional. Like a fancy hood ornament.

"Hey, Bryn. You ever see one of these?" Sasha was squatting in front of a rusty metal box near the head of one of the beds. I went to look. The critter started to follow but got distracted by his tail. He pounced at it, missed, then hissed at it, snorting out blue smoke.

Sasha frowned at him. "Hey there, Mr. L. We're in nonsmoking. Just so you know."

The writing on the box said MAGIC FINGERS. Sasha pushed two fifty-centers into the slot. The bed began to hum and vibrate. Even the floor was vibrating. I lifted the critter onto the bed, and he began to knead the bedspread with his talons. He began to thrum.

"Beam me up," Sasha said. "He thinks it's the mother ship."

The three of us sat on the bed, snacking on the McThingies, vibrating together. Sasha had talked the guy at the fast food place into giving us some extra processed cheese, which the critter gobbled up. When he was done, he sighed, stretched his wings, then folded them like paper fans. He leaned against me, pillowing his head on my leg, and kenned me a contented little hum.

"You're definitely the fave," Sasha grumbled.

"You jealous?" I tickled under the critter's chin.

"It's a lizard," she said. "Why would I be jealous?"

After the critter fell asleep, I wrapped him up in the fireproof blanket and put him in the shower next to the litter box. The tiles were mungy, and the grout had some kind of mold growing on it. One good thing: it looked fireproof, with the glass door and the tiles going all the way up across the ceiling.

"Excellent location for the Tylenol test," Sasha whispered.

She had a theory. It had to do with sleep. She'd read some-where that sleeping drugs disrupted REM patterns. So maybe, she hypothesized, if we drugged the critter, it might disrupt something, some sleeping pattern connected with fire.

I wasn't nuts about her theory. First off, it seemed farfetched. Secondly, how did we know Tylenol PM wasn't poisonous to dragons? I mean, *parsley* is poisonous to birds. And even if it wasn't poisonous, how would we know how much to give him? What if he got really sick? What if he OD'd and died?

But the deed was done. We'd put a quarter of a caplet in a hunk of McMeat, and he'd gobbled it right up.

"The Tylenol still makes me nervous," I said.

"Bryn. You're going to be riding on the ferry with Mr. Lizard. You're going to be on it for three whole days. What if he flames? What will you do?"

No idea. Not a clue.

I tried to sleep while Sasha dug through Mom's boxes, which she had brought in from the trunk. She picked out books and notebooks, stacking them on a nightstand, skimming through. After a while, she said, "Bryn? You awake?"

I sighed, sat up.

"Look at this." She held up a sketchbook with pictures of dragons, or flying lizards, whatever. The paper was yellow and the ink was brown. It looked ancient.

Where did Mom get this stuff?

"It reminds me of something," I said.

"Yeah, like Mr. L."

"No, something else. But I can't think of it."

"Bryn?"

Something different in Sasha's voice.

"Yeah?"

"Do your parents, like, read at night?"

"What do you mean, read?"

"I mean read. Not just watch TV."

"Yeah." We hardly ever watched TV.

"Did they buy you lots of books when you were little?"

I nodded. Remembering something Gandalf had said. *She's too smart for the rest of us. National Merit whatever.* "Why?" I asked.

She shrugged. "Mine think I read too much. 'Too big for your britches. Miss Smarty-Pants.'"

Wow. I didn't know what to say.

"Do you ever feel like you were switched at the hospital and wound up in the wrong family?"

I shook my head. "Wrong planet, maybe. But the family fits."

Two hours later, I was wishing I had taken that Tylenol. Sasha was sound asleep, but I lay wide awake on the lumpy mattress, staring up at the rusty stains on the ceiling, thinking about our Plan.

It would have to be the ferry. We'd figured out that much. In a car or a bus, I'd have to cross the border into Canada. There would be inspections. I'd need a passport. Which I didn't have.

With a plane, there'd still be way too many issues. No, the ferry seemed best, as far as Skagway. Tons of people going. I could get lost in the crowd. Plus, they had, like, pet accommodations.

There'd been a ferry brochure in a rack where we registered, and that's what it had said: pet accommodations.

Sasha knew a guy who had moved to Skagway two years before. They texted sometimes. We figured he could maybe link us up with a bush pilot who could fly me to Anchorage. One who wouldn't ask too many questions. She'd get hold of him somehow tomorrow. Ask him to meet me where the ferry docked in Skagway. She was pretty sure he would.

I lay there listening to the night noises—the cars swishing by on the highway, a door slamming, a TV droning somewhere above. Trying not to think too much about the gaping suckholes in the plan.

All at once, I dropped down into a hollow, aching place, and I couldn't climb out again. I missed Stella, missed her there beside me, missed the comfort of our kenning conversations. It pierced me to think of her back there at Aunt Pen's house. Waiting for me. Lonely. Lost.

And Piper. How could I have left her without telling her a thing? *Dropped off the face of the planet.*

I could call her now. I could use the motel phone. They'd never trace it back to me. Aunt Pen would have her hearing aid out. Maybe Piper would answer.

I slipped out of bed, tiptoed past Sasha. I picked up the phone handset off the nightstand. Took it into the bathroom. Shut the door. Dialed Aunt Pen's landline.

Ring.

Ring.

Ring.

I clicked off.

What would I say to her, anyway?

I'm alive. I'm okay.

I could come home, but I'm not going to?

I'm leaving you there, just to deal?

No matter what I said, that's what it would sound like. I wouldn't blame her if that was what she thought. It would be true, but not what I really intended.

Take care of Stella. Ken with her, if you can. Tell her I'll come back to her. Soon. I will, Piper. I will come home.

I swear to you, I will.

 24
SPIFFY

The next morning, when we were brushing our teeth, I caught Sasha looking at me funny in the mirror.

"What?" I said.

"Nothing."

"No, what?"

Sasha spit, rinsed her toothbrush. The critter leaned against the backs of my legs. He'd made it through the night okay—no scorch marks on the shower. So maybe the Tylenol worked?

"So what color would you call your eyes?" Sasha asked.

"What?"

"They're not even hazel, right? They're just full-out green."

I shifted uneasily. "What are you talking about?"

"Well, I was reading last night."

"Yeah, I know."

"I'd actually read one of those books before. When I was in middle school, I think. It's part of an old series about dragons. Dragons that float in their sleep. They flame when they want to come down."

"You're kidding."

"What I want to know is, how would the author know that? That dragons float?"

I shrugged. "They're all just guessing, right? Just making stuff up. And there's a truckload of books out there about dragons. Somebody's got to get it right."

Sasha shrugged, looked sidelong at me. "So, in this book, some people can talk to them telepathically. To dragons, and to birds."

Birds. I froze for a second, then reached for a plastic cup, filled it with water. Swished it around in my mouth.

"This girl, like, summons birds—makes them come. Or sometimes sends them away to certain places. She can feel what they're thinking."

I choked, spit out the water. "Really?" I said.

"And this other book in there talks about the language of birds. It says that in mythology, when people understand the language of birds, it's symbolic of sort of understanding and bonding with all of nature. If you can do that, you're, like, an ecomensch."

"An *ecomensch*? Did it say that?"

"Well, no. Not exactly. They didn't have 'eco' way back in the old mythology times. At least, I don't think so. But it's like that John Muir quote? 'When we try to pick out anything by itself, we find it hitched to everything else in the universe.' You've heard that, right?"

I wiped my mouth with my hand. "No," I said, "I haven't."

"Yeah, well. In that novel? The one where dragons float?

If people can do that thing with birds, they can do it with dragons too. They call them 'dragon-sayers.' And guess what color their eyes are? The people who can talk to birds—every single one."

I'd never read those books, but I'd known the answer for years.

Turns out, there was a problem with the ferry.

I sat on the bed with the critter in my lap while Sasha called about reservations. She started taking notes, but then she put the pencil down. "Twenty-one?" she said. "Honestly? Because—"

She listened for a second, then, "That's just faulty. Why not eighteen? Why not sixteen? Why not twelve?"

Listened.

"That is so flagrantly ageist," she said. "It should be illegal. You should—"

She pulled the phone away from her ear. Looked at it. Looked at me. Beeped off. "Twenty-one," she said. "Someone in your party has to be at least twenty-one. You are so totally fragged."

We went back through the options. Car—no, we'd both need passports. Bus and train—no. I'd need a passport. Walking— same deal. A plane wouldn't necessarily stop in Canada, so I wouldn't need a passport. But commercial airplane security was brutal. Besides, if the police were looking for me, the airports would have my information. And I'd need a photo ID.

"If we found the right private bush pilot, you might be okay," Sasha said. "I hear those guys are sometimes pretty lax."

"How would we know the right one, though?"

Sasha shrugged. "And the wrong one would report you."

The critter butted my hand. I scratched beneath his jaw.

"Do you want to go home?" Sasha asked.

The critter thrummed. The corners of his mouth turned up in a kind of smile. He was warm. Warm-blooded, for sure.

Did I want to go home?

Yeah. I did. And if home were an option—my real home, with everybody in it—I might have gone.

I sighed. "I'm not ready to give up. We might have to, eventually. But not yet."

"Okay, then," Sasha said. "Maybe we'll think of something."

It was the pet carrier that got us going again. If you thought of the critter as a pet—as opposed to a dangerous, probably illegal, and gravely endangered and/or mythological beast—there were certain things you were going to need. A carrier, for sure. A collar. A leash. So we called the front desk and got the address of the nearest pet store.

I wanted to go, see what-all was there. But Sasha and the critter weren't exactly simpatico, so I stayed at the motel and baby-sat.

By now the drugs had worn off, and the critter was feeling frisky. He jumped off my lap and chased his tail for a while, then got a megaburst of energy and went pinballing around the room. I made like I was going to chase him; he zipped under the bed. I tiptoed into the bathroom and hid behind the door. Soon, I could hear him, walking, his little talons plucking at the carpet loops. He sent me a questioning ken. I kept my mind blank. Slowly, he neared the door.

At the last second, I jumped out at him. "Boo!"

He jumped straight up in the air, snorting smoke. Then he galloped to the foot of my bed, tunneled under the spread, and speed-burrowed all the way to the top. He poked out his head and looked back at me. He kenned: Fizzy. Buoyant.

Laughing!

"I return triumphant," Sasha said, setting down a pet carrier and a bag full of stuff.

The critter had settled down on the bed with his hairbrush. Sleepy again.

"What's in the bag?" I asked.

She pulled out a collar. "For your medium-size dog," she said. "Alternatively, a harness." A harness appeared. Then came a leash. "Note the retractability feature." She demonstrated. "And you're going to love this."

"What?"

She pulled out something baby blue, beige, and brown, printed with an argyle pattern. Soft and fluffy, like a sweater.

"Spiffy, huh?" she said.

Spiffy? Who knew Sasha would be into spiffy? I looked over at the ugly yellow/orange coat she'd bought me. All those zippers and grommets. Not so much with the spiffy.

"It's microfleece," Sasha went on. "Machine wash, tumble dry." She did the spokesmodel thing with her hands. "Collar," she said, pointing to a thin band at one end. "Leg holes," she said, pointing to two round openings. "Handy Velcro closing underneath. I had to guess the size," she said, "but I think it'll work."

"Yeah, that's good," I said, trying to be appreciative. "It'll probably be cold in Alaska."

She frowned at me. "I don't think you fully appreciate the blinding genius of this purchase."

I shook my head. Guess not.

"Wings," she said. "That's how you know Mr. L's not, like, your basic monitor or Gila monster. But if you can't see the wings—if they're covered—this guy's just another lizard."

Ah!

In the end, we parked under a couple of trees outside the ferry terminal and scoped it out. We'd splurged on a late lunch in a nice restaurant, fed and pottied the critter, dressed him up in his spiffy new jacket, and buckled the harness over that.

Reluctantly, I'd drugged him again, on the assumption the Tylenol would keep him from flaming. Now he lay sleeping in his carrier at my feet.

All I had to do was get on the boat. I'd ridden ferries before. Once you got on, they never checked tickets. When you were on, you were on.

Just get on the boat.

We stared at the long, winding line of waiting cars and trucks. It was just after five; the ferry wouldn't leave until six, but they were supposed to get in line way early. To the west, beyond the ferry, the sky had gone yellowish and celumbral.

"Hey, that might work," Sasha said. She pointed at a UPS van. "If you could somehow sneak in there."

"But they'd lock it, right? Even if we did somehow get in, we'd be stuck for like three days."

"Hmm," Sasha said. "Drawback."

I searched the line, looking for something, some way in. Pickups, SUVs, cars, delivery vans, semis, busses. Petrol, biodeez, hybrid, electric.

"Hey, Bryn. Look there."

School bus. Three women stood just outside the door. They looked like moms, like parent helpers. One of them was pacing, talking into a cell phone. "Flat tire," Sasha said.

I saw it now. The bus listed to one side. As we watched, the rear bus door swung open and a couple of kids climbed out, then a few more. They milled around. One of the PHs came around and shooed them back inside.

Now the line ahead of the bus had begun to move. The people in the cars behind it started up their engines, but they had nowhere to go. The PH with the phone walked over and talked to some of them, but soon the drivers farther back began to honk.

"Chaos," Sasha said. "Opportunity."

Two things happened then. Someone in an official-looking uniform moved the cones that marked the lanes; the cars began to edge around the bus. And a tow truck pulled up to the curb behind us. The tow truck driver walked through the lanes of traffic and said something to the PH with the phone. She motioned for the kids to get out. They poured out both doors—front and rear. Most of them looked middle school to high school age, but a few were younger, too, maybe fifth or sixth grade. A couple of 'tants, a couple of Goths, but mostly just straight-looking kids in jeans. The PHs started yelling at the kids, motioning them to stay close to the bus, but the kids weren't paying attention.

Party time.

"Check out the camper," Sasha said.

An old woman climbed out the side door of a big trailer camper, a little way behind the bus. She dug around in her purse, pulled out some keys. The driver of the car towing the camper must have said something, because she looked up, walked to his window, and talked to him. Then she shuffled around the front of the car and got in the passenger side.

"She forgot to lock it," Sasha said.

"Maybe it locks from inside."

"Then why did she get out her keys?"

The tow truck driver was jacking up the left front corner of the bus. Going to fix the tire. Somebody honked. A bunch of other drivers joined in. A Subaru pulled out of line and tried to take cuts. The Toyota just in front of it tried to pull out too; I heard the crash, a metal-on-metal crunch.

Lots of people got out of their cars to look. Toyota man started yelling at Subaru man. The bus kids drifted over toward the accident. The PHs were calling, trying to round up the kids, but it wasn't working.

"There it is," Sasha said. "What we've been waiting for."

It was. I knew it. Nobody would notice if I opened that camper door and got in right now.

Don't think about it. Just go.

I pulled a note out of my pocket. "Could you give this to my sister, Piper? Just somehow get it to her?"

Piper would give it to Aunt Pen to read, but I wanted Piper to know it was *hers*.

"Sure," Sasha said.

I gave her a second piece of paper. "Here's an e-mail address for Taj, Mom's grad student. Could you tell him I'm okay? Not anything else, though. Not where I am. He might feel morally obligated to tell the cops."

"Okay," Sasha said. She reached over, stuffed a huge wad of cash in one of my pockets.

"No," I said. "You don't have to—"

"Shut up and take it. I'll put my Skagway guy on alert—his name is Bruce. But you're probably in way more expensive trouble than either of us knows." She slugged me softly on the arm. "*Nobody* has problems like you, Bryn."

I swallowed. No words came out.

"Now get moving," she said. "I don't want to have to schlep your sorry butt back to Eugene."

There was a thank-you in my mouth, but I knew she wouldn't want to hear it. Especially since it might come out funny. All pasty-soft and shell-less. I nodded at her again.

Just go.

I opened the car door, skootched out with the pet carrier, turned back to pick up the duffel from the floor. I had to lean all my weight against that messed-up door to close it.

Then I turned and walked away.

25  JUST RUDE

BELLINGHAM, WASHINGTON

Nobody seemed to be watching as I made my way along the line of cars. Plenty of other people to look at. People milling around, walking their dogs, gawking at the accident. The honking had pretty much died down, and so had the yelling, though every so often someone lost it and laid on the horn.

I could see the camper trailer, not far ahead. My heart was knocking around inside my rib cage. One part of me was thinking, What are you *do*ing? You're insane. While another part thought, Just *go*.

What would I say if I got caught? *Oops, I thought it was ours. We have a trailer just like this one.* Or, *I got separated from my parents and I can't find them, and I need to get on the ferry.*

As if anybody would ever believe me.

Coming up behind the camper, I saw the driver in the rearview mirror. He leaned forward, fiddling with the GPS. I set down the duffel and reached for the door handle. I pulled.

It didn't budge. I pulled again.

Locked.

I grabbed for the duffel and stumbled backward, praying the driver hadn't seen me.

"Ouch!"

It was a kid. I'd knocked him flat on his butt. I set down the duffel and reached to help him, but he ignored my hand and got up by himself.

"Sorry," I said. "You okay?"

He shrugged. "You should watch where you're going." He brushed himself off. Didn't seem hurt, though. He was maybe a fifth- or sixth-grader. Kind of early Harry Potterish. Short and skinny. Glasses. Short, dark hair that cowlicked in the back. He turned to go.

I glanced at the camper trailer. The driver wasn't fiddling with the GPS anymore. He was looking back at me. Not suspicious, really, but noticing.

So much for that idea. There were other campers and vans around here, but I couldn't just go around testing doors. I was about to give up, head back to Sasha so she could schlep my sorry butt back to Eugene, when I noticed the kid hadn't gone anywhere. He was stooping at my feet, peering inside the pet carrier.

"Whoa," he said. "What is *that*?"

"Um," I said, "it's a lizard."

"Like a *huge* lizard! Is it your pet?"

I nodded.

"What's its name?"

"Ah, Mr. Lizard."

"Mr. Lizard? That's the best you could do?"

Little twerp. "Gotta go," I said. I picked up the duffel, headed back toward Sasha.

But the kid tagged along. "What kind of lizard is it?"

"They call it"—I vamped—"a Burmese water dragon. They're very rare."

"Does it bite?" he asked.

"Um," I said, "yes. Better not get too close."

Behind me, I heard a shout from the direction of the bus. "Anderson! Get back here. We're leaving!"

"Be right there!" the kid yelled back. Anderson, apparently. But he stuck to me, still on about the critter. "Are you taking it on the ferry?"

I stopped. Looked at him. Drew in a slow breath. Maybe I had one more chance.

"I, uh, got separated from my parents and I can't find them," I said. "I've got to get on the ferry somehow. I can meet up with them on board."

"They wouldn't get on the ferry without you, would they?"

No. Of course they wouldn't. That didn't make sense at all. Stuff like this always happened when I lied. "I'm not sure they know I'm gone," I said. "I've got a really big family, and they get involved in their own activities, and they're very kind of focused, uh, on their own, uh, activities, and then . . ." I trailed off.

Anderson looked disgusted. "You're lying," he said.

I swallowed. Nodded slowly. "Want to know the truth?"

He frowned, suspicious. "Go ahead."

"I can't tell you everything, but . . . I've got to get the lizard up to a professor in Alaska. He'll know how to take care of him, or anyway, he can find out. I'm feeding him, like, junk food, and I don't have anyplace to keep him. Nobody wants to take him—nobody I can trust. My family . . . you wouldn't believe it if I told you about my family, but everything I just said about the, uh, animal is true."

"Could it die?"

"It could. Seriously. It really could."

Another shout from the bus. Anderson squatted to peer in the pet carrier again. He was thinking, I could tell. He stood up. "I can get you on," he said.

"On the bus?"

"Yeah. Let's go."

Anderson and I were the last ones in the rear door. Some of the bigger guys yanked it shut behind us, and then we were moving. We found a seat near the back; I set the pet carrier on the floor in front of me. The PH at the front of the bus was taking a head count. "Get down," Anderson said. I scooted the pet carrier toward Anderson and crouched on the floor beside it. Anderson skootched over to my side of the seat and planted his feet on my back. He got out his phone and started texting or gaming or something. Hopefully, not ratting me out.

The floor was sticky. It smelled like Cheetos and dust and some kind of fruity gum. "Is she still counting?" I asked.

"Yep." Anderson shoved his phone down in front of the pet carrier grill.

"Cut it out," I said. "No pictures."

He pulled the phone away and grinned at me. "Too late!"

Twerp.

"Okay, you can get up now," he said.

I did.

No one seemed to notice. They were all talking or texting or gaming or plugged in to their tunes. Some of them sucking on inhalers. "What kind of group is this?" I asked Anderson, real soft.

"Methodist," he said. Not looking up from his phone. I peeked. He was surfing the Net.

"Where are you all going?"

"Camp in Skagway."

Skagway. Me too.

"Are you all from the same church?"

"Nope."

Good. So maybe not everybody would know everybody else. An outsider wouldn't be so obvious.

Three kids in the seat in front of us turned around and checked me out. I smiled. Tried to look like I belonged. One of them smiled back—a boy. Then they all turned around again. I wasn't that interesting, apparently.

I looked out the window, tried to catch sight of Sasha's car, but we were facing the wrong direction. I could see the ferry, though. Coming near.

Yeah, it would be bad to get booted off the bus, but it was scary to be here too. Going to Alaska. To Skagway. Everything hinging on some guy named Bruce, some guy I'd never met.

What are you *doing*, Bryn?

"Hey!" Anderson poked my arm. "Hey, I can't find Burmese water dragon."

"They're really rare," I said. "Not many people know about them."

Anderson glared at me, indignant. "I've used five search engines already. I bet you made it up."

"That's right," I admitted. "I did. It's really a dragon. A baby dragon. The jacket covers up its wings."

Anderson blinked. Then shook his head. "That's just rude," he said. "If you don't know what kind it is, you should just say so."

The bus jolted; the tires hummed beneath us. It got darker all at once, and I could feel that we weren't on solid ground anymore. I looked out the windows. A parking structure, with water at the far end and metal walls on both sides.

I'd made it onto the ferry, after all. If I didn't get caught, I'd be in Skagway in three days.

Though after that . . .

Hopefully, Sasha's friend Bruce would meet me there. Hopefully, he could link me up with a pilot. Hopefully, the pilot wouldn't ask too many questions. Hopefully, the critter wouldn't flame. Hopefully, I'd be able to find Dr. Jones, and hopefully, he'd help. Hopefully . . .

Cut it out, Bryn. Breathe.

I breathed.

It helped, a little.

But there were way too many *hopefully*s in this plan.

26 STRANGE TIME

INSIDE PASSAGE, OFF CANADA AND ALASKA

There was a dicey moment when I stepped off the bus and one of the PHs looked at the pet carrier a little too long. "I didn't know we had pets with us," she said.

But Anderson said, "Oh, yeah, we're good. Come on, Ashley." The woman eyed me doubtfully but let me pass.

"Hope you don't mind, *Ashley*," Anderson said when we were out of earshot. "There's a bunch of Ashleys on the bus."

"Works for me," I said. "Thanks."

"What are you going to do with your lizard?"

Sasha had found out that you had to leave your pets on the car deck, either in your car or truck or whatever or in a special spot up near the front. They had "pet call" three times a day, when you could go down and take care of them. The rest of the time, the doors to the car deck stayed locked.

I looked around. "There," I said. I pointed to a row of pet carriers near a man with a uniform who was talking to a lady holding a cat. A girl set down a carrier at the end of the row. Uniform man didn't even look.

"Here goes," I said. Walked on over there. Set it down. Walked away.

Nobody said boo.

I didn't like it, though. It wasn't heated down here. The critter might get cold. Yeah, he had his jacket and his SolarSox. But still. He was bound to get chilly, wasn't he?

And what would he do when he woke up and I wasn't there?

But I didn't have a choice. Pet call. I'd check on him then.

Anderson caught up to me on the way up the stairs.

"He never noticed," he said.

"Phew."

He held out his hand, a funny, formalish, adult-like thing to do. I shook it. "Anderson Brown," he said. "And you are . . . ?"

I almost told him my name. I felt like I owed him something. But I caught myself. Don't be stupid. Don't let him in. The cops were probably looking for me, and if he let my name slip . . .

"Ashley," I said.

He dropped my hand in disgust. "What's wrong with you?" he said. "Can't you at least be civilized?"

It was a strange time, those days on the ferry. The first morning, we cruised through a dense, wet bank of mist; it felt like the world had shrunk to the size of the boat itself plus a narrow rim of heaving gray water. When the mist burned off, though, it was like we'd warped into a fantasy landscape. Mountains, veined with snow, towered on either side of the narrow strait. Moss green forests sloped down to the edge of the water, which mirrored the mountains and the clouds that streamed across the sky. Every so often, we headed for a tiny toy town, its buildings crowded into the thin strip between the mountains and the strait. Fishing boats nuzzled at the docks, and seaplanes buzzed overhead like dragonflies—bright-colored, glinting in the sun.

The feedings went okay. Three times a day, a loudspeaker announced pet call. A steward unlocked the door, and the pet people trooped on down. You could feed your pets in your cars, or you could feed them in the pet area with the carriers. There was a handy little peeing and pooping area, complete with scoops and plastic baggies.

Some of the pet people looked seriously stunned when they first saw my "lizard." Couldn't say I blamed them. He'd grown to the size of one of those huge tomcats that terrorize small dogs. But I told everyone he was old and harmless, and after a while they calmed down. Anyway, they were so into happy reunioning with their own little critters, they didn't have all that much energy to spend on mine.

I'd run out of ReliaVite, which would have been awkward anyway. Good thing the critter loved junk food. Hot dogs, chili, burgers, nachos. Most things with peanut butter. Anything with cheese.

The only thing he absolutely refused to eat was vegetables.

Sometimes he was asleep when I got there. Happy to be awakened. Even happier to be fed. But other times, I found him wide awake and desperate. He flung himself at me, climbed up my arm, draped himself around my neck. Seemed like he wanted to crawl right inside my skin.

I worried about the Tylenol. I wanted to keep him dopey enough that he wouldn't panic at being alone, but not so completely out of it that he'd miss meals or get sick. So I kept with the quarter tab, twice a day. It wasn't perfect. But I didn't know what else to do.

Anyway, I didn't find any burn marks in the pet carrier. So far, so good. Maybe Sasha's theory was right.

Except for pet call, there was nothing I had to do—just hang out and keep a low profile. But it wasn't good for me to have too much time to think. Whenever I sat down for too long, a wave of loneliness swept over me and settled around my heart. A couple of times I forgot myself and reached to ken with Stella.

Nobody there.

If you've never had a bird to ken with, you can't know how lonely that feels. You just can't.

I tried listening for the critter in the kenning way, tried to feel him down through all the decks. Mostly, I didn't get anything. But sometimes I felt a faint, buzzy hum that told me he was still alive. Alive and antsy. Lonely. Scared.

It pulled at me. Pulled hard.

So I kept busy. I explored every corner of the ferry—the inside parts and the outside parts, the upper and middle decks. I kept track of where people were, tried not to stick out in any way. I never, ever, ate in the restaurant. I bought food from the snack bar or the vending machines and ate it outside, on deck, where I could duck out at a moment's notice. I avoided the PHs, especially the one who'd asked about pets. I stayed away from the security guard, who fortunately gave off warning *clink*s from the assorted paraphernalia hanging off his belt: flashlight, phone, handcuffs, keys, gun.

But Anderson made a habit of appearing out of nowhere

and scaring the spam out of me: "Hey, lizard girl!" Very phaging funny. Holding up his phone and taking pictures when I jumped. He pestered me to let him come along with me on pet call. I seriously wanted to strangle the kid. Alternatively, I'd liked to have grabbed that phone of his and thrown it overboard.

Once, Anderson actually managed to sneak down with us at pet call. When I caught him taking pictures, I ratted him out, and the security guard took him upstairs. After that, I worried that Anderson might rat *me* out—tell that I'd sneaked on the bus. Good thing I hadn't told him my name.

The first night, I rented a blanket and a pillow, then took them outside, away from everybody else, and curled up on a deck chair. The engine vibrations rumbled up through the deck, into my bones. I heard the swish of water gliding past; I felt the rocking of the waves. I lay there, looking up at the stars. Which were monster bright. Not just pinpricks, like in Eugene, but spreading blots, like when you touch a marker pen to a damp paper towel.

The cold woke me in the middle of the night. I moved my stuff inside and made a nest for myself on the heated sleeping deck, as far as possible from the bus people. I pulled my coat over my head. It creeped me out to think of people looking at me while I slept. Especially since there might be some kind of alert out on me. *Missing girl. If you see her, notify the cops.*

But in between pet call and eating and sleeping, impossible to ignore, was the jaw-dropping beauty of the Inside Passage. Rain squalls went floating past, dragging purple shadows across the mountains and the sea. They pelted hard, cold drops on the deck, then drifted off again. And afterward, the sun streamed down through the clouds in liquid gold shafts, piercing the waters with their light. There was a rainbow every time. Seriously. Every single time. And then the sunsets: turning everything the color of peaches or of copper or of blood.

The first day, a pod of Orcas swam alongside the ferry. They stayed with us for miles. The second day, it was dolphins. They partied in the water beside us as if the ferry was a friend of theirs—a massive, dorky dolphin with embarrassing chugging noises and fumes.

The third day, it was three bald eagles soaring overhead. I'd never kenned with wild birds—it's not allowed, for kids. It could be dangerous.

But I was so lonely for Stella, I couldn't help it: I shyly reached out and listened. Felt a vibrating thrill of connection. Sensed the pull of their wings, the supporting firmness of the air. Something stirred inside me, something that wanted to push out to the edges of the sky and listen to it all, wanted to know as much of this world as I could possibly take in.

Nighttime was when it was hardest to leave the critter. After the final feeding, he would curl up in my lap and thrum. I'd scratch his eye ridges, his jaw. I felt like telling him things. I used words, in my mind, but I knew it wasn't words he understood. It was the things behind the words. The promises. The hopes.

Each time, I felt a faint, fizzy thread of *something* wending back to me. Something warm and happy and comforting.

Taj, now, he might call it imprinting, that *something*. And you could legitimately call it that. You could.

Alternatively, though, you might want to call it love.

27 MACROECONOMICS

ANCHORAGE, ALASKA

Quinn glanced at his phone, balanced on the arm of the recliner. It was ringing. He checked out caller ID.

That Gandalf guy. From Oregon.

What kind of bivalve would name his kid Gandalf?

The guy had e-mailed Quinn earlier. Said he had information about the egg fossil Quinn was selling online. Of mutual interest. Said he wanted to talk.

Quinn doubted the guy knew anything. Probably on a fishing expedition, trying to pump *him* for information. Quinn had given him his number, just in case, but he didn't feel like talking now.

Didn't feel like studying, either. Economics. He made a face. Could anything be more boring than that?

He cranked up the game on TV. Seattle versus Arizona. Spawn. He downed a swig of Alaskan Amber and let her ring.

Two minutes later, Gandalf called again. Quinn could see he wasn't going to get any peace until he talked to him. He muted the game. Picked up. "Yeah?"

"You the guy with the fossil egg?"

"Maybe. Why do you want to know?"

Turned out, this was way more interesting than Quinn had thought.

Gandalf claimed he'd seen another egg just like Quinn's. He wanted to trade information, maybe partner up. He asked where Quinn had gotten his egg, but no way was Quinn going to tell.

He was still ticked about that. Cap had distributed the eggs back there in the cave. Not all of them had broken clean, but they'd wound up with four good ones: one egg per person. Quinn's egg was his payment for leading them up there. Which was fine. Except that Quinn had wanted to be *in*. Like a partner. Cap had squashed that plan. Even though they wouldn't have any eggs at all if it weren't for Quinn.

"Where did *your* egg come from?" Quinn asked now.

Gandalf danced around it, hinting, but wouldn't tell. Then he said, "Have you seen the dragon?"

Okay. That did it. The guy was a loon. Quinn clicked off.

But he was curious, he had to admit. So when Gandalf called back, he picked up again. "I got a URL for you," Gandalf said. "Check it out."

Quinn thumbed it in.

It was a dim photo. You were looking through a wire mesh screen into a pet carrier. Bad lighting, but you could see some kind of lizard in there. Some kind of big lizard. It was wearing maybe a pet jacket, like old ladies get for their fluffy little rat dogs.

Quinn had seen quite a few big lizards on TV. This one didn't look familiar, but that didn't mean anything.

Still, it was spooky. Quinn remembered the cave, that little skeleton he'd seen. What would it look like if it hatched?

He scrolled up. The picture was part of a blog. Anderson Blogs the Universe. Quinn skimmed through it. This Anderson claimed the lizard belonged to a girl he'd met, and she'd told him it was a Burmese water dragon. There were some pictures of the girl. Anderson had looked everywhere on the Net and hadn't been able to find anything quite like the lizard. No such thing, he said, as a Burmese water dragon. Could anybody identify it? he wanted to know.

"That's the dragon," Gandalf was saying. "The one I saw. It phaging flamed at me. And that's the girl."

Quinn sat up straight. "Flamed at you?"

"Yeah. I'm trying to tell you—"

"You're not trying hard enough! If you want to be my partner, you have to be straight with me right now. Everything. From the beginning. Where did this thing come from? Where did the egg come from? Who is that girl, and how does she fit in?"

Then Gandalf spilled: told Quinn a story he would never have believed if the blog didn't back it up. About the girl—the friend of Gandalf's cousin—and her . . . whatever it was. In the crate with its ridiculous jacket.

"I'm still having trouble with the flaming thing," Quinn said. "You said the shed behind them was burning, right? Are you sure you didn't—"

"I know what I saw! I'm telling you, it snorted out smoke and sparks."

"And what about the wings? I don't see any wings."

"They covered them with the jacket."

Yeah, right.

On the other hand, though, the bidding on Quinn's egg was huge. It had shocked him, no lie. Some fools thought it was an actual petrified dragon egg.

At least, Quinn had *thought* they were fools.

And then there was that other egg. The new one, not petrified. The one Dr. Jones had talked him out of. Claimed it was illegal to possess it.

What if these things were actually hatching? What would they be worth?

Donald Trump money. Bill Gates money. Jeff Bezos money.

Now, that was the kind of economics Quinn could get into. Macroeconomics.

He looked down at his phone, scrolled through the school files directory. Textbooks, articles, syllabi. They went on and on. Waiting for him, making him feel guilty. He was so far behind, it seemed like he could never catch up.

"Screw you," he told them.

"What?" Gandalf sounded upset.

"Hey, not you," Quinn said. "Listen, partner. Tell me all about your cousin and her friend. Anything that could help. I'll see what I can find out and get back to you."

28 A DARKER DARKNESS

Sometime in the middle of the night, I jolted full awake. I lay listening to the sounds—the engine humming, the water swishing by. Moonlight laid long, pale stripes across the lumps of sleeping people. No one stirred. I could sense the faint, trailing echo of something I had heard in my sleep. But I couldn't quite drag it back.

There. A muffled noise, drifting up from below.

Barking?

Dogs?

Maybe. I probably couldn't have heard them in the daytime, with all the other sounds to mask them.

I listened, in the kenning way, for the critter.

Faint. Very faint. Seemed like he was sleeping.

Still, I felt uneasy. *Had* it been dogs barking? What was that about?

I shoved aside the blankets, drew on my coat and purse, and threaded my way among the heaps of sleeping bags, backpacks, bodies. When I came to the door to the stairs, I pushed on it. Testing.

It opened.

Unlocked.

I nudged the door wider. It creaked. The engine noise pulsed louder.

I hesitated. I'd left my duffel back with the blankets. Nothing especially valuable in there, except to me. But maybe I should get it.

A surge of barking, clearer than before. Something happening. Better go now. I slipped through the doorway and tiptoed downstairs.

The car deck had a dim, greeny, underwater look to it, and also the scary vibe of parking ramps at night. Light from the overhead fluorolamps glinted off the humped shapes of cars and trucks, campers and buses. But darkness lurked at the edges of things: on the floor between the cars, in corners, in the high deep hollows of the ceiling.

The dogs had stopped barking. I could hear the ferry's engines grinding—louder, down here, than above. I could hear the slap of water against the hull of the boat. I could smell the sea.

Another smell too. Faint. A burning smell. Petrochemical, sort of, with an aftertaste of metal.

I moved toward the pet carrier area, then stopped. Footsteps from over there. *Clink*s. The security guard.

A shaft of light swept low across the deck.

I slunk backward, away. Squeezed into the space between a van and an SUV.

A tongue of blue flame shot out, high in the darkness. A quick burst; then it was gone.

Oh, no.

The dogs started barking again. The flashlight beam swung wildly around and up, searching.

I searched too, in the maze of pipes and ductwork above. Lots of nooks and crannies where a small, floating critter could hide.

I listened for him, in my mind. Found his wavelength. Synched with him.

Still sleeping.

But I could feel a shifting in the ken. I could feel him slowly waking.

Hush, I begged silently. Be calm. Be still.

How had he escaped from his carrier? Had the security guard opened it, or . . .

That smell. Burnt plastic, maybe? Hot metal?

Had he *burned* his way out?

Footsteps again. Coming closer. If I tried to move, the guard would see me, he would hear.

Slowly, I unzipped one of my pockets. Felt around in there for the biggest coin I could find. Ah. A fifty-center. I threw it side-hand away from me, as far as I could. It clanked, bouncing off something metal, then clattered onto the deck and rolled away.

The footsteps moved away, fast. Stopped again.

Silence.

A cool breeze raked through my hair. I heard the creaking of ropes, the rattlings of chains. I searched up in the ceiling and at last found what I was looking for, a darker darkness in the hollows between the ductwork and the pipes.

The critter.

He wanted to come to me. I could feel it. He wanted to be held, be fed.

I kenned him happy thoughts. Happy, floating thoughts.

A staticky crackle—a little way in front of me. Then a voice, perfectly clear, from down here on the car deck: "Can't tell you that. Don't know."

A walkie-talkie?

Static again. Then, "Nope. Whatever it was, it's over. Nothing going on. Quiet as the grave."

Static.

"Yep."

Static.

"Nope."

Static.

"Nothing. Don't smell it anymore."

The static went on for a longish time.

Then the guy seemed to lose it. "What do you want from me, man?" he said. "Maybe somebody sneaked down here for a smoke."

Static.

"I don't know how! Maybe—"

Static.

"What d'you want me to do, break into every single car down here? There's only one of me. Can't be everywhere at once. If the captain's so agged, maybe *he* should come down, look arou—"

Static.

"Okay, okay. I'm just saying—"

Static.

"Yeah, whatever. Be right up."

His footsteps moved away from me. There was a *creak*, and a heavy *thump*, and a *clang*.

What was that?

Silence. I strained to hear the ring of boots on metal stairs, but nothing.

What was he doing?

Then, "Freakin' weird" I heard him mutter. "They don't pay me enough for this."

29
THINGS THAT HAD TOUCHED FISH

INSIDE PASSAGE, OFF ALASKA

I heard the door *snick* shut behind the guard. I stood waiting in my hiding place for what felt like a monster long time. He might be coming back. Maybe with someone else. Maybe the captain. I sent a stream of kennings up to the critter, trying to calm him, keep him floating up there, out of sight. But I could feel his yearning, seismic fierce. To come down. To be with me.

At last, I couldn't hold out any longer. I went to stand beneath him and kenned him down. He belched out a crackling flame ball and dropped into my arms.

He felt tense, all knotted up and twitchy. His little heart was fluttering. He climbed up my arm and draped himself over my shoulders. In a minute, he relaxed into me and began to thrum, a liquid vibration that softened my own clenched body clear down to my bones. He tipped his head and nuzzled my chin; I scratched behind his jaw.

"Critter," I said.

Something funny about his jacket. Patches of . . . stuff, stuck to the fleece. Something rigid and smooth. Like plastic.

Melted plastic.

The carrier.

So *had* he burned his way out?

Had he gone too long between Tylenols? Or maybe that stuff had never worked at all.

I needed to see the carrier, find out if it was useable. But going into the pet area right now . . . maybe not the best plan. If the dogs started barking, the guard might come down again.

Though clearly he didn't want to. Clearly, he'd been spooked.

Right before he'd gone upstairs, there'd been those noises. The *creak*. The heavy *thump*. The *clang*.

Hmm. Could it be?

I looked around and found it, a small Dumpster in a corner near the stairs. I shifted the critter to one arm. Opened the lid.

And pulled out what was left of the carrier.

Melted. Grotesquely warped and twisted. The door had dropped off, and most of the top was just gone.

I dropped the thing back in the Dumpster.

Useless.

Now what?

The critter was hungry; I could feel it. And I had to find a place for us to hide.

I wandered up and down the rows of cars and trucks, testing doors. Most of them were locked, but not all. And whenever I got inside, I found food.

People travel with food. They just do.

Car food: trail mix, amino bars, corn chips, jerky. Apples,

oranges, bananas. Processed cheese and crackers, turkey sandwiches, PB and J. Water in bottles, pop in cans, electrolyte juice in boxes. MoonPies, Frisbee Bars, Oreos, Peanut Blasts.

I didn't take everything—just a little from every stash. Not so much that you'd notice. Not more than like 10 percent.

Next, I considered evicting a dog from his carrier, maybe the yappy Chihuahua. Tying him up someplace. Repossessing his little home away from home.

Harsh.

And it wouldn't make sense, not really. First of all, the noise. Plus, the dog's owner would make a stink. Might demand a search.

I sighed, thinking of all the useful things inside my duffel. Wishing I'd gone back for it when I'd had a chance. But we were stuck down here now. Locked in until the next pet call. And I couldn't show my face even then. How would I explain that my pet's carrier had disappeared?

No, the duffel was history. I'd never see it again.

The red-and-black slide-in camper was crammed with equipment and smelled like fish, but it was the best place, by far, to hide. In a car or a van, you'd be right in there with everybody else. You couldn't even sneeze, much less, say, snort out the occasional puff of smoke. The camper, though, was a separate *thing*—a cozy little nest on the back of a pickup. It had two windows, which were tinted. You'd have to open the door to see us.

I cleared out a space inside the camper, then crawled inside with the critter and moved more stuff around. Fishing gear:

some poles, some nets, a couple of coolers. Two pairs of neoprene overalls connected to rubber boots. Camping gear: two sleeping bags, a propane stove, and two duffels full of guy clothes. When I was done, I had enough room to lie down, knees drawn in, with the critter snuggled beside me. I could even sit up if I wanted to.

We settled in for an early breakfast. The critter snarfed the cheese, the PB and J, and the jerky, but the Peanut Blast stuck in his teeth. He shook his head, snorted out smoke, and basically looked annoyed. It kept him busy, though, licking and smacking his mouth.

I rooted around in one of my many excellent zippered pockets for the half tab of Tylenol I'd put there earlier. Found it. Good. I'd left the rest of the Tylenol in the duffel. But I hated to drug him again. It couldn't be healthy. Plus, I felt less lonely when he was awake. I checked my watch. Morning pet call in two hours. I waited as long as I could, then bit the half tab in half, carefully pocketing one piece, and shoved the other deep into the squishy middle of a MoonPie. I held it out to the critter; one gulp, and it was gone. "Sweet dreams," I said.

By morning pet call, he was out cold. I could hear the pet people talking, kind of muffled from in here. I could hear the dogs barking and yipping and whining. I watched the critter, snuggled up against my belly. His jacket didn't look so spiffy anymore. It was grimy and had those plastic drips. The Velcro seemed to be holding, but the whole deal had gotten wolly-jobbered. The harness looked a little tight, and his wings bulged between the straps. Maybe they were growing. It hit me again:

A dragon.

Really? Are you *kidding* me?

An actual dragon.

Maybe it shouldn't be so surprising, given everything else that's out there. Platypuses and vampire bats. Armadillos and octopi. Bioluminescent plankton and hydrothermal vent worms. You couldn't make that stuff up. Plus the outer-space phenoms—the red dwarfs, the black holes, the quasars. Dragons weren't really all that extreme, considering.

But still.

A dragon.

I sighed, then shifted around, tried to find a comfortable position. We'd hit Haines around two p.m., and Skagway an hour later. If we made it to Skagway. This truck might get off in Haines.

Then what?

I'd just have to think of something.

Some stuff you have no control over. None. It's almost a relief, actually. There's not a thing you can do.

After a while, the fish smell got seriously rank. I doubted there were actual fish in here. Just probably things that had touched fish.

I wished I could pop a window, but I didn't want to risk it. Also, I was beginning to cramp up. Pins and needles prickled in my thighs and butt, and my right shoulder full-out hurt.

I'd slipped out to pee after pet call. But the pressure was building again.

Just when I thought I couldn't stand it anymore, I heard

voices. I looked at my watch. One forty. The Haines people would be coming to their cars. I pulled the guy clothes out of one of the duffels—the one with the camo pattern—and eased the sleeping critter inside. I packed in a few wadded-up T-shirts to disguise his shape. I squashed myself down, trying to keep every part of me as flat to the camper shell floor as possible.

The pickup rocked and squeaked as someone got in. Maybe two people. The engine rumbled to life.

So. Haines it was.

I could feel that friend of Sasha's drifting away from me, drifting north and east, shrinking into the cold distance. That Bruce guy. I hadn't realized how much I'd believed in him. Counted on him.

Haines.

We were going to Haines.

I kenned the critter, halfway hoping to feel a friendly thrum. But no. Still sleeping.

For the first time, I felt totally alone.

 30
COCKATIEL GIRL

HAINES, ALASKA

Josh pushed open the grocery door and headed for his pickup, squinting out beyond the rooftops of Main Street. Gray clouds boiled up from the horizon in the west. But it didn't look like they were going to get here for a while, and they might not have much water in them anyway. If he hurried home, he could probably get in a ride. He'd been tinkering with the mountain bike all winter, and now it was finally ready.

He beeped open his truck door and had just settled the groceries on the passenger seat when he heard some kind of ruckus up ahead.

What was that about?

He shut the door. Looked around.

There. Half a block up, across the street, a girl was jumping out the back door of a pickup with a red-and-black slide-in camper. A big man towered over her, yelling. She started to run away, but the man grabbed for her, caught her by the arm.

She struggled to escape, looked wildly around.

Hey. Not cool.

Josh didn't know either of them. And he knew everyone in Haines. Must be tourists.

Wait a minute. Josh looked hard at the girl's face. Maybe he did know her. Well, not exactly *know*, but he might have seen her before. Her picture, to be exact. With a cockatiel on her shoulder.

No. Couldn't be.

The man was reaching for a duffel that the girl held clasped to her body. He was still yelling. Josh heard the word "thief." The girl made a quick twisting, ducking movement; the man swore, let go of her, started shaking one of his hands. "Ow!" he yelled. "She bit me!"

The girl took off across the street, straight into traffic. Brakes squealed. Horns honked. She kept on, running in Josh's direction.

A second guy joined the yelling man; they lit out after her. More careful about the traffic, but still. Unless she had somewhere to hide, the kid was toast.

"Hey!" Josh called to her. He opened the truck door. "Get in!"

She slowed, looked at him, wide-eyed and scared. She glanced behind her—the men were closing in—and seemed to make a decision. She lunged for the truck, pushed the grocery bags to the floor and scooted into the passenger seat. Josh jumped in, started the engine, gunned it into the street. More horns and squealing brakes. Yelling Man caught up to the pickup, banged his fist on it, yelled some more.

Josh turned onto 5th, then glanced over at the girl. She was staring straight ahead, clutching the duffel on her lap.

Same girl. Wasn't she? Definitely a lot dirtier than in the picture. But this was the cockatiel girl . . . or her identical twin.

What were the chances of *that*?

On the other hand, Haines was a really small town. If you had to come here, you were going to wind up on Main Street at some point. And Josh came through here almost every day.

"Where to?" he asked.

The girl shrugged, not looking at him.

Her hands were shaking, Josh saw. Really scared. Scared of those guys. Maybe scared of him, too.

He turned onto Union. Checked the rearview mirror, hoping that Yelling Man and his friend weren't following.

They weren't.

"Look," Josh said. "I don't know what happened back there, and I don't care. Unless those were bad guys, guys who were trying to hurt you, in which case I can take you to the police station—"

"No!" she said.

Well, at least she could talk.

"Okay. So then, where do you want to go? I can drop you off somewhere or . . . whatever. Just say the word."

Shrugged again.

That was helpful.

If he headed toward home, or anywhere outside of town, she might think he was a rapist or something. Trying to get her off somewhere alone. He might get bit.

Josh was beginning to wish he'd minded his own business. What had he gotten himself into?

He couldn't just drive up and down the streets in the main

part of town all day. Plus, it was starting to smell in here. Something rotten. Like old fish.

He turned south on Front, checking the rearview mirror. No Yelling Man. No red-and-black camper. He looked at the girl again. Long, dark hair. Ugly orange coat. A little bump at the bridge of her nose that somehow managed to look cute. Maybe thirteen years old, fourteen max.

Could she really be the daughter of the woman whose phone he'd found? The woman who had disappeared?

What was she doing in Haines?

"I need to find a bathroom," the girl said. "I have to pee." Still looking straight ahead.

"Uh, okay," Josh said.

"But first I have to go to a drugstore. And then get something to eat and drink."

Josh would have gone for the bathroom first, but that was just him.

"I can pay," she said, turning to look at him for the first time. "I can pay you for gas, too."

She had nice eyes. Like in those pictures: very, very green. They seemed sad, though. Sad and scared.

"You don't have to," Josh said.

"But I will," she said. "I'll pay."

She said this so fiercely that Josh nodded. "Okay," he said. "Thanks."

This was one strange girl, Josh decided. She spent ages in the drugstore—doing what, she didn't say—while Josh waited in the truck. Hoping Yelling Man and his pal wouldn't spot him parked right out there on the street. Thinking about maybe leaving her there. But somehow not able to do it.

And then she took a way long time in the sandwich shop, deciding what kind she wanted. Which made Josh more than a little nervous, to be honest. He kept looking out at his truck, half-expecting to see one of Alaska's finest pulling up behind.

Aiding and abetting. How much time do you get for that?

She took her duffel with her everywhere she went and was extremely picky about bathrooms. Extremely. The one in the drugstore didn't suit her for reasons she didn't go into. The one in the sandwich shop was too dark, she said, and small. Gave her the creeps, she said. Didn't Haines have, like, a highway rest stop, something like that?

Best thing he could think of was Chilkat State Park. Josh headed out Mud Bay Road, explaining what he had in mind. It was a secluded, bumpy road, but she didn't seem especially worried. Not inclined to bite. In the parking lot, he sat in the pickup. Again. And waited. Basically, forever. It started to rain, lightly at first, and then hard. Those clouds he'd seen—they were full of water, after all. So much for the bike ride.

There'd been a couple of other cars in the lot, but now they cleared out.

He ought to take her back to town, just drop her off. This girl was a major pain. How did she get to be *his* problem? Let her sucker somebody else into chauffering her around.

Josh sighed. But if she was who he thought she was, she'd lost her mom. And that voice on the phone when he'd called?

He was pretty sure it was hers. The saddest voice he'd ever heard.

Dad? Are you there? Dad?

Josh twisted around in the seat, checked out the women's room door. Still closed. What did girls *do* in bathrooms, anyway? Besides the obvious. No wonder their lines got so long.

But in this case, he was beginning to get an idea. Because there was something funny about that duffel. Every once in a while, it had moved. Swear to God, it twitched. Once, it out-and-out squirmed.

Each time this happened, the girl had clutched at the bag and developed an interest in the scenery. Pointing out the window. Asking questions. Super-talkative, all of a sudden. What's that mountain called? Is Skagway over that way? Look, is that a bald eagle? Once, when the duffel twitched, he'd asked about it. She'd started scratching her knee—violently—claiming she'd moved the duffel, claiming she had an itch.

One thing Josh could tell about her, she wasn't a thief. Or at least, hadn't been for long. Because only a basically honest person would be such a terrible liar.

31

FULL-OUT SEISMIC NUTCASE

HAINES, ALASKA

I fed the critter, sitting on the toilet seat with my clothes completely on. He lay on my lap, chewing, making happy little grunchy noises.

For a little guy, he could really put it away.

While he was busy, I punched a Tylenol caplet out of its plastic bubble. I bit off about a quarter. I shoved the large piece into one of my many attractive zippered pockets, along with the bubble pack. I opened the hoagie the critter was eating, tore off some of the processed cheese product, wrapped it around the smaller piece of Tylenol, and molded it all into a rubbery little cheesefood ball. I pushed it back inside the sandwich.

Hate to do it, buddy. Have to, though.

He took another bite, chomped down on a good three inches of salami and cheese.

"I'd actually planned on eating some of that sandwich myself," I told him. Which was why I'd bought a foot-long. But at the rate he was going, there wasn't going to be anything left for me.

It was quiet in here, and dark. I could hear rain tapping at the roof. That, and the critter's happy chewing noises. The whole time I'd been here, no one else had come in. Maybe in summer this park would be full of people, but now it was deserted.

Excellent.

That bathroom in the drugstore where I bought the Tylenol— that wouldn't have been private enough. Not for this. It had been fine for me, but to feed the critter, I'd needed a really private place.

I sighed. I knew I should hurry, maybe wrap up the rest of the sandwich, zip the critter back inside the duffel, get out of here right now. That guy was there in the parking lot, waiting in his truck. Or maybe he was tired of waiting. Maybe he'd gone.

But I couldn't make myself move. Not yet. I was a mess. Sleep deprived and hungry, with mostly just corn chips and trail mix floating around in my bloodstream. Coming down from a massive adrenaline high.

God, I'd been scared. Shaking. I'd actually been Shaking With Fear. That one big man grabbing me, then two of them chasing me, and then the cute guy with the truck rescuing me, like a fairy-tale prince. But even he was a total stranger. My kindergarten programming kicking in, nearly impossible to override:

Stranger-danger! Run!

And I still wasn't thinking right, even now. I knew that. I needed to sit here a little while longer.

And think. Try really hard to think.

The critter chomped down again. Nearly got me with those

teeth of his. Those razor-sharp baby incisors. "Watch the fingers, fella," I said.

Could I trust that guy out there? If he was still there. I wouldn't blame him if he left.

If he'd been going to try something sketchy, he would have done it way before now.

Why was he being so helpful?

True, some people were helpful for no reason. But this guy . . . I didn't know anything about him. High school. Tall, with muscles. Long, straight, sandy-colored hair. Probably a junior or a senior. Maybe a football player. An athlete, for sure.

In Eugene, a guy who looked like this one would be dating a cheerleader or, alternatively, one of the perkier lacrosse girls. Way out of my league.

If I had a league. Which I didn't.

I cringed, remembering the first actual sentences I'd said to him. *I need to find a bathroom. I have to pee.*

Good going, Bryn. That was so way cool.

The critter was looking at me. He cocked his head, sort of questioning. As in, *Why aren't you offering me the rest of my sandwich?* He snorted out a puff of smoke. As in, *Hurry up!* He wasn't so desperately hungry now. Wasn't lunging and chomping.

I let him have the last of it.

Back to the important question: Could I trust this guy?

The critter stiffened. He tossed back the sandwich in a single gulp. Then, before I could stop him, he leaped straight out of the duffel and off my lap. He shot under the stall door, scrabbling his sharp little talons on the concrete floor, and disappeared from view.

"Hey!" I said. "Come back here!"

I grabbed the duffel, undid the latch, and took off after him. He was leaning into the restroom door, pushing it, opening it a crack. He wriggled through.

Who knew he could do that?

I found him outside, crouching behind a bush. It was good that he was house-trained, but still . . .

What was that on the ground beside him? A little mound of yucky *something*. Not pellets: something that looked like barf.

Had he puked up some of his dinner?

What about the pill?

I glanced at the parking lot. The pickup—still there. But the guy couldn't have seen the critter; he was screened by a row of bushes.

I gazed out over the bay. Rain dimpled the waters and rattled on the eaves above me. I breathed in the clean smell of it.

I was going to have to trust him. At least, halfway. I was going to have to apologize. I'd behaved badly, like a full-out seismic nutcase. After that, I was going to have to confess about stowing away and stealing the duffel. And then I was going to have to ask him to help me get to Anchorage. Skagway, at least.

It would be best if he didn't find out about the critter. Whose wing bulges were looking kind of suspicious. Who was blowing out smoke too often for comfort. But if I had to show him the critter, so be it.

At this point, I didn't have much choice.

 32

SECRETS

HAINES, ALASKA

"Luggage," Josh said, "doesn't usually move all by itself."

The girl looked down and sighed. Bryn, she'd said her name was. Which started with a *B*. Supporting Josh's theory that she was the one he'd called.

She'd come running back to the truck, splashing through the puddles in the parking lot, and straight off apologized for being rude. She'd confessed to her recent crime spree—stowing away in the camper, stealing the duffel. She'd asked Josh to help her get to Anchorage. Said she needed to see someone there. Some professor. Didn't say why. But when Josh had asked her about the duffel, she'd lied again.

Badly. Just her luggage, she'd claimed.

Now she admitted, "It's my pet."

"What kind of pet?"

"He's a lizard."

Yikes. Big lizard. And she didn't strike Josh as the lizard type. He'd thought it must be a cat, maybe, or a ferret. "Can I see?"

Bryn shrugged. "Okay."

Slowly, she unzipped the bag. Peeked inside. Then spread the edges so Josh could see.

The pet coat threw him at first. Argyle microfleece. Truly hideous. Lumpy, sort of. A long, spiny lump down the middle of the back, and two oval-shaped humps on either side. Then Josh got a look at the tail—long, pinkish, with spiny ridges all the way down. The thing seemed to be asleep; its head was mostly hidden under its claws, which looked strange. Not exactly lizard-like. But familiar.

Just then, the thing raised its head, yawned, stretched, and curled up again.

Josh drew in a sharp breath.

Quickly, Bryn zipped up the bag.

"See? Just a big old lizard," she said.

Josh tried to arrange his face so that his shock didn't show. Which was hard. Because he had chills. Actual chills. Because what he really wanted to do was unzip that duffel and stare.

Just a lizard?

Yeah, right.

He'd never thought he'd actually see one. Not alive. Not sleeping in a duffel in the front seat of his truck.

Not in his wildest dreams.

Josh started up the engine, just to give himself something to do.

"Where are we going?" Bryn said.

"I, uh, I'm kind of hungry," he said. "I could use one of those sandwiches myself."

"Me too," Bryn said. "The one I bought was for my lizard.

Well, I was going to share it, but he ate the whole thing."

I'll just bet he did, Josh thought.

By the time they got back to the deli, the downpour had ended. Josh waited in the truck while Bryn went inside to order two more foot-longs—one for herself and one for him. She'd almost left the duffel in the truck, but at the last moment she reached back for it, slipped the strap over her shoulder, and took it along with her.

So she didn't quite trust him yet.

Just a lizard.

Uh-huh.

If he hadn't seen the fossils up there in the cave, he might have bought it. But Josh could trace the memory of those bones in the living shape of the animal in Bryn's duffel. This animal was familiar to him, like the face of an old friend.

Maybe it was the bony ridges above the eyes, which made them look fierce, even when they were closed. Maybe it was the proportions of the head—the mammalian-looking nostrils, the high forehead—that gave the animal a look of intelligence. Hinted at the possibility of a good-size brain cavity in there. Josh couldn't put his finger on it exactly. But he knew. Beyond a doubt, he knew.

He'd known it even before he grasped the significance of the twin bulges beneath that pet coat, on either side of the animal's spine. Where wings would be.

No—where they actually were.

And Bryn knew. She had to. Wings were the reason for the coat.

A flying lizard.

Dinosaur.

Cap would love this. Josh remembered the time when he and Zack were little and Cap had taken them out in a tundra buggy. They'd come across a mother polar bear and her two cubs. One of the cubs had caught its paw in a fox trap. Cap had run at the mother with the buggy to scare her off, then moved the buggy away from the cub. Josh and Zack had watched while Cap went out alone and worked like crazy to release the rusty trap before the mother bear came back to maul him. It had been close, but he'd sprung it just in time.

Cap would know what to do to save this animal, too. He could use his connections to get them a flight.

Josh pushed Cap's speed dial number, then hit END.

Pushed speed dial. Hit END.

Sat there, feeling funny.

He hadn't talked to Cap in a while. And their conversations were different, since the cave. Cap seemed cautious now with Josh. Holding back. And truthfully, Josh felt different too. He couldn't believe Cap had been in on the break-in at the professor's. But what if he had? What if he'd changed that much?

Still, this thing was *alive*. Not a fossil. A totally different deal. Cap didn't poach live animals. He just didn't.

And if Josh didn't help Bryn, what would happen? Realistically, it was a miracle she had gotten this far, but her luck couldn't hold out much longer. Clearly, she was a runaway. She'd as much as admitted that. So the police would be looking for her. And if word got out about what was in her duffel, the poachers would come swarming. Sooner or later, someone was going to catch up to her. Depending on who it was, she could be in a load of trouble. Depending on who it was, he might be brutal.

So brutal, Josh didn't even want to think about it.

Cap, though, he'd protect her. He'd protect that animal of hers—just like he'd protected the cub.

Josh hit speed dial again.

Cap picked up. "Josh," he said. "What is it?"

Josh clicked off as he saw Bryn push open the sandwich shop door. The call hadn't lasted long. Cap could process things fast, grasp all sides of an issue, see past the parts of it that seemed to make sense to the problems that lurked in logical bends and blind alleys. Josh hadn't told Cap everything, but enough. Enough, probably, to get himself on a plane to Anchorage, along with Bryn and her duffel.

Enough to hear Cap say, "Good work, son."

Cap had mentioned a blog. Word was out, apparently, about Bryn and her so-called lizard. There were pictures of the thing. Vid links. Pictures of Bryn too. People were looking for them. Posting comments. The crazies were in on it, going on about fire-breathing dragons.

So he'd been right to call.

Bryn opened the door, handed Josh a sandwich, settled the duffel on her lap. "You said mustard, right?"

Josh nodded. He started the engine, headed north toward the Haines Seaplane Base on Portage Cove. Cap was going to call some pilots he knew: Stan Howard first, then Ron Lehman. Last resort: Sam Mills.

Josh hoped it wasn't Mills. Mills could be difficult.

Josh explained the plan to Bryn—that his father would hire a pilot and meet them on the dock in Anchorage. He, Josh, would be coming too, he said. He explained about his family, that his parents were divorced, that his father lived in Anchorage and Josh lived with his mom in Haines.

Bryn nodded. Said thanks. He couldn't tell if she was happy or not that he might be coming along. Mostly, she seemed to be eating. Really chowing down. Poor kid. She was probably starving.

Late-afternoon sunlight reflected off the wet roads, making it hard to see. Josh pressed his right elbow against his side, felt the shape of the sat phone in his pocket. Bryn's mother's sat phone, presumably. Which he hadn't told anyone about and hadn't thrown away.

There were a lot of secrets, come to think of it. Josh usually thought of himself as a straight shooter. What you see is what you get. But he hadn't been exactly straight with this girl. If he told her he knew the truth about the animal, she might get spooked.

In fairness, there were things she hadn't told him, either. Completely bogus parts to her story. Where had she gotten the thing? Josh wondered. Her mother, who had gone missing . . . had she poached it?

He looked over at Bryn. She'd finished her sandwich now and leaned back against the seat, still clutching the duffel in her lap. Her "pet."

Had she run away from home because of it?

How much had she sacrificed to protect it?

She probably loved it. She must.

It would all work out, Josh told himself. She might be upset at first, when she found out what Josh knew and that Cap was in on the secret. But she'd thank him in the end.

33  CRYPTOMAN

EUGENE, OREGON

Taj had the graveyard shift. Every night at midnight Jasmine came into the bedroom and tapped him on the shoulder. "Yours," she would say. She would slip under the covers as he rolled out the other side of the bed and stumbled into the nursery to pick up the screaming baby.

Daria. That was her name. Daria Antonia. Lovely, lovely name. Lovely, lovely baby . . . in the daytime. Truly. Taj could have stayed home all day, stared into that sweet face for hours.

But at night, it was a different story. Colic, the doctors said. Nothing much to worry about. Lots of babies have it. Gets better all by itself. Four months—six max. No cure for it; all you can do is hold her, rock her, gently rub her back. Talk to her softly, let her get used to your voice. Let her know she's loved in the middle of the night.

But Taj felt so helpless, holding her, when he knew that she was hurting.

It usually started around dinnertime, about six. Their beautiful, smiling, joyful baby would begin to whimper. Her face would wrinkle up and turn red; she would draw up her tiny knees. Taj could tell she was in pain. Before long, she was full-out screaming. Jasmine would pick her up; Taj would head for the bedroom, wedge the wax plugs into his ears, try to sleep until his turn. All too soon, it came. Graveyard shift: midnight to five a.m.

Tonight, Taj felt especially groggy. It had taken forever to get to sleep, and it seemed like he'd just dozed off when Jasmine had come in to wake him. Handed him Daria. Who was screaming.

Taj rocked her. Rubbed her back. Hummed to her. Logged onto his e-mail, cradling the small, wailing Daria in one arm. It surprised him how much he could do, in a sleep-deprived state, with a baby crying on his chest. When he saw the message from cryptomano1, he blinked. Cryptoman. Who was that? He scrolled to the bottom of the message. It was signed *Mungo*.

Slowly, through the screaming and the haze of fatigue, he put it together. Mungo. Dr. Mungo Jones. He was a friend of Robin's. Taj had met him several times. Mungo was the one who had invited Robin to Anchorage, before she'd disappeared. He'd had a skiing accident in his twenties that confined him to a wheelchair. Taj liked the guy. Mungo had been trained as a zoologist at Cambridge. He came from money. He didn't really need a job, but Alaska State gave him a light teaching load and let him do the work he loved: finding overlooked species. Cryptids. He'd discovered several previously unknown species of lizards and mammals, plus one new bird, as Taj recalled.

Cryptoman. Must be some reason he didn't want to use his Alaska State e-mail account.

The subject line read: *Robin's daughter?*

Taj clicked on the message. Read it. Mungo had surfed his way to a blog with a picture of something that looked like a cryptid lizard. Apparently, it belonged to a girl. A girl whom Mungo suspected, for reasons he didn't say, was Bryn.

Bryn?

Daria eased back on the screaming. Just fussing now. Maybe she'd go to sleep.

Taj clicked on the link: www.andersonblogstheuniverse.com.

And there she was. Bryn.

The picture Mungo had linked to was kind of blurry. Scrolling up, Taj saw a dim photo of a lizard. *The* lizard, Taj was pretty sure. In a pet carrier, looked like. Taj scrolled up again. More pictures, pictures of Bryn on some kind of ship.

A ship?

What was she doing on a ship?

Taj clicked on a short vid of Bryn feeding the lizard a piece of cheese. It was making that funny noise, like purring. Bryn smiled down at it, then something caught her attention, and she looked up. "Anderson!" she said. "What are you doing here? Get that thing out of my face. Ander—" The vid went black.

Bryn!

Taj began to read the posts, starting with: *Burmese Water Dragon? I Think Not!* He read all the way up—through the descriptions of and links to Komodo dragons, Gila monsters, and Chinese water dragons; through the story of Anderson's encounters with Bryn. Apparently, Anderson had met Bryn on a ferry on the Inside Passage to Alaska. Anderson was heading for

Skagway. But Bryn and the lizard had disappeared from the boat one night. And hadn't been seen since.

Taj groaned, cradled his forehead in his free hand. Daria ramped it back up to a scream.

Taj clicked on the comments. Some people interested in lizards in general. Way more people interested in this one in particular. And in Bryn. Though Anderson never referred to her by name. "Lizard girl," he called her.

The most recent picture, which Taj had missed the first time through, was of a strange, semi-squarish, plastic-looking thing sitting on top of a Dumpster. *The pet carrier,* Anderson had written. *Melted. Burned up from the inside. Dragon fire?*

Of course that would get Mungo's attention. He probably searched "dragon" every day.

Bryn!

Taj had totally let her down. He'd been texting back and forth with a herpetologist he knew, trying to find a safe place for the lizard. But there were times when he hadn't even looked at his messages. Days, actually. The days surrounding Daria's birth. Days when he'd just been too dragged out. Days when he'd been preoccupied with the lab. Reynolds wanted him out of there, but Taj had found something, something that could be huge. He needed someone to confirm his findings before he packed it in.

Preferably, someone who'd had some sleep.

Taj hadn't seen the news for days, had no idea what was going on in the world. He searched now, found what he was looking for: *Local Teenager Missing.*

Bryn!

He'd just assumed, since he hadn't heard from her, that she was holding down the fort.

What was she doing? Where was she now?

Was she all right?

He looked at his watch. Two a.m. Couldn't call anybody yet. He clicked back on Mungo's e-mail, hit REPLY. *You're right. It's Bryn. Help me find her, please! Call me on my cell and I'll tell you everything I know.*

Mungo called just as the graveyard shift was ending and Daria was winding down. Taj handed her off to Jasmine and took the phone out into the hall.

"So it's she," Mungo said.

It's she. Only Mungo talked like that. "It is," Taj said.

"There's an APB out on her. I've made inquiries. Apparently, her people are frantic. Do you know anything about this?"

"I didn't know she'd left. But that lizard she's got . . . I've seen it."

Silence on the line. Taj could hear Jasmine crooning in the bedroom. Then, "Do tell," Mungo said.

Taj told everything he knew about Bryn and the lizard. He told what he'd learned by carbon dating some of the shell fragments. One hundred years old. That thing had hatched from a hundred-year-old egg! But he held back about the microbes. The microbes from the Alaska dirt with the shell fragments, which acted exactly the same as the microbes on the lizard's shell, droppings, and saliva. Microbes that were doing things no known microbes had ever done before. Eating up endocrine disruptors lickety-split—so fast, Taj still couldn't quite believe it.

"We have to find her," Mungo said.

"Or tell the police."

Mungo was against this, for predictable reasons. The authorities would take the lizard, possibly destroy it. Or give it to someone who had no idea what it was or how to take care of it. Anyway, the whole episode would reflect badly on Robin. It might be considered poaching even to possess the thing. He, Mungo, would find Bryn, get her back with her family. By hook or by crook.

Taj believed him. Or at least, he thought it likely. Mungo was honest, first of all. A man of his word. Plus, Taj had heard stories about Mungo from Robin, and he knew that Mungo was competent in all sorts of surprising ways. He had an amazing network of connections, and if he said something would be done, it would. You might never see Mungo's fingerprints on it—he'd probably never tell you what had gone on—but a little while after you talked to him, things would happen. Problems would get fixed.

Still, Bryn was out there all alone, nobody knew where. Her friends and family must be out of their minds. And it was Taj's fault. At least, partly.

"I received a phone call," Mungo said, "from a friend. I think I know where Bryn is. Or, not precisely where she *is*, but where she may be soon. We have some contingencies to work out. My friend is . . . reluctant, but I suspect she'll come around. Meet me up here. I need someone Bryn will trust on sight."

Taj sighed. "I'd do anything for Bryn. But *that* . . . Jasmine would never forgive me." He explained about Daria.

"You old devil!" Mungo said. "I had no idea."

"Right," Taj said. He had no desire to discuss his personal life with Mungo. "What about Bryn's father?" he asked. "Do you know if he's come back? Or what about her aunt?"

"The father, no," Mungo said. "He's still away. The aunt . . . not someone I'd care to deal with. Not likely, from what I hear, to be cooperative. Might there be a friend? A mutual friend?"

Mutual friend. That triggered something in the dim caverns of Taj's brain. There'd been an e-mail. . . .

"Just a sec," he said.

He scrolled through his "deleted" folder. He'd trashed it without reading it, he was pretty sure. Subject line: *A mutual friend.* It had sounded like a solicitation. Like one of those "Russian girls" looking for a "friend."

Wait a minute. There it was.

He opened it. *I'm a friend of Bryn's. She's fine. So is Mr. Lizard. Can't tell you anything else, but she wanted you to know.* It was signed *S.*

Taj rubbed the bridge of his nose, tried to ease the headache that was radiating out from his sinus cavities. Maybe it was the sleep deprivation, but Mungo's plan was beginning to make sense. Taj's judgment must be seriously impaired.

He could always call the police later if it didn't work out.

Taj reread the "mutual friend" e-mail. Hit REPLY.

"I might be able to find someone for you," he told Mungo. "I'll call you back."

"Very well," Mungo said. "But hurry. If you find this person, we'll have to move hastily in the extreme."

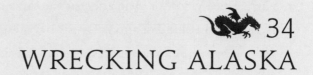 34

WRECKING ALASKA

HAINES, ALASKA

I must have dozed off. When I woke, the truck was rattling down a two-lane highway, and I could see the inlet a little way ahead. I glanced at the cute guy, relaxed at the wheel. Whose name was Josh, he'd said.

He turned to me. "You're awake."

I nodded.

"Got a text from my father. He's found a pilot for us, set it all up. We're flying to Lake Hood, the seaplane base in Anchorage. Do you have someplace to stay?"

"No," I said.

"You can stay with us, if you want. At Cap—er, my father's house."

I hesitated.

"Or we can take you to a motel."

A motel might be better. More private, with the critter. And I wasn't sure how close I wanted to get to Josh and his dad. I didn't know them. Not even Josh, not really.

I synched a quick ken with the critter—still zipped inside

231

the duffel on my lap. He kenned back to me. Awake. So he'd probably upchucked the pill. But there was a funny texture to the ken. Queasy, sort of. And antsy at the same time. I'd learned to recognize that kind of antsy.

In a perfect world, you could spend all day riding around in a pickup truck with a good-looking guy without ever once having to mention bathroom stuff. But we're stuck with the world we have.

"Do you think we could pull over?" I asked. "My lizard has to go."

Josh parked at the side of the road. I wished I still had that retractable leash, but the critter didn't seem inclined to run away. He snuffled slowly up through the tall, wet weeds at the side of the road, searching for a spot he liked the smell of, until he came to a place where the weeds were mashed down in a wide swath that went on forever.

What was that about?

In the outdoor light, I could see that the critter was kind of pale. At least, paler than before. And splotchy looking. I kenned him again. Something *off*. He felt weaker, maybe. A little shaky.

The critter's poop didn't look right, either. Kind of runny and greenish. Eesh. The sooner we linked up with Dr. Jones, the better.

I folded some of the long weeds over the stuff. Biodegradable. Good to go.

I debated giving him another quarter tab. I really ought to. We were going on a *plane*. What if he got all frisky? What if he flamed?

I kenned him again.

Not right. Not right at all.

I just couldn't drug him now. Hopefully, I wouldn't live to regret it.

Back in the truck, I asked Josh about the mashed-down weeds.

"It's the swarms," he said. "Porcupines, mice, different kinds of insects. Started happening a few years back." He started the engine, pulled onto the highway.

"We've got swarms too. My mom . . ." I swallowed. "Some people think they're maybe caused by toxins in the environment. Endocrine disruptors. They mess with hormonal systems, cause chromosome damage. Monster hard to clean up. But that wouldn't explain it up here. It's pristine."

"Oh yeah? PCBs float up here on the wind. They concentrate up here. Some of our sea mammals are so poisoned, their own bodies qualify as toxic waste."

"You're kidding."

"No! We're under siege. And they're not even *our* poisons. They're"—Josh glanced at me—"yours. Down in the Lower forty-eight. Like the North Pacific gyre, all that plastic swirling around in the ocean? It'll never biodegrade, just break into smaller and smaller pieces. Poison the fish forever and move on up the food chain. We didn't do that. You did."

Ouch.

"And the warming. It's worse here than anywhere, but we didn't do that either. The beetle populations have exploded. They're eating our forests, killing the trees. And after that come the wildfires—huge ones. Then you guys, you send your big-city lawyers up here, try to tell us that hunting and drilling are wrecking Alaska."

Whoa. What set *him* off? "I don't actually have a lawyer," I told my knees.

"Yeah." He looked at me. Sort of ducked his head. "I know," he said. "I mean, not you personally, but . . . people don't understand. They don't understand Alaska."

Maybe not. But I felt something between my shoulder blades, a funny little itch.

Definitely I would stay in a motel.

Josh turned onto an unpaved road that wound down toward the water. At the dock below, a red seaplane rocked gently in the chop. Set against the mountains and the wide, gleaming expanse of the inlet, it looked as fragile as a kite.

He parked the truck in a gravel patch in front of a small shack at water's edge. A faded sign on the shed read SAM MILLS, PILOT. ALASKA SAFARI AIRLINES. I kenned the critter. Not quite asleep, but feeble, muddled.

Uneasy, I hitched the duffel strap over my shoulder and followed Josh inside.

It was a tiny space, crowded with beat-up furniture: a wooden desk facing the door, two metal filing cabinets against one wall, two plastic visitors' chairs in front of the desk.

A small, white-haired woman, seated behind the desk, looked up from the computer screen and peered at us over a pair of narrow glasses. She nodded. "Josh," she said.

He nodded back. "Ma'am."

Ma'am? Wasn't that a Southern thing? Did anybody actually

say "ma'am" anymore? I had to admit, though, she kind of looked like a ma'am. Her hair was pinned up in a loose, wispy bun, and a black satin cord looped around the ends of her glasses and wound behind her neck. But the "ma'am" was in her expression more than anything else.

She turned to me. "You the other passenger?"

"Yes," I said. Biting back the "ma'am."

She looked me over, then picked up a clipboard from the desk and handed it to me. "Fill this out," she said.

I looked at it. Name. Address. Phone. Age. All things I didn't necessarily want to give her.

Josh took the clipboard from me. "Didn't Cap tell you?" he said. "We're not doing that."

The receptionist leveled her eyes at him. Severe. "Your father," she said, "does not determine what information this enterprise requires."

"What about that time with those environmentalists? The enterprise didn't require it then. Ma'am," he added.

"You, young man, are teetering on the very precipice of insolence." She rose from her seat, snatched the clipboard from him, then sat back down and turned to me. "Do you have any disabilities that would cause you to be unable to fly safely?"

"Uh, no," I said.

"History of seizures?"

"No."

"Heart attack? Stroke? Dementia?"

"Hey," Josh said.

"Are you currently pregnant?"

"That's way out of line!" Josh said.

I felt myself redden. "No! I don't see what that—"

"How old are you?" the woman asked.

Uh-oh. Was this going to be like the ferry? I hesitated. What would be plausible? "Sixteen?" I said.

She just looked at me. Josh groaned.

The woman turned to Josh. "Sorry. No can do."

"What do you mean?" he said.

"I'm not taking her. You, I'll take. If you can keep a civil tongue in your head. Not her."

"What! Cap already worked it out with you; you can't just cancel us like that."

"That was before I knew she was a runaway."

Josh glanced at me. My face felt hot.

"Look me in the eye and tell me you didn't know," she demanded. "You young people, tuned in twenty-four/seven. I saw her on the news, so don't even try to feign ignorance."

The news?

"She's on the *news*?" Josh said.

"And you," the woman said to me. "What about your poor parents? They're probably sick with worry."

"They're gone," I said, feeling a sudden, sharp surge of anger. "Missing. My mom first, and then my dad. Last I heard from either one, they were in Anchorage. I'm only trying to fin—"

I stopped. Pursed my lips. My whole mouth had started trembling. I couldn't get the words out.

"Trying to find out—" Stopped again.

"Oh, God. Don't tell me. Your mom was the one who. . . .

Last fall. That university professor. From, where was it? Idaho?"

"Oregon," I said.

"Lord help me." She slumped over her desk, rested her forehead in one hand. "He didn't tell me that." She sighed. "I'm going to get arrested for this. Kidnapping, aiding and abetting, transportation across state lines—"

"It's not across state lines, it's just Alask—" Josh said. The woman sat up, silenced him with a look. She turned to me.

"When's the last time you went to the restroom?" she asked.

Oh, please. Not this again.

"It's a four-hour flight," she said. "There's a funnel and a jar in the plane, it's all the same to me. But maybe you'd prefer to take care of that beforehand"—she jerked a thumb toward a door at the back of the room—"rather than in the air." Then, to Josh, "You too. Think about it."

I thought fast, then headed for the back door. When I reached it, I turned. "When will the pilot get here?"

"The pilot?" The woman glowered at me. She stood, plucked a leather jacket from the back of her chair, and shrugged it on. "The pilot's been here all day."

35  DOOMED

"Have you seen it?" Mills asked.

Josh had to strain to hear her above the vibrating drone of the engine. He felt the air currents beneath them, tugging them this way, nudging them that way, bumping them up and down as they crossed the branching veins and arteries of the sky. Mills glanced at him, then looked back out the cockpit window.

"Seen what?" Josh said. He didn't know what she meant—not for sure. He had an idea it was about the stowaway in the duffel, but he was hoping he was wrong.

It had taken them a while to get airborne, while Mills readied the plane, a sweet little de Havilland Beaver. Now they flew low over Glacier Bay Park. Over the mountain peaks, marbled with snow, and the flowing glaciers. Josh sought out that blue he loved, the light-filled blue visible in rifts in the dirty glacial ice. You couldn't describe that blue. It was electric, unreal. No matter how many times he saw it, it always knocked him out.

Mills made constant little corrections with the controls, always moving, never still. To Josh, she almost seemed like a different person up here. The tight, disapproving line of her mouth had relaxed; she seemed completely at ease and focused. You wouldn't think it to look at her, but people said she was one of the best bush pilots around. Ancient—yes. Prickly—yes. But good.

"Oh, come on, Josh," Mills said. "It's not sweaters and underwear in that duffel. Clothes do not move of their own volition."

"Shh," he said. "She might hear you."

"You know she can't hear," Mills said. "The engine's way too loud. Anyway, she's dead to the world."

He twisted around to peer into the backseat, where she sat with the duffel on her lap.

Still asleep.

She had zoned out right away. Must have been exhausted. He could study her now in a way he couldn't when she was awake. The curve of her lashes. The little bump at the bridge of her nose. The smooth, dark hair that reached halfway down her back. A twisted strand had gotten hung up in her lashes. Josh itched to sweep it back across her cheek and tuck it behind an ear.

But he didn't.

Again, he wondered: She'd come up here, alone, all the way from Oregon? Taking care of that "pet" of hers? Feeding it? Hiding it?

How had she *done* that?

She was definitely flaky, but you couldn't do what she'd done if you weren't pretty smart . . . and really brave.

Could *he* have done it?

Was *he* that brave?

She'd draped one hand protectively across the duffel. Josh could make out the shape of the animal inside—a lump where the snout pressed up against the fabric, a bulge where the belly was, the hint of a curve above the spines of the tail.

Mills spoke again. "We both know what your father and his cronies are into. This is better than a fossil, though, isn't it?"

How did she know that? Had Cap said something?

Mills went on, as if Josh had responded. As if they were having an actual conversation. "The thing I don't understand is, how can you be so all-fired sure you're *right*? You and Cap and all your ilk. What if the genetic material in that girl's bag could save us, one way or another? Or even just a few of us? What if it could cure prostate cancer, or Parkinson's disease, or diabetes? What you're doing is irrevocable. You can't change your minds later—none of us can. When the genome's gone, it's gone."

"Cap's not going to hurt it," Josh said.

Mills turned to look at him. "Do you really believe that?"

"Yeah. He's just doing fossils. He's strict about poaching live animals."

"If you say so. But ten bucks says he'll tell you something like this: 'They're not viable. There's no ecological niche for them. They'd just screw things up.' And if you press him, he'll say, 'What do you want to do, bring back the woolly mammoths? The giant sloths? T. rex? How well do you think that would work, environmentally? Where do you draw the line?'"

"You're wrong," Josh said. "You don't know him."

"Do you?"

Josh shifted, uncomfortable. He remembered when he'd been to Cap's place earlier this spring. Dirty dishes heaped in the sink. Stacks of bills on the kitchen counter. The truck ran rough, and the house looked like it was molting strips of yellowish paint.

So unlike Cap. "Shipshape" used to be his motto.

"It's a good point about the ecological niche," Mills said. "In case you didn't notice. How big is this animal going to be? How dangerous? Where do you put it so it doesn't wreck everything in the environment? That's definitely a problem. On the other hand, it's *here*. It wasn't cloned from prehistoric amber. It hatched out of an egg. Which was *here*, not manufactured in a lab. So it's not extinct. Not yet. It's in our care."

How did she know all that, about the egg? Who had she been talking to? But Josh kept his mouth shut. If he didn't argue, eventually she'd run out of steam.

"And another thing: I don't want that girl getting hurt," Mills said.

"Cap would never do that!"

"No," she said. "I know he wouldn't. Not physically. I'm sure Cap will see she gets home or wherever she needs to be. But mark my words, her 'pet' is going to disappear. And that's going to hurt her. Anyone can see it. Once Cap gets his mitts on that thing, it's doomed."

Doomed. Josh flashed back to the cave, to those fossils in the eggs. A word popped into his head: *Exquisite*. Those tiny, curled-up claws. The rib cage, as perfectly drawn as the circuits on a computer chip. The precise little knobs of the spine and tail. He remembered that feeling he'd had there, a feeling of expanding inside—huge and calm.

He looked back again at Bryn. At her hand moving up and down with the animal's breathing. She looked so unprotected, so vulnerable.

Mills broke into his thoughts. "You sure you want me to take her to Anchorage? I could take her somewhere else. In fact, I've got half a mind to."

"No," Josh said. Absolutely not. Cap would be waiting. Josh remembered his voice on the phone. Even now, the memory warmed him. *Good work, son.*

No, it would be fine.

"Okay, then," Mills said.

Clouds crept in, thin strands at first, then long, white sheets of them, streaming past the windows. Blotting out the mountains and the sea.

Mills cleared her throat. "*Does* it have wings?" she asked.

Josh hesitated. What the hell. "Yeah," he said. "She's got it in some kind of jacket-looking thing. But you can see the wing shapes beneath it."

"Wings." Mills shook her head. "I'd better not see it, then. If I saw wings, no matter how much damage the animal could cause, there's no way I could turn it over to your father."

PART IV
DRAGON

Why do you think
I've made myself scarce,
Hid from you year after year?
So you can name me?
So you can claim me?
Now I've gone and I won't reappear.
—from "Cryptid Rant," by Mutant Tide

One hit, another hit—
It starts with such a little bit.
But soon there's just no stopping it:
Gone viral!

Every person that you know
Sends your tidbit, makes it go
Across the World Wide Web, oh ho!:
Gone viral!

Fifty, a hundred grand
A million, billion, trillion, and
A googolplex links cross the land:
Gone viral!
—from "Gone Viral!" by Pixel Slippers

36
CELEBRITY LIZARD

ANCHORAGE, ALASKA

I woke in the thrumming dark. The critter's back rose and fell beneath my hand. I could tell that he was sleeping. I kenned him. Still weak and shaky. Something not right.

I blinked, stretched up, looked out the cockpit window between Josh and Sam Mills. Samantha, she'd said. Ms. Mills, to you, she'd said.

There was Anchorage, framed by snowy mountains, glittering with lights, speeding toward us across the darkness. The tallest buildings, mirrored in the inlet, stretched wobbly, luminous ribbons across a sheen of mud and water, drawing us in.

Anchorage. Where Mom had gone, and Dad. I leaned toward it, wishing I had like satellite vision, so I could zoom in on every avenue, every back street, every space between every building.

The plane banked. Now I could see the airport lights below, and the dark, empty space of a lake. Seaplanes clumped around lighted slips near the shore. I felt a thump as we touched down, then a solidish floor of water moving beneath us. Twin plumes of gleaming spray rose up on either side.

We taxied in. Ms. Mills was talking on the radio; Josh was talking on his phone. The engine had throttled down; I could hear some of what Josh was saying. "Yeah," he said. And, "You're kidding." And, "How many?"

I rubbed my eyes. Checked my watch: just past eleven. I'd need to be alert now. I'd ask Josh to take me to a motel. I could call Dr. Jones tomorrow. Or no, not call him. Sasha had said I should show up on his doorstep, and she was probably right. I could take a bus or a cab.

Josh turned around. Smiled at me. "That should work," he said into his phone. "Okay. See you in a minute."

He beeped off. "Cap says there's a crowd there, on the other side of the fence. We'll have to go through them to get to the car."

"What's going on?" I asked.

"Don't know," he said. "But Cap says it won't be a problem."

Ms. Mills cut the engine. She slid out to stand on one of the plane's floats and tossed a line to a tall man waiting in a puddle of artificial light at the edge of the slip. Josh's dad? Ms. Mills stepped onto the dock; Josh scrambled out behind her. I could see the crowd at the shore end—a dark mass of people behind a chain-link fence. Before I could get out, though, Ms. Mills ducked back into the plane and fiddled with the controls. "A friend of yours is here," she murmured. "She'll find you. Go with her."

A friend? I started to ask who, but Ms. Mills said, "Shh," and tipped her head for me to go.

Josh's dad, a graying, square-jawed man, introduced himself as Cap. He reached to take my duffel but I clutched it to my chest. The critter had wakened. I felt his ken: jittery and thin.

Cap's hand stayed out there. "No, really," he said. "I'll take it."

I shook my head.

"Cap," Josh said. "It's okay."

Cap shrugged. Let the hand fall. "Suit yourself," he told me.

Ticked. I could tell. He smiled, though, hiding it. A smile that didn't reach his eyes. "Let's go, then," he said. "Stay close. We're going to have to navigate the crowd."

I followed Cap down the dock. Glanced back at Ms. Mills. Who was watching us. *She* didn't smile.

A friend? What friend? And how did she know?

"Mr. Lizard!"

I whirled around. The fence was shaking, making a ringing sound.

"Mr. Lizard!"

"Mr. Lizard!"

I stopped. Stared. People were climbing the fence. "Let's get a move on," Cap said. He grabbed the duffel, yanked it out of my hand, and marched on up the dock.

"Hey!" I said. "Give it back!"

"Just *move*," he called over his shoulder.

"Make him give it to me!" I said to Josh.

"I will," he said. He looked straight into my eyes, reaching toward me, as if to take my arm. Then hesitated. Didn't touch me. "I will. But first, let's get out of here, okay?"

A *clang*. A *thump*. I tore my eyes from Josh. People dropped over the top of the fence, poured down the path, onto the dock. They surrounded Cap now, blocking him. Chanting: *Mr. Lizard. Mr. Lizard. Mr. Lizard.*

Somebody yelled, "Bryn!" A bright white halo of hair in the crowd, just ahead.

Sasha.

I gaped at her.

"Don't just phaging stand there," she said. "Snag Mr. Lizard!"

Josh said, "Wait! It'll be fine," but all at once people were forcing their way in between us. I cut through the crowd, which actually seemed to be yielding, giving way before me. I reached Sasha and kept going as she ran interference. I could see Cap now, clutching the duffel against himself, pushing back against a clump of people who were trying to take it away. Like a huge old bull caribou, harried by wolves.

I kenned with the critter. Jaggedy. Off balance.

Combustible.

Somebody lunged for the duffel. Cap jerked it away.

A blinding blue flash. People screaming, running, jumping into the water. Smoke bloomed up, swirled in the dock lights, surrounded us. For a moment, I couldn't see anything: not Cap, not the duffel. Then Cap reappeared in the thinning blue haze. Holding his arm, as if it hurt.

"There it is!" Sasha pointed to where the duffel lay charred and smoking on the dock ahead.

I ran to the critter, kenning him not to flame. I tried to unzip the duffel, but it was hot—too hot. Parts of it were melting.

High polyester count. Why didn't they make these things out of cotton?

I pulled my shirtsleeves over my fingers and tugged at the zipper. The critter slithered out and hooked his talons into my coat. He climbed up a sleeve until his head pushed into my neck, until I was breathing his smoky breath.

I looked up. People had formed a silent circle around us; I blinked in the glare of their flashing phones. Josh stood toward the back, looking stunned.

Sasha smiled. "Quite the celebrity, your Mr. Lizard," she said.

"Josh! What are you doing? Get it!"

Cap shoved toward us through the crowd; Josh didn't move. People jumped in front of Cap, tried to block him, but he was strong. They couldn't hold him forever.

We ran.

37  VIRAL

ANCHORAGE, ALASKA

The crowd opened up, letting us through. I heard a siren, coming near. I followed Sasha toward the gate—now open. But something jerked me backward. Someone was holding me, an arm clamped hard about my waist.

The critter stiffened, hissed. "Sasha!" I called.

"Hey!" She appeared at my side. "Let her go!" I heard some *thud*s, a *crack*, some *oof*s. "Help!" Sasha yelled. "They're after Mr. Lizard!"

And the crowd thickened all around us. Someone swore. A yelp of pain. Then I was free again, running, holding tight to the critter and following Sasha through a dark parking lot. She opened the back door of a black car with tinted windows. "Get in!" she said.

I did. She jumped in after me, yanked the door shut. I settled the critter in my lap; the driver peeled out onto a frontage road and headed toward the highway, going fast.

Behind us, the siren cut out. I looked back and saw flashing lights, back near the gate.

"Woo hoo!" Sasha said. "We busted out in a blaze of phaging glory."

I blinked at her. I had so many questions, I hardly knew where to start. The most obvious one rose to the surface. "What are you doing here?" I asked.

Sasha laughed. "I'm everywhere!"

Not helpful. I was so confused. "Where are we going? Who were all those people? Who is . . ." I nodded toward the driver, in the seat in front of me.

"Long story. Mungo, here—" The driver flicked his eyes at me in the rearview mirror and nodded. "Mungo sent for me."

Mungo? "Dr. Mungo Jones? From the university?"

"At your service," he said. We squealed around a corner; I clutched the grab bar. Dr. Jones said something into his earpiece; he was making a call.

Dr. Jones! I leaned back, breathing in the leathery smell of the seats, feeling safer, somehow, than I'd felt in weeks. I hadn't had to find him at all. He'd found me. He'd know what to do.

The critter had melted into my lap. Not sleeping. More like tapped out, completely drained. We accelerated onto the highway. I relaxed into it, let the g-forces squish me back against the seat.

Another question surfaced. "How do you two know each other?" I asked Sasha.

"I'm getting to that," she said. "So, Mungo saw you on the blog and called Taj."

"What blog?"

"You don't know about the blog?"

"What are you talking about?"

"Do you know a guy named Anderson?"

"Anderson! He's not a guy; he's a kid."

"He's a blogging kid. Anderson Blogs the Universe dot com. He's put up pictures of you—you and Mr. Lizard. Lots of comments. Mr. L's got quite the fan base. New Zealand. Sweden. Japan."

Anderson! That little twerp!

"Those people with their phones tonight?" she said.

"Yeah?"

"They're taking pictures. Uploading to the blog. Mungo put out the word to his students, and it went viral. You know that pet carrier I bought?"

"Yeah?"

"There's a picture of it, all wrecked and melty and stuff."

"Anderson found that thing?"

"And posted it. *That* energized the base."

Anderson! I was going to strangle him.

And yet . . . that blog of his might have saved the critter's life.

I looked down at the little guy, curled up in my lap.

Listless. Not right.

Hopefully, he was saved.

"That guy you were with on the dock?" Sasha said. "He and his dad are poachers! Mungo knows all about them."

Poachers. So Josh had meant to rat me out. Had he ever wanted to help me—even when he rescued me in Haines? Or had he known about me from the blog? Planned it all along?

The painful part was, I'd liked him. I'd thought he maybe liked me. Not girlfriend liked, but still. I felt all twitchy, halfway mad and halfway mortified.

"Phew!" Sasha said. "Do you smell that? It's, like, dead fish."

Superb. That would be me.

The critter flicked his tail. Beneath my hand, his breathing felt different. Labored.

"Can we turn on the light for a sec?" I asked.

Sasha flipped on the overhead. "What is it?"

"Something's wrong with the critter."

He looked even worse than before. Super-pale, speckled with funny white spots. He lay limp, like he was sleeping, but with eyes half-open. Even when I scratched his jaw, he didn't thrum. I kenned him. Felt a feeble, sickly tingle in my mind.

"Is that normal?" Sasha asked.

I looked at her.

"Right," she said. "Normal, not so much."

"Maybe he's dehydrated," I said.

"Try this." Dr. Jones handed back a small, metal water bottle. I wedged the nozzle between the critter's jaws and tipped the bottle. A thin stream of water trickled out of his mouth and onto my jeans.

Usually, he'd at least try. He'd lick at the nozzle and if that didn't work, he'd bite it.

"Think he's hungry?" Sasha asked.

"Could be." But definitely he was sick. I thought about all the junk food I'd given him. I should have been more careful. Even the cheese could have been bad. What if he was, like, lactose intolerant? I'd been lazy. I should have stuck with the ReliaVite. And on top of everything, I'd been drugging him. That stuff was way toxic if you overdosed.

"Hey, little guy." I stroked the tips of my fingers across his eye ridges. "We've got to stop," I said. "We've got to feed him. He isn't right."

We stopped at a grocery store. Dr. Jones handed Sasha some money. "We're going back to the ReliaVite," I said.

"Strawberry, right?"

I nodded. "And the baster and the cup. You know the drill."

The door shut behind her. Suddenly quiet in the car. Dr. Jones had hardly spoken to me at all—he'd been talking on the phone—but now he turned around. I scooted to Sasha's side of the seat, to see him better. Green eyes. I remembered them from his website.

"How is Samantha?" he asked. His voice was deep and somehow comforting.

Samantha: the pilot, Ms. Mills. "She's, ah, fine," I said.

"Friend of mine," Dr. Jones said.

"Oh." That explained some things.

He leaned toward the critter. Drew in breath. "Will you look at that," he said. He reached his hand toward him, then hesitated. "May I?"

I nodded.

He moved his hand along the critter's jacket, tracing the ridge of the spine. Gently, he stroked a talon, then picked it up, examined it.

I kenned the critter a wave of calm. Thinking that a stranger's touch might upset him. But he seemed too sick to care.

Dr. Jones pointed to the bulges under the jacket, on the critter's sides. "Wings, I presume?"

"Yes."

"I've known about these creatures for years. But to actually see one . . ."

Something clicked. The sketches on his wall, in the website photo. "Those sketchbooks Mom had. Were they yours?"

"I gave them to her for safekeeping, along with the egg. I do have other sketches, but . . . They're evidence, you see. Old eyewitness reports. Substantiation that they've been here before." He brushed his fingertips across the critter's eye ridges. I sent another calming ken.

Dr. Jones looked at me. Cocked his head. Something different in his face, a kind of listening. "You're doing it now, aren't you?" he asked.

"Doing what?"

"Kenning."

Kenning. He knew.

"Do you know any other kenners?" he asked. "Outside of your own family?"

I shook my head. *Other kenners?*

"There aren't many of us," he said. "Though perhaps more might ken but don't know it. But, yes. We're a small band. And every so often, more of us turn up."

I sat perfectly still, astonished at the crashing relief I felt, to hear that there were others.

Dr. Jones looked down at the critter. "Is it different with . . .
a dragon?"

"A little. There's a deeper under-vibe, like a bass guitar. But
sort of jaggedy sometimes. A little bit . . . hot. That's not a good
description, but . . ."

He nodded. "Words won't do, for kenning."

"Do you want to try?" I said.

"I couldn't possibly presume. The bond is yours." He studied
me for a moment. "I have to admit, though, I'm envious."

"It hasn't exactly been a picnic."

He laughed, low and rumbly. "No, I can't imagine it has." He
sighed. "Much has transpired," he said. "Events you will need to
know of, and a favor I must ask. I wish I had longer to explain,
but we're in a bit of a rush."

In the short time while Sasha was gone, I learned a truckload of
stuff.

I learned that Anderson's blog had the scientific community
buzzing: cryptozoologists, zoologists, wildlife biologists. And
also, unfortunately, poachers.

I learned that Dr. Jones had first heard about the critter's
egg from a student last fall. Dr. Jones had talked the student
into giving it to him and had passed the egg to Mom because
he'd feared that poachers were out to steal it from him. And as
it turned out, he'd been right. Both his office and his home had
been raided.

I learned that Mom had paid the student to take her to the
mountain cave where the egg had been found. She'd taken the

dirt samples and found the fossilized egg. She hadn't known what it was until she'd chipped it out of the rock. She was going to turn it in. It's illegal to take them out of Alaska. But then, a little while later, she'd disappeared.

I learned that several weeks ago, Dr. Jones had hired a different student to search the cave and set up a camera trap— a motion-activated camera in a tree outside the cave entrance.

Now Dr. Jones pulled out his phone. A sat phone. "Would you care to see what we recorded?"

I hugged myself, uneasy. "I guess."

He tapped at the screen, handed the phone to me. It was running a vid. I watched.

I couldn't tell what it was at first. A large, moving *something*— black or super-dark green—seen from a camera above. The air around it shimmered like hot pavement on a summer day. I made out the shapes of things that could be nostrils, things that could be eyes, things that could be ears, or maybe horns. Then came a long neck and back—sharp ridges along the spine.

At first it was like those old bogus vids of Nessie or Bigfoot: the thing could possibly be what they claimed it was, but it looked completely fake.

The scales were what started to get me. Chipped and broken pieces along the ridge of the neck and spine. Variations in the color—veined and mottled, darkening around the edges like maybe they were tarnished.

I shivered, drew in a sharp breath. "Is it . . ."

Dr. Jones said, "Watch."

The thing kept coming. Enormous. It didn't move like you'd

expect, not powerful and smooth. No, it hobbled, sort of. Stiff. Like an old guy with arthritis. And then, incredibly, wings: folding as I watched, turning from stained-glass translucent green in the slanting daylight to flat black in the shadows of the cave.

The vid ended. Dr. Jones took his phone.

I leaned back in the seat. Laid my hand on the critter's back and felt him breathe. Something was squeezing on my chest; tears sprang into my eyes. "His mother?" I asked.

"We think so."

"Where's she phaging *been*?"

He shrugged. "Not all egg-laying animals stay to incubate. Some leave, and return for the hatching. Some never return at all. In this case, the incubation period may have been extremely long."

"Like years?"

"Or decades. Perhaps many decades. Tests have shown that the one live egg"—he nodded at the critter—"was nearly a hundred years old. I'm guessing these creatures live for centuries."

I sat there a moment. Breathed.

I'd always assumed there wasn't a mother. Not alive, anyway. I'd assumed that if he'd had one, she'd have been with him. I'd assumed that if there was a full-grown phaging *dragon* cruising around Alaska, I'd have heard about it. Everybody would.

Dr. Jones's eyes met mine. There was something that had to be done—something megahard—and it filled up all the space between us.

The critter's mother would know how to care for him. Could save him, maybe.

"If only I could go," Dr. Jones said. "I'd give anything to see, but—" He pointed to a folded metal contraption leaning against the front seat.

A wheelchair.

I swallowed. "You mean, it would be just me and—"

"Sasha has volunteered to go up there with you."

Oh, God. I looked at him, pleading. "I can't. No, I really can't. That dragon—you saw her—she's . . ." A monster. A full-out seismic *monster*.

"You wouldn't have to go near her, or even see her," Dr. Jones said. "You could merely leave her baby at the mouth of the cave."

Merely?

The critter moaned, snorted out a puff of smoke.

And what if some wild animal found the critter at the cave mouth? What if his mother rejected him? What if she caught me messing with her baby and burned me to a crisp? All kinds of bad things could happen.

"Don't you have a safe place we could keep him? I could help you ken with him or whatever, and—"

"Bryn," he said. "He should be with his mother. Only a dragon can properly raise a dragon."

I knew that. I did. Nobody should be separated from his mother. And I'd never meant to keep him. From the very start, I'd been running around trying to figure out some way to off-load him. But now that I had, it seemed impossible to let him go.

"Anyway," I said, "people will come after them, try to kill them. How can we be sure they'll be safe?"

"The mother came here from somewhere. She must have a home. The world is still big enough, Bryn. There may even be others."

But for how long? With satellites taking pictures of every square centimeter of the planet, putting them up in cyberspace for everyone to see. With all the people who knew about the critter now. Thanks to Anderson. Little twerp. Now they'd all be searching.

Sasha opened the door, tossed in a bag of groceries, jumped inside. I scooted back behind Dr. Jones. Her phone rang; she checked it. "Gandalf again. What's with him, I wonder?"

"Sasha, it's best you turn off your phone at this juncture," Dr. Jones said.

"Okay." She did. "Did you tell her?" she asked.

"Yes," I said, and at the same time, Dr. Jones said, "No."

No?

I looked at Sasha, puzzled.

"We have one more matter to attend to," Dr. Jones said. He dialed. Waited. Then said, "It's Mungo. Is she there?"

He held out his phone to me. All at once, I was afraid.

"Go on," Dr. Jones said. His voice was very, very gentle. Which scared me even more.

I took the phone gingerly, between my forefinger and my thumb. "Hello?" I asked.

"Bryn? Is it you, Bryn?"

And then I began to weep.

 38

MAGIC MAN

EUGENE, OREGON

Gandalf tried Sasha's number again. Got the recording. Left another message. Beeped off.

What was going on? Was she dissing him on purpose? Still miffed about the little incident with the egg?

And what was she doing up in Alaska, anyway?

If she didn't pick up soon, Quinn was going to be ticked. And that would be bad.

Gandalf went back to the client, still straddling the chair. It was a standard flash design—an eagle, on the biceps. Not exactly art, but it was a living. If this thing with Quinn worked out, he'd never do flash again. It would be his own designs or nothing. Freehand. Forget the stencil—just pick up the marker and vamp. Imagine in red, refine in blue. Clients standing in line, totally stoked to be getting a piece of his work. Gandalf: Magic Man!

"Sorry," Gandalf told the client. "Had to make a call."

The client shrugged. "No worries."

Gandalf set his phone faceup on the shelf beside him. He

washed his hands again, drew on new gloves, wiped the tat with green soap and a paper towel. He picked up the machine, hit the foot switch, buzzed the needle into skin.

He was still into the line work. With flash, line work was basically just tracing. Nothing to trip out the imagination. Once you got to the shading, though, all sorts of factors came into play—dimensionality, intensity, luminescence, blacklight reactives. It was hard for clients to micromanage shading. And even with some spam flash design, even with gray work, you could shade it into something totally spawn. You could make that tat pop right off the skin.

His phone rang again. He looked to see who it was.

Quinn.

Crap.

Gandalf had had to talk fast to convince Quinn that the dragon was for real. But now Quinn was a full-out fiend for it.

"Gotta get this," Gandalf said. "Be right back."

The client frowned at him. Not so happy this time.

Gandalf drew off his gloves, tossed them in the bin, grabbed his phone, and left the room. He picked up. "Yeah," he said.

"Did you raise your cousin yet?"

"No, man, she's not picking up."

Quinn groaned. "We had them. Your cuz and that girl from the blog. We were seriously *that close*. But they took off too fast. We missed a turn or something, and now we can't find them."

"What about the dragon?" Gandalf asked. "Did she still have it?"

"It was right there. Right before our phaging eyes. Keep calling. Get her on the line. Get her to tell you where she's going."

And how was he supposed to do that? Gandalf wondered. He didn't see how it was his fault if Sasha didn't want to talk to him or kept turning off her phone. She was in Alaska; he was in Eugene.

"Gandalf?" Quinn said. "Talk to me: are you with me here? 'Cause—" He broke off. "Wait a minute. Don't go away." He put Gandalf on hold.

Gandalf plucked nervously at his beard. Another thing he hated: Quinn didn't seem to respect his time, didn't seem to consider that he might have something else to do. Might, just for instance, have a client in the chair.

He sighed, flopped onto the couch. Something else was bothering him. Quinn wouldn't even know about Sasha if it weren't for him. Somehow, he'd told Quinn more than he'd meant to. It had just slipped out. He'd described what Sasha looked like, and Quinn had recognized her.

Gandalf wanted his share of the dragon money—no question there.

A dragon!

What would that be worth?

Gandalf: Magic Man!

On the other hand, he'd never thought it would lead to this. To Sasha all the way up there in Anchorage, with those poacher friends of Quinn's tracking her down.

Sasha could be annoying. But still. She was his cousin. He'd known her like forever.

Quinn was kind of creepy. The more Gandalf talked to him, the creepier he got. Reminded Gandalf, for some reason, of a fox.

And poachers, Gandalf knew, could be brutal. Sasha wasn't the type to back off, which could make things worse.

Maybe it was good they couldn't find her.

The phone beeped back. "We thought we saw them, but we were wrong," Quinn said. "We'll keep looking, but you better do your bit. We're counting on you to raise her."

 39

A FALL

ANCHORAGE, ALASKA

It was a long time before I could talk. Coherently, anyway. At first I could only choke out a few words into the phone.

To Mom.

Who was alive.

I was able to choke out a few words to Dad. Who was there with Mom.

And also alive.

Some choking-out on the other end of the line too. We all sort of choked there together for a while.

Dr. Jones started the car, took the ramp to the highway. Driving like a sane person this time. I leaned back and watched the lights from night traffic wash through the dark, rumbling space we were in—the snug hollow of Dr. Jones's car. They swept across Sasha, who sat there smiling. They flowed over the critter, draped across my lap.

Finally, I asked, "What happened?"

There had been a fall.

I could hang on to just parts of what they told me, one at

a time, taking turns with the single phone they had between them. Dad's voice, gravel-edged, and Mom's fluty-bright one. I couldn't take it all in. Not right then.

Mom had stepped off the edge of something, and there had been a fall.

This was after Dr. Jones had given Mom the critter's egg, and she'd put it in the storage locker. Then someone had taken her to the cave where the egg had been found. She'd taken some samples her first trip—including the petrified egg. But she'd wanted to go back alone.

And there had been a fall.

Two teenage boys, on a hunting trip, had found her unconscious. They'd somehow managed to get her to their borrowed truck. The boys had wanted to help Mom but had made a bad decision. They drove right past the hospital in Seward. A friend of theirs, or maybe a relative, had died suddenly in a hospital. They didn't trust hospitals. The boys had lifted Mom into their little motorboat and had ferried her all the way to the tiny island where they lived, to the healing woman who was there with Mom now.

"No one knew who I was," Mom said, and for a long time, she couldn't tell them. For a long time, even after she woke up, she couldn't remember anything.

The healing woman had found Dr. Jones's card in Mom's coat pocket, but they hadn't been able to reach him. No electricity on the island. No phone service. Bad storms. It had been a while before a skiff could safely make it to the port on Kodiak Island, where they could call. But at last, a messenger had made it to Kodiak. He had called Dr. Jones. Who had called Dad.

"'Onto something,'" I said. "Was that what it was?"

"Yes," Dad said. "I didn't realize it would be so long before I could call again. But your mother wasn't ready for travel, and after I found her here on the island, I couldn't leave her." Eventually, Dr. Jones had managed to get them a sat phone with a solar charger. The phone they were talking on now.

A truck whooshed past, making the car rock. Sasha reached to scratch the critter's eye ridges. He opened his eyes and watched her warily but seemed too weak to hiss.

"How is Piper?" I asked. "And Stella?"

Holding up, Dad told me. Hanging in.

"Tell me about you," Mom said. "Tell me about the dracling."

Dracling: baby dragon. So there was a word for him.

I didn't know where to start. I told them he was sick, told them that he flamed, told them that he floated in his sleep.

"Bryn, please start at the beginning," Dad said.

So I did. I ended with now, with the sick dracling breathing shallowly on my lap, with my fear that he would die, and soon.

Mom got on the line. "I think he needs his mother," she said.

Right. I knew all about that.

Dad got on the line. "Listen, Bryn. Wait for me. We're arranging things here. We can be back in Anchorage in a couple of days. I'll take the dracling up there."

"He might not last a couple of days. I think he's really sick."

Dr. Jones caught my eye in the rearview mirror. "Tell him the word is out," he said. "Tell him we don't have time."

I did.

"I'm not letting you go up there without me," Dad said.

It would be good to have Dad with us. So good. If only we could wait.

But if the critter died, or the poachers got him . . .

How could you live with that, if you could have prevented it?

The critter had bonded with me. No one else could do this. Only me.

I sighed and felt something deep within me unclench. In a weird way, it was freeing to know that. To accept it. To quit scrambling around looking for someone else to take over, and just know it would have to be me.

"Sasha will be with me," I said. "We're going, Dad. We'll be fine."

Muffled murmuring on the phone. Dad came back on the line. "We don't like this, Bryn. Not at all. But we're trusting you to do as Mungo says. Don't get within sight of that other dragon, do you hear me? Just set the dracling at the opening of the cave and leave. Promise me."

"Okay," I said.

When we finished, I handed the phone back to Dr. Jones.

"What now?" Sasha asked. "Where to?"

"To a little inn in Seward." Dr. Jones glanced back at me. "I was hoping you would agree. We've been heading in that direction all along."

40
PET SMUGGLERS

SEWARD, ALASKA

Millie Penobscot was wise to the ways of pet smugglers. You wouldn't believe the shenanigans they pulled. You had your Coat Stuffers, who zipped their parkas over their pets, supporting them with their arms, figuring that hotel desk clerks were maybe blind as well as stupid. You had your Pocket Poachers, who tried to cover up the telltale yaps and squeals of their little darlings by coughing, or laughing, or talking really loud.

Then there were your Midnight Skulkers, who waited until late, when the front desk was closed. You'd think, in this day and age, they'd just *assume* that the inn would have security cameras. But apparently it never crossed their minds.

Your Satchel Stashers could be more challenging to detect. In her twenty-three years at the front desk of the Seward Inn, Millie had dug pets out of purses, duffel bags, fishing tackle boxes, backpacks, briefcases, musical instrument cases, baby carriers, cardboard boxes, suitcases, and trunks. Satchel Stashers sometimes drugged their pets, so there was considerably less to go on.

Still, over the years, Millie had developed a nose for smuggled pets. Literally. Most people didn't actually educate their sense of smell, but Millie had worked at it. It was possible, she'd found, to train your nose to identify smells most people would never notice.

You'd be amazed.

It wasn't that the pet smugglers didn't know what they were doing. Though some of them feigned innocence when caught. *Really? No Pets? I had no idea!*

Unfortunately, there was a sign on the front desk, large as life: NO PETS. Could it be any clearer than that?

Excuse me? I don't think so!

But usually, all Millie had to do was look hard at the smugglers' faces. Guilt, in Millie's experience, was exceedingly hard to hide.

This man tonight—the black man in the wheelchair—had come in with two girls. He'd booked two rooms. Claimed to be a family friend. Honestly, you never knew. Millie used to try to find out if guests were who they said they were. Mr. and Mrs. "Smith."

Really? Don't insult me. Could you at least try to be a little bit plausible?

But management frowned on Millie's efforts to get at the truth. And if management didn't care who was staying here under false pretenses, why should she?

One of these girls was very, very strange. Millie had heard about this fad. What did they call themselves? Oh, yes. 'Tants. But she'd never actually seen one before. Webs between the fingers and hanging off an ear. Fake skin-cancer tattoos. Bleached-white hair. It hurt Millie's eyes to look at her.

What was this girl's mother thinking, to let her carry on like that?

But the other girl was the smuggler. A Coat Stuffer, and not an especially skillful one, at that. If people only knew how ridiculous they looked, it would stop them in their tracks.

It didn't seem like a dog in there, under the girl's parka. Could be a cat, maybe. More likely, to Millie's practiced eye, it was a ferret.

Millie had sniffed, tried to get a whiff of it.

Fish.

Dead fish.

That was strange.

Millie would have stopped the girl right then and there. Would have come out from behind the desk, stood directly in front of her, and asked what in the world she thought she was doing.

But there had been something familiar about this girl's face. Millie had seen it before, and recently. If only she could remember where.

Millie was good with faces. People had noticed this about her. She never forgot a face. Lately, though, more and more, she forgot where she'd seen the face.

Millie let the girl pass. Usually, she preferred to catch the smuggling right away, nip it in the bud. Before the fur and fleas and heaven knew what-all else had a chance to infest the rooms. But she could always do it later. Come up to the room with some extra mints or towels. Listen to them scramble when she knocked.

Just when the three guests stepped into the elevator, it came to her. Channel 2. Alaska's News Source. It had been on when she was checking in some other guests. Millie hadn't heard what the announcer was saying, but she'd seen the girl's picture. She remembered the face.

Now she logged onto the Internet, found the Channel 2 site. And there she was. The very one. Millie clicked on the link and read the article. Then clicked on the link to a blog. When she was done reading, she leaned back in her chair.

Well. That was a first.

It didn't surprise her as much as you'd have thought. Millie made a point of not being surprised by much. She'd actually heard about something like this before. There had been rumors around here for years. Earlier this spring she'd heard someone mention them, talking about eggs. It was a young man who'd stayed here before. This time he'd checked in with an older man and his two teenage sons.

The older man had hushed the younger one—but not before Millie had heard quite a bit. She remembered the older man's face, all right. An extremely handsome face. Graying at the temples. Strong, masculine jaw. Distinguished. Rugged yet refined. He was well-spoken and had been very polite to Millie. He had looked her in the eye—not looked right through her, the way most of them did. He had such a remarkably handsome face that Millie had made an exception and broken the rules herself: she'd searched for him online.

Apparently, he was divorced.

He had a bit of a limp, poor man. And with no wife to take care of him!

What was his name? Oh, yes. They called him Cap. Cap McVey.

She searched him now. Hmm. He ran a hunting guide service; the cell number was right there on the site. Millie would bet anything that he'd be interested to know who—or what—was here right now.

It was the least she could do.

She picked up the phone and dialed.

41 SUBWOOFER VIBE

SEWARD, ALASKA, TOWARD RESURRECTION PEAKS

All that night—while Dr. Jones drove us to Seward, while we checked into our rooms at the inn, while he gave us equipment and instructions and advice—during all of that time, nearly every single second, a private sound track went running through my head.

Mom's voice. From the phone call. Alive.

She'd sounded softer than she used to. Or at least, than I'd remembered. Not quite so quick and energetic. But she didn't seem fused out or anything. She seemed totally *Mom*.

Alive.

Dad too. Though I hadn't doubted so much with him. Hadn't let myself.

Sasha and I roomed together. Dr. Jones stayed down the hall, but he came in with us for a while. He pulled out a second sat phone and looked up Mom's island online. A tiny island, in the far northeast corner of the Kodiak Archipelago, population twenty-seven. He captured the coordinates, then handed the phone to me. "Here," he said. "You've got them. You know exactly where they are."

It was a comfort, somehow. To have them marked right there on the map.

Dr. Jones watched as I tried to feed the critter. I coaxed him to swallow half a basterful of ReliaVite, but after that he turned his head away, refused to eat. He dozed on the bed, not curled up like he used to, but all stretched out and limp. My heart hurt when I remembered how he'd been in the motel in Bellingham. Full of mischief. Chasing his tail. Burrowing under the spread.

Laughing.

Had I done *this* to him?

"Maybe he just needs his mother's milk," Sasha said.

Milk? I turned to her. "Dragons don't have milk."

"They might! I read it in those books, the ones with the floating dragons."

"But dragons lay eggs," I said. "Eggs: reptiles, amphibians, and birds. Milk: mammals. They don't go together in the same animal."

"Do you hear yourself? We're talking about an animal that breathes actual fire and floats in its sleep. Who's to say it can't have both eggs and milk?"

"In point of fact," Dr. Jones said, "the spiny anteater has eggs and milk, as does the duck-billed platypus. Monotremes: eggs and milk. So milk is at least a possibility."

Okay, so milk would be good, I thought. Mother's milk could maybe help.

Nobody mentioned the fact that some mother birds reject their babies if humans have touched them. No point in going there.

The next morning at the trailhead I unzipped the backpack Dr. Jones had given me. I lifted the critter inside. His eyes, dull and glazed-looking, didn't seem to actually see. I tried to ken him and felt only a faint, stuttery buzz. Panic pushed up inside me.

He could die. He really could.

I zipped him in and shouldered the pack while Dr. Jones repeated instructions for the new sat phone. "Keep it off until you need it," he said. "Do you know how to navigate the GPS? I've got the cave mouth marked under 'favorites,' and the trail-head as well. And I'm on speed dial, number one."

"Due respect, Mungo," Sasha said, "would you chill? We get it, already."

He frowned, then turned to me. "Remember," he said, "leave the dracling just inside the cave. His mother will find him there."

"Right," I said. That was the plan. That was the hope.

We set off.

A chilly breeze had swept away the clouds, and, even in the pale first light, the high crests of the mountains stood crisp against a dark gray sky. The trail started out easy, following the chalky waters of the Resurrection River.

Before long, we found the narrow track Dr. Jones had told us about, the one that followed the course of a little tributary stream. We hiked up through the sweet-smelling forest—snagged by trailing underbrush and whipped by branches, the sound of running water constant in our ears. The ground was muddy, with patches of snow in the shadows of trees and shrubs and boulders.

It was going to be a long, hard slog. Several hours, at least, Dr. Jones had said. Sometimes bushes swallowed up the track; my hands got all scratched and sticky, and prickers embedded themselves in my clothes. We crossed a long, grim stretch where the trees looked sick, their needles orange or gray; and then an even worse one, with just blackened earth and stumps.

The beetles and the fires. Like Josh had said.

About forty minutes in, the sat phone buzzed. I picked up. "There's been a complication," Dr. Jones said.

"What?"

"A car just drove past, quite slowly. I couldn't see inside; the glass was tinted. Possibly they're just sightseeing. Or perhaps, if they intend to hike, they'll follow the river trail. But just in case, you should be watching."

"Okay."

"And if there's any sign of hikers behind you, you're going to have to hide the dracling deeper in the cave."

"Okay."

"You'll have to hide as well. Wait for them to pass, then come back down."

"Okay."

A pause. "Bryn, are you all right?"

All right? All right as in, I'm schlepping my sick critter up this stupid mountain and the best-case scenario is that I'll lose him forever and never know for certain what's happened to him? All right as in, there are so many worst-case scenarios that I can't even allow myself to *think* about most of them?

"Yeah," I said. "We're fine."

So now we were constantly looking behind us.

Higher up, the trees fell away, the sick ones and the healthy ones. We scrambled up rocky slopes dotted with scrubby brush. Twice, we had to ford the stream, groping for footholds in water that was heart-attack cold, leaning against the current so it wouldn't knock us on our butts, grabbing onto roots and branches to haul ourselves out. Then it was alpine meadows. Clouds bulking on the horizon, pierced by shafts of light. Mountains behind mountains behind mountains. Eagles, moose, and bear.

But no one following.

So far.

After a while the track veered away from the stream and got steeper and narrower, sometimes winding along the sides of cliff faces, sometimes cutting up through the crevices between crags. My shins hurt, and I had a blister on one heel, and my lower back ached. And the critter was fading from my ken.

Just walk.

More snow now, sometimes deep on the trail. More piles of loose rocks and gravel. In places, the rock piles crusted over the track, so high and so unstable, we had to scramble up the steep hillsides and go around.

Dr. Jones hadn't warned us about this. Maybe there'd been a little earthquake or something. Maybe he didn't know.

Before long, we could see the whole huge Harding Icefield to the south, with that blue-blue naked ice in the folds of the ancient glacier, a blue that didn't obey the rules of other colors.

And farther south, I knew, was the Gulf of Alaska. Where, on a tiny island marked on my phone, Mom and Dad waited for a boat to take them to Kodiak, so they could catch a plane to Anchorage.

I would see them soon.

And the critter . . .

I touched him with my mind. This time, I felt his answering thrum, fluttery and weak.

What would become of him?

I blinked back tears, halfway relieved and hopeful, halfway terrified and grieving.

We were high up in the rocky crags when Sasha stopped. "Rat piss!" She pointed downhill.

Four men, hiking up the trail, maybe a quarter mile back.

Oh, no. My legs went soft and rubbery; my knees buckled.

"Come on." Sasha grabbed my arm; we stumbled around a bend to where the cliffs blocked us from sight.

"Do you think they saw us?" I asked.

"Don't know."

"Did you recognize them? Was it Josh and his dad?"

"Couldn't tell," she said. "But Mungo said to hide."

"Yeah, but where?"

"That cave's got to be around here somewhere."

To our left, the cliff rose straight up, dotted with scrub, boulders, patches of ice. To our right, the hillside dropped straight down.

"There," Sasha said. A little way up the path, I saw a tall, wide gap in the cliff face.

Was that it?

We edged up the track. I stopped at the opening. Peered inside.

Dark in there. And cold. I felt a thin, frigid breeze, exhaled from the depths of the mountain.

The cave.

I didn't like the idea of being stuck in there, between whoever was behind us and whatever was in front. I wished I could stay right here, where the sun sparkled off patches of snow and warmed the stones at my feet.

There's only me.

I stepped inside. Blinked until my eyes adjusted.

It was bigger than I'd expected. You could fit an entire hemlock tree in here. I'd hoped the cave would have a complicated shape—lots of offshoots and nooks and crannies. But no. Just the one megacavern, narrowing, farther back, into a tube like a freeway tunnel. No place to hide that I could see.

We had flashlights, but we couldn't use them. Not if we didn't want to be seen. I followed Sasha, deeper.

The cave smelled metallic and damp. The walls grew closer, squeezed in tight. After a while, it grew so dark, I couldn't see at all. I held tight to Sasha's jacket so I wouldn't lose her.

"Ouch!"

Sasha tripped, and I went down with her, crashed into a pile of rocks. We groped blindly over the top of it. My palms stung; they were slick with blood. Pretty sure one knee was bleeding too.

"We could stop and hide here," I said, when we reached the other side.

"We can't. They'll have flashlights. If they're looking for us, or for something in the cave, they'll have to come right by here."

I listened for the men behind us.

I listened for whatever was in front of us.

Nothing. Which was scarier, almost, than *something*.

Soon, though, the tunnel began to widen. I could actually see a little again, by the thin gray light that seeped in from somewhere ahead.

More heaps of rock and gravel. We threaded our way through. The cave walls drew in close again, but the light kept growing stronger. Then suddenly, Sasha stopped.

Just ahead, the cave seemed to end at a huge berm of rocky rubble. Above the rubble: a jagged strip of light.

And air. An actual breeze.

Noises, behind us. Voices.

"Crap," Sasha said. "That must be them."

Something in the breeze: a smell. Alien, and scorched. Something in my body: a deep, subwoofer vibe.

In the backpack, the critter stirred. Coming awake. Alert.

The vibration was making me tremble, was humming in my bones.

"Do you feel that?" I asked Sasha.

"What?" she asked. She turned to look at me. "What?"

A shiver passed over me, like ice water down my back.

I didn't wonder anymore if the mother dragon was here.

I knew.

42  NOT THE BORG

Josh paused on the trail. He hitched up the rifle he'd slung across his back. Feeling kind of shaky.

Everything had changed so fast. The whole unbelievable scene at Lake Hood, with all those people surging over the fence. And the moment when Bryn's "lizard" had flamed.

Actually *flamed*.

He was still having trouble wrapping his mind around that.

Then there was bumping into Quinn in the crowd, after Bryn and her friend had disappeared. And Quinn claiming to know Bryn's friend's cousin, saying he could find out where she'd gone. And later the random phone call from the clerk at the inn, and the late-night drive to Seward with Cap, Zack, and Quinn.

The worst thing, though—the very worst—had been right after Bryn got into the car, when Cap had started yelling at Josh, raging at the crowd, cursing whoever took Bryn away. Josh had never seen him so out of control. In that moment, Josh had understood without a doubt that Cap didn't intend to save the animal after all. He wanted to collect it. Preferably alive, but dead if necessary.

Josh wanted to kick himself. Stupid! How could he have been so stupid!

Now he took a swig of water and fell in beside Cap, behind Zack and Quinn. No point in arguing with Cap. Arguing would get him kicked off the team. Josh's only hope was to go with it, pretend to be on board. Swallow the sour bile that pushed up in his throat.

And try to find a way to help Bryn.

The morning sun had tipped over the mountains, but at the moment they walked in shadow, headed into the steep part of the climb. Cap had taped his knee, which seemed to be doing fine so far; it had held up even while they'd forded the stream. He was in high spirits, energized by the hunt—and by the fact that he'd guessed right about where Bryn's group was headed.

The car at the trailhead had confirmed it. The car the desk clerk had described.

"Want me to go on ahead?" Josh asked Cap now. "I could pinpoint their location and call it down."

"I'll go," Zack said. "Cap and me do this tag team thing when we're hunting. We—"

"Not yet," Cap said. "We're sticking together for now."

If Zack said "Cap and me" one more time, Josh was going to deck him. He really was. All last night it had been "Cap and me." *When Cap and me went fishing . . . When Cap and me were out snowmachining . . . Cap and me think . . .*

Cap had stopped him on that one. "We're not the Borg, son. You think for yourself."

Josh leaned into the trail, remembering. The Borg. Those

hive-mind guys from *Star Trek* reruns. But he couldn't help wondering if what Cap really meant was that Josh and Zack were supposed to think independently but come to the exact same conclusions as Cap did.

Like for instance: It's not okay to poach wildlife, but poaching fossils is a completely different matter. And: That animal isn't viable, so it doesn't count as wildlife. And: Your little friend will be fine.

Mills had been right. On the drive to Seward, Cap had used the exact same arguments she'd said he would.

Josh should have seen it coming. But maybe he'd been desperate not to see. Not to admit to himself how much Cap had changed.

Or maybe he'd just wanted to hear *Good work, son.*

Cap's knee was bound to start slowing him down soon; maybe then Josh could go on ahead. Help them hide or get away.

Cap wouldn't hurt Bryn. Josh was certain of that.

But as for that "pet" of hers . . .

Mills was probably right. More than likely, the little guy was doomed.

A while later, above the timberline, Zack stopped and pointed up the trail. "Look," he said.

Movement on a stony ledge above. Two girls. Running. One with weird white-and-purple hair. The other in an ugly orange coat. As Josh watched, they disappeared around a bend.

"They've seen us," Cap said. "Now we split up. Quinn and I will follow them. They'll probably go into the cave. Zack, you and Josh head off trail. Find the rear cave opening and wait there for us. Cut off their retreat."

Josh seized his chance. "Why don't you take Zack with you, too? I can cut off their retreat myself, then you guys can . . ."

Cap leveled his gaze on him. Glacial. "If I were you, son," he said, "I'd be very, very careful. Zack's going with you. It's your chance to redeem yourself. You missed the animal last night. Don't hurt the girl, but do what you have to do."

43 DRAGON'S MILK

RESURRECTION PEAKS, ALASKA

I wasn't thinking well. The deep vibration had come into my head and was crowding against my thoughts. The critter sensed it too; I could feel the tug of his longing.

I shrugged off the backpack. Unzipped it. Reached inside. The critter was warm and thrumming. He leaned into my hand and arm as I lifted him out. He snuggled against me, hooked his talons into the fabric of my coat. I scratched his eye ridges, then rubbed the length of his rubbery crest down to his jacket.

"Bryn," Sasha said. "What's the plan here?"

The jacket. All at once, it seemed wrong for him to wear that thing. Like we were trying to diminish him, make him seem cute. When he was so much more than *cute*. So much more . . . I groped for the word. That one from before, meaning powerful and awesome and miraculous and huge. The Mr. Franzen word.

Oh, yeah. *Sublime.*

Sublime in argyle microfleece? You don't send someone to meet his mother dressed like that. You just don't.

Another shout, from way back in the cave behind us.

I slipped off his harness, then ripped open the jacket Velcro and pulled out one of the critter's front legs.

"Uh, Bryn?" Sasha said. "Can I ask what you're doing? You're starting to creep me out."

I pulled out his other legs, dropped the jacket on the ground. Done.

"Whatever that was about," Sasha said.

A deep rumbling sounded from behind the rock heap. The rocks shivered.

"Did you hear that?" Sasha asked.

"Yeah."

She looked at me. Sort of squinted. "You know what it is, don't you?"

"Pretty sure."

"It's, ah, the mother ship, right?"

I nodded.

"You're not going over there, are you? Over the rock pile?"

I was, actually. I had to. They were pulling me, someway. Both of them. I knew I ought to be meltdown scared. And I was—almost. But at the same time, I felt weirdly calm. That vibration . . . it was familiar, down deep. Maybe something with the kenning . . .

"Just to the top of it," I said. "I think the critter'll go to her when he sees her. They're, like, connecting. I'll come right back down after that."

"You can feel them, can't you? Connecting."

I hesitated. Shrugged.

"Bryn. You remember that shell thing I told you? At school, the day we met?"

"Yeah?"

"Sometimes it's wrong. Sometimes you have to, you know, trust. Let people in. It's too lonely otherwise. Anyway, if you're scared I might, like, unfriend you for being different and strange . . . just think about it. How dumb is that?"

I smiled. Then searched her face, memorizing it. The face of a friend.

"We call it kenning," I said. "We do it in my family. With birds, like in those books. But you can't tell anyone, ever."

"Okay, then," she said. "Okay."

I started toward the berm.

"What happens when those guys catch up to us?" Sasha asked.

"You could hide. But I don't think they really care about us. I think they're after dragons."

"Right."

I headed up. The loose rocks shifted under my feet.

"Hey, Bryn."

I turned back.

"You want company?"

She looked scared. It was clearly a big deal for her to offer. And, yeah, company would have been nice. But I knew this was something for me to do—just me.

The critter was thrumming, thrumming loud. Still clinging to me with his sharp little talons.

"Be right back," I said.

It was hard to keep my balance on the rocks. They kept

moving, sliding. A big stone clattered, echoing, down the heap to the cave floor. A couple of steps farther up, some smaller rocks dislodged, and my feet slipped out from beneath me. I came down hard on one hand, breathing dust, trying to lever myself up so I wouldn't squish the critter.

The rumbling in my mind trembled deeper, and now everything seemed to shudder—the rocks, the air, the cave walls. I got to my feet, unsteady. Climbed higher.

I could go back down now. No one would blame me.

But, strangely, I wanted to *know*. Not just about whatever was in there. It had to do with me. With some mystery that had haunted me all my life.

I stretched up, peered over the top of the heap.

And there she was—staring at us from across another cavern.

I couldn't take her in all at once. I had an impression of great size, black and looming, bulking out to the edges of my peripheral vision. Green eyes, as long as my forearms. Older than anything; fierce and wise and sad. Framed in fold upon fold of black skin—wrinkles, pouches, bags.

She began to move, limping away from the back opening of the cavern, toward us. Making dry, scraping sounds, like rustlings of dead leaves blown by wind across a sidewalk.

Something shrunken about her. Something wizened. Things were broken. Broken scales, I saw—some with ragged, chipped edges and others full-out missing, leaving black, naked patches of skin. One of her wings jutted out at a weird angle, wouldn't fold in all the way.

She was totally alone.

Outsider.

Outside of *everything*.

"Go on now," I said to the critter. "That's your mom. Go." I tried to unhook his talons from my coat, but he clung to me, wouldn't let go.

She drew nearer. The air shimmered in the heat of her breath. I could feel it now, her hot breath on my face, lifting my hair, drawing out beads of sweat on my forehead. It smelled like campfires, like barbecue coals, like pots with metallic glazes firing in a kiln.

My whole body wanted to run, get away, slide back down the berm. I forced myself to stand still. The thrumming ramped up, began to vibrate the rocks beneath my feet. A stream of gravel trickled down. The critter lifted his head off my shoulder. Seemed to be listening.

And now, all at once, he changed his mind. He struggled to get loose, to unhook his claws from my coat. I helped, hands shaking. When finally the last toenail snicked free, he lunged toward the big dragon with more spirit than I'd seen in him in days. He tumbled down the far side of the berm, flapping his flimsy little wings and scrabbling uselessly with his claws. At the bottom, he collided with a *thump* against a great, black talon—knobby, warped, arthritic.

Right away, he started rooting around underneath the dragon. Looking for something.

For milk.

The dragon bent down her head to nuzzle him.

I couldn't see exactly where he found it, but I could tell that he had—by the eager way he pushed into his mother's leathery belly, by the warm, contented thrill I felt when I kenned him.

So she had milk, then.

Dragon's milk.

I could feel them talking to each other in some thrumming language I could only partway grasp. I sensed a deep, lonely pulse in her kenning. She had a name for the critter, but nothing I could put into words. It was like *Fire*, but more precise than that. Some particular kind of fire. Lively. Happy. A laughing kind of fire.

I kenned the critter good-bye, but he wasn't listening. My heart swelled in my chest.

Time to go.

I started to back away—then pain shot through my head: white-hot, explosive. I flinched, closed my eyes, pressed my palms against them. The flood of pain cooled, ebbed back to a dull, aching throb.

I looked up. Those old, old eyes held mine. I felt a second kenning, milder this time, and understood that she wanted something from me.

Help. With the wing. The gimpy one, the one that wouldn't fold.

I tried to hold in my thoughts, but I could feel my fear seeping out. She lifted the wing, still gazing at me, and the kenning softened to a plea.

I stood breathing, unmoving. Caught by her eyes and the deep, rhythmic throb of her ken.

Slowly, I edged myself over the crest of the berm. Slowly, I clambered down.

Into the heat of her breath.

It was like standing at the edge of a bonfire. Waves of hot air washed over me; sweat ran down my face.

The dragon shifted her weight, brought the sticking-out wing to hover just above me. It looked like a bat wing—but seismic huge—with leathery skin stretched between many narrow, bony ribs. I reached up, felt the skin. The wing twitched, as if in pain. I pulled my hand away.

Those eyes again. Looking at me.

I swallowed. Reached out again. Touched the wing.

It didn't move.

I wiped the sweat from my face, then began to explore the wing with my fingers. Gingerly, at first. The skin between the wing ribs felt thin as paper, crinkly. Parts of it were tattered and ripped; other parts seemed to have fused together, like an old umbrella I'd once left too long on the heater vent to dry. Some of the ribs had twisted, buckled. Others had snapped; they poked out from the wing in ragged splinters.

It smelled musty here, under the wing. Like ancient, leather-bound books, brittle with age, their pages yellow and torn. The dragon looked away, her breath heat suddenly less intense. But sweat still trickled into my eyes, and, under my coat, my shirt clung damp to my body.

I ran my fingertips along one of the crooked wing ribs until I came to the bend, then tugged gently on either side of it. I was afraid it would crack, or the skin would tear. But the rib bent back, mostly into shape, though a little flat where the bend had been.

I straightened more ribs, then went to work on the parts where layers of skin had fused. I peeled apart the gummed-up edges and carefully picked at the larger areas, like pulling price tags off plastic packaging.

My fingers went on working, bending the ribs back into shape, teasing apart the fused layers of skin, straightening, smoothing, mending. The dragon began to thrum again, quivering the rocks, spilling runnels of sand down from the berm, from the walls of the cave. The thrumming deepened, filled me up. It trembled in my mind, and I felt some boundary between us dissolving. The thrumming became a song, a mother's song, mournful and old.

I could feel that she was dying.

My fingers froze.

I forced them to move again, to pull apart the fused skin layers, to straighten the bent ribs.

Dying.

What would happen to the critter when she died?

"Bryn!"

I turned around. Sasha peered over the edge of the berm.

"Those people are coming. I can hear them." She eyed the dragon warily and crept over the top of the pile, as far from us as possible.

The dragon turned, leveled a hard gaze at Sasha. Then, seeming to sense something else, she lifted her head, sniffed at the air. She picked up the critter in one foot and limped away from us, toward the rear cave opening.

A clattering behind. I looked back. Two men climbed over the rocks.

A *crack* of gunfire. A loud *clank*. I threw myself to the ground, saw the dragon twitch. She swiveled her head around, spat out a gout of blue flame. A roaring sound. A shout. Smoke stung my eyes and filled my lungs. In the dissolving haze, I looked for Sasha. Found her.

Not hit.

Two men, still coming. More shots. A hail of *clank*s. I got up and sprinted toward the critter, caged loosely in the massive gnarled talons. Beside me now, the dragon swiveled her head and flamed at the men again.

Someone screamed.

A tiny ledge jutted out beyond the cave, into the sky.

Birds. The sky was black with them. Circling, crying.

The dragon tensed, seemed to gather herself together. Her wings unfolded, the gimpy one and the good one.

I looked down. There, on the steep slope below, was a guy with a rifle aimed at us.

And Josh.

A *crack*. I felt it hit her, high above me. Not with a *clank*, this time, but with the soft, wet *thud* of lead burrowing into flesh.

Shouting, from the cave behind us. The dragon rocked back, stumbled. She roared, belched out flame, then gathered herself up again. She leaned forward, into the air.

In the back of my mind, I heard the whine of the scaredy-cat kid, distant and thin. But it was drowned out by the shouting, by the roar, by the cries of the birds, by the commotion in my head.

She couldn't protect him if she were dead.

I lunged for one of the dragon's front legs, braced my feet on her toes. I held on.

With a sickening lurch, the ground dropped away beneath me.

44 UGLY ORANGE COAT

"Josh. Check it out."

Josh looked up where Zack was pointing: the back entrance of the cave.

Finally!

It hadn't been easy to find. They had the coordinates, sure. But that didn't mean they could get there, even when they'd been there before. Distances were fluky with GPS. GPS didn't tell you about things like brambles and boulders and cliffs. GPS hadn't warned them about that creek they'd had to ford or the rock slides they'd had to climb over. Racing against time. The whole while, Josh had kept wondering about Cap and Quinn. Where they were. If they'd found Bryn. The more time passed, the heavier the dread weighed in him.

Now Josh squinted at the cave mouth, up a steep, rocky slope from where they stood. He untied his bandanna, wiped the sweat off his face. Lots of birds in the sky here. Ravens, eagles, hawks.

"We should go in," Zack said.

"Yeah. Listen . . ." It felt different, being with Zack when Cap wasn't around. And maybe Zack was having as much trouble with this as he was. Now that Zack had seen Bryn and the dragon on the blog. "Look," Josh said, "this is going to be rough on her. On Bryn."

Zack gave him a sideways look. "What's the matter? You like her?"

Josh shrugged. She was a strange girl, no doubt about it. But she'd grown on him, somehow. He wished she were a little older, maybe a harder kind of girl. Tougher to bruise.

More than anything, he really didn't want to see her hurt.

"If we find them first, couldn't we just let them go?" he said. "The thing's alive, not a fossil. This doesn't feel right to me."

Zack shut down. It was a physical thing; Josh could see it in his eyes, in his face.

"Stop," Zack said. "Just shut up. I don't want to hear that kind of talk. Not now, not ever."

Halfway up the slope, Josh heard a deep, throbbing sound. Felt it too, up through his feet, like the far-off rumbling of a train. He stood still, listening. Uneasy.

The flat *crack* of a rifle shot startled him. Josh hit the dirt; Zack thumped down beside him, already unslinging his rifle.

A shout from the cave. A deep, roaring, crackling sound.

Fire?

More rifle shots above, from the cave. The birds were calling now. Hundreds of them.

Zack gasped, pointed up at the cave. Something moving there. Almost completely blocking the entrance.

Josh tried to make sense of what he was seeing.

Somehow, he had never quite grasped the scale of them, how enormous they would be, full-grown. It seemed more tree-size than animal-size, with those gnarled talons rooting it to the rocky ledge. Its body, shingled over with rows of broken scales, was all shades of faded black, except for a wash of emerald where sunlight seeped through the membranes of its crippled-looking wings and bled green across its belly. Wisps of smoke trailed out through its nostrils into the sky. Its great, long eyes gleamed green.

Intelligent.

Aware.

Zack raised his rifle.

"Don't!" Josh said. "Look."

And there she was, in that ugly orange coat, under one of the dragon's wings:

Bryn.

What was she *doing?*

Near her, clutched in the dragon's foot: her "lizard."

Zack fired.

Was he *crazy?*

The dragon lurched backward, roared, spit a sizzling blue flame ball in their direction. Josh ducked. Zack raised the rifle again. The dragon unfurled its wings—wider than the de Havilland's. It gathered itself to fly. But something was happening, some kind of scramble there near its feet.

"Hold your fire!" Josh said, but Zack was aiming again; he was going to shoot.

Josh flung himself at his brother. The rifle discharged just as the dragon tipped its body forward, off the lip of the cave. It plummeted toward them; its massive tail scraped against the hillside, sending rocks and gravel flying. Josh ducked, but looked up as it passed on his left, in time to see the smear of color go whizzing by.

Ugly orange coat.

The dragon dropped down past the cliffs, toward the valley: down and down and down.

45  FREE FALL

RESURRECTION PEAKS TO THE GULF OF ALASKA

We dropped. My stomach lurched up into my throat. I thought I heard another shot, but the wind was howling in my ears. I could sense the riffle and snap of wings above me, the calling of birds, the wild beating of my heart. Then a jolt: a harsh, rasping noise. Flying rocks and gravel. I looked back. It was the dragon's tail, scraping along the slope.

I hugged the dragon's leg tighter, locked my arms and legs around it. We bounced away from the slope, into the air beyond.

Free fall.

The valley rose up to meet us, zooming in. My eyes stung. My nose ran. Tears streamed sideways into my hair.

I closed my eyes. *Dropping down and down through black nothing.*

Something changed. G-forces, shifting. I opened my eyes to see the horizon tip sideways. We were still falling, but some-how not as fast. The horizon righted itself again and we were soaring—a shaky kind of soaring—out over the icefields, ice that went on forever, studded with the massive, craggy tips of hidden mountains. And nearer, in the air all around us: a rock-star entourage of screeching birds.

It was cold. Prickly, biting cold at first, then numbing. Tears and snot froze solid on my cheeks; my ears burned. I shivered all over. The rough knobs and ridges of the dragon's leg dug into me, and then I began to slip. My arms had morphed to rubber. I couldn't hang on . . .

The great talons beneath me stretched, spread wide. My arms gave out; I slid, with a spasm of panic, between the dragon's toes. The talons snapped shut beneath me; I sat cradled and caged within them.

They felt solid, the talons. For now. I turned my back to the wind and gingerly leaned against their bony curves. I pulled up my hood. The cold still penetrated, though not so painfully. I looked for the critter. The dragon's belly blocked him from view, but I kenned him, felt him. He seemed stronger. He seemed . . . happy.

Where were we going?

Would she take me someplace safe?

Or would she drop me, like a gull with a clam, and crack me against the ice?

I brushed her with a quick ken—wary of the white-hot pain from before. I couldn't sense what she intended, only a wall of bass vibration that throbbed all down through my body.

A great weariness came over me. I was too tired, or too numb, for terror. I tucked my head, huddled myself into a miserable ball, and just endured.

A while later, maybe a long time, I lifted my head. Something seemed different. I felt the huge wings teetering and quaking above me. No longer soaring but struggling. Currents of frigid air tossed us up and down and sideways. I peered through the ribs of my cage and saw seabirds among the mob of ravens and hawks. The wrinkled sea stretched out below. I could smell the brine; I could see foam blowing off the whitecaps; I could make out the shape of each separate wave.

Too low now. Weren't we? Too low to the water.

Tilting hard one way. Correcting. Tilting too far in the other direction.

The sea crept up beneath the tips of the talons. They scored it, drilled into it, sent out sheets of frigid water. The waves lunged up, swallowed my feet.

I screamed.

With a tortured, heaving groan, the dragon wrenched us up out of the sea and back into the air.

Rising now, slowly, up through the throng of birds. Dragon wings creaky, straining. My eyes streamed with tears, and the pounding of my heart made a roaring sound that filled my head.

I kenned the critter:

A little hum of worry. A whole rock concert of bliss.

It struck me that I was the only one in this entire crowd who couldn't fly or float on air.

A drop of something warm and wet hit my forehead, splashed onto my hands.

Bright red.

Blood?

I looked up, saw masses of it streaming across the dragon's chest.

Blood.

Dying. Sooner, rather than later.

A long coastline stretched out to my right, amber in the late-afternoon sun. I could see islands to my left and some others, faintly, farther on.

Islands.

Mom's island?

I dug through my pockets for the phone. Found the sets of coordinates. If the dragon would turn a little . . .

I kenned her again. Opening up to her. Trusting. Letting her feel my longing, see the map in my imagination.

Her thrumming presence filled me. My mind went huge and still and spacious. I tasted fire in my mouth; I leaned into the arms of the wind. I blinked, and saw back from forever—from when forests stretched clear to the sea, and the only hint of humans were the faint twists of smoke in the sky. I felt birds, great waves of them, inside me. They made a song of many threads, buoyed me up with a strange, wild joy.

The dragon banked south and, in a while, the sea rose up to meet us. The island rushed in, shore and trees and hills, then a patch of grassy weeds with a village in the distance.

The talons unclasped. I dropped a few feet, thumped down safe on solid ground beside the critter.

The dragon wheeled and came to hover above us, rowing her wings in the air among the circling birds.

Blood on her chest—an open, bleeding wound.

The critter strained up toward his mother. I gathered him in my arms. The dragon brought her head down to him, breathed her smoky breath on him. I could sense the kenning between them.

Then she turned the kenning on me.

It wasn't words, but I caught her meaning. She wanted something from me. A promise. A promise to tend, take care. To protect her baby from the world. A promise that took in the whole of his lifespan, hundreds of years.

I promised—and meant it—though I had no idea how I would keep it.

But I would. I *would*.

Something moving, off to the side, at the top of a small rise. A man running. A big, bearlike man. I would know that run anywhere. More people coming now, some running, some walking. I searched for her and, among the stragglers, found her.

Mom.

The dragon gathered herself up, spread her wings wide, and skimmed above the shoreline to the sea. The birds followed, trailing away in a long line behind. She was low to the water, listing to one side. I was afraid she would falter, drop out of the sky. But she pumped her wings, laboring hard, and slowly lifted her ancient, broken body over the waves. She veered to the south, coasted low out toward the horizon.

The critter was keening for his mother. The critter whose name meant some precise kind of fire, a kind of fire we have no word for. I held him tight and watched his mother shrink and fade in the distance.

How could he survive without her, without her milk? How could I find him enough food when he was grown? How could I keep him safe from the people who wanted to use him, to kill him? How could I keep others safe from him? How could I protect him all those years he'd live after I was gone?

I'd have to find a way.

I turned toward the people coming toward me. More slowly now. They were clasping hands, Mom and Dad. Dead serious: not smiling, not angry, not afraid.

I waited, holding the critter close. Stepping off the edge of the world I knew, and dropping free-fall into a whole new life.

EPILOGUE

Windsong and smolder-breath,
Plummeting gyre,
Bloodscent and thrumming joy:
Heartful of fire.
—from "Dragon Dreams," by Ghost Meridian

Hush little darlin', don't you cry.
Mama's gonna buy you a nice MoonPie.
And if that pie don't make you thrum,
Mama's gonna buy you some bubble gum.
And if the flavor do not last,
Mama's gonna buy you a Peanut Blast.
And if that nut bar fails to please,
Mama's gonna buy you some processed cheese.
—from "Dracling Lullabye," by Heart-Kludge

 # FLYING LESSONS

ONE YEAR LATER
SOMEWHERE ON THE OREGON COAST

At twilight, on an evening late in May, Dad backs the van into the old blimp hangar and throws open the rear van doors. I ken the critter to jump inside. Piper, with Luna on her shoulder, scoots onto the front seat with Mom and Dad; Stella and I ride in back with the critter. We drive through the little town where we live and out to a deserted spot by some cliffs on the coast. We wait there until dark.

The critter is excited. He knows something is about to happen. Something new. He bounces around, chasing his tail, crashing into the sides of the van, making it creak and shudder. Then he offers me his new rope toy and, at the last moment, snatches it away. Like a puppy, except he's seven feet long now and those pointy spines of his aren't so flexible and rubbery anymore. They're hardening up—sharp and seismic treacherous. He butts my stomach, buzzing me with hyper, twitchy kens, until at last I coax him to lie across my lap—head and shoulders off to my left, tail and back legs off to my right, and wings right there in front of me.

When I massage his wings, he settles down. He loves it when I massage his wings.

Stella hops off my shoulder and alights on his neck, greeting him with a whistle. I smooth the translucent skin between his wing ribs, rubbing Vaseline into the rough spots, kludging the little tears on the edges with stretchy surgical tape. I sing to him, trying to hide how scared I am, and he begins to thrum.

Now that he's calmer, it's safe for Piper and Luna to come back. Luna perches next to Stella; Mom passes around little chewy treats—dragon treats and human treats. We sit there, chewing, thinking our own thoughts.

The critter loves his chewy treats. We know what to feed him now, to keep him healthy. Mom did some research, and through trial and error we figured out what he should eat and what vitamin and mineral supplements he needs.

Piper leans into him now. They're kenning, I can tell. "Good, Kindle," she says. "Good boy."

Kindle. We had to call him something. Mom got the name from one of those old dragon novels she has, the ones with the floating and the kenning.

But for me, *Kindle* isn't big enough. It's not ancient and powerful and joyful. It's not, like, sublime. It's just a watered-down translation of the name I felt in the cave that day, eavesdropping on the critter and his mother. Failing that, for me, he's *the critter*.

Now he's really relaxed. Piper and I ken the birds back to our shoulders, and I slip the critter into his harness, the one with the GPS tracker. I ken him happy flying thoughts, the way I used to, before he knew how to fly on purpose. Before he knew that flying was a thing that—being a dragon—he probably ought to learn to do.

Dad turns to me now. "Ready?" he asks.

Ready? I'm scared out of my phaging mind. I want to say, *Do we have to do this now?* I want to say, *Let's just go home.*

"Yeah," I say.

Dad turns on the headlights. Mom hops out and opens the van's back doors. It's dark, a moonless night. Wind seethes in the fir trees, and I can smell the sea. A mist is rising; it swirls in the headlights like milk.

The critter bounds out, sniffs at the air. Piper and I climb out with our birds. I squat beside the critter at the edge of the cliff. When I synch with him, I like buzz all over. I can feel it; he wants to fly.

I tell him: *Go.*

He gathers himself together, spreads his wings, and drops straight off the cliff.

Free fall.

I hold my breath.

He reappears in the mist over the water, soaring.

It's magic to watch him fly. He wings straight out west, over the waves. Soon, he's swallowed up by darkness and fog. I stay with him, kenning. He's in bliss mode, surfing on full-out joy.

Does he know now that there's no cable attached to his harness?

Does he know now that he's free?

The kenning fades. Out of range.

"He'll be back," Mom says to me. "I know it."

Dad holds out the GPS monitor for us to watch.

Still heading west.

We wait.

It's only a tiny circle of us who know where we are, know what's happening here tonight. There's Mungo, who raises funds. Taj, doing good work with the microbes, so maybe someday we can clean up a small part of the mess we've made of the planet. Aunt Pen, who loves us and knows how to keep a secret. And Sasha. I let her in, and I refuse to close her out.

Way too many people found out about the critter last year. We've had to move, we've had to hide, we've had to go mostly off the grid. Mungo bribed Anderson to close his site. He promised him something, but he won't say what. The buzz is dying down, but the blogosphere's still humming with talk and pictures and even songs about our journey.

Sometimes I wonder about Josh. Sasha told me he saved us, up there on the mountain.

I wonder what he thinks about the critter now. If he's glad he escaped.

I wonder if he ever thinks about me.

I used to think we were outsiders, before, keeping the kenning secret. But I had no idea.

Sometimes I like to imagine those little kids with their birds. Stretching back in time, who knows how far.

They knew all about lonely.

They knew all about scared.

Still they nurtured it, the kenning. Cherished it. Kept it alive—something rare and seismic strange. Not for any practical reason. Just purely out of joy.

"Look," Dad says. "He's turning around."

He is. I can see it on the monitor. Piper claps her hands, jumps up and down. Mom squeezes my shoulder.

I breathe.

I *will* him to keep coming this way. Soon, I feel Stella stretch up, alert, on my shoulder. Then Luna lets out a little chirp. A second later, *I* can feel his ken. His high spirits have dissipated. He seems lost and a little scared.

Good. A little scared is good.

I ken to him, and he greets me with relief, lets me guide him back in our direction.

I know he won't be like this forever. He's wild—a *dragon*—and he won't always consent to being told what to do by the likes of me. Someday, he'll want to be free.

But where?

Is there a place for him—a place where he'll fit in, where he won't harm what's already there, where he'll be safe?

Are there others out there, others like him?

I have no idea. None of us do.

We're all pretty much in free fall around here. All learning how to fly. Making it up as we go along.

We stand together now, at the edge of the cliff. Staring out over the Pacific—into the fog, into the dark—waiting for the dragon to reappear.

ACKNOWLEDGMENTS

It was a lizard that got me going again with dragons. For years I'd toyed with the idea of a near-future sequel in the Dragon Chronicles series, but nothing really popped until my daughter, Kelly, a microbiologist/environmental engineer, told me about a rare lizard whose saliva has microbes that might be able to degrade environmental toxins into compounds that are completely safe. Lizard spit! That was it, for me: a way to return to my Chronicles and re-explore, through dragons, what we may lose when a genome disappears.

So many people helped me with this book! My agent, Emilie Jacobson, shored me up with eloquence, loyalty, and determination. Kelly Fletcher spent hours on the phone teaching me science and exploring alternatives; she vetted the manuscript twice for accuracy. My editor, Karen Wojtyla, was ever perceptive, wise, and kind.

Tricia Brown and Ryan Fisher shared their expertise on Alaska and showed me the location of the dragon's lair. Bill Lewis gave me insights into flying; Jack DeAngelis, into beetles; Jesse Olmsted, into tattoos; Joanne Mulcahy, into the Kodiak Archipelago. Mark Kullberg showed me how to dig out a petrified dragon egg and crack it open with a rock hammer. Many thanks as well to Anita Fore and Richard Crone.

I'm seismic grateful to all my smart and generous draft readers: Ellen Howard (double thanks!), Bruce Clemens, Hannah Fattor, Jerry Fletcher, Pamela Smith Hill, Cynthia Whitcomb, Laura Whitcomb, Emily Whitman, and Kate Whitman; and to the challenging and helpful comments of my critique group, including Margaret Bechard, Carmen Bernier-Grand, Nancy Coffelt, David Gifaldi, Becky Hickox, Eric Kimmel, Winifred Morris, and Dorothy Morrison.

Thank you, one and all!

THE DRAGON CHRONICLES

"I loved each one of Susan Fletcher's dragon books.
She makes the dragons as real as the people."—JANE YOLEN

"An intricate blend of humor, adventure, and sadness. . . .
A satisfying fantasy set in a world that could be yesterday—or tomorrow."
—*VOYA* on *Dragon's Milk*

"Readers empathize with the deftly crafted characters, always aware
of the struggle between good and evil, honor and dishonor. . . . Fletcher pens
some of the best yarns around."—*Booklist* on *Flight of the Dragon Kyn*

"An absorbing fantasy."—*Horn Book Magazine* on *Sign of the Dove*

———————

Don't miss the newest adventure,
Ancient, Strange, and Lovely

EBOOK EDITIONS ALSO AVAILABLE
From Atheneum Books for Young Readers][KIDS.SimonandSchuster.com

On the trail of a squeal and a squeak,

Isabelle Bean opens a door . . . falls through the opening . . . and tumbles into a very different world, right into the middle of a wild adventure. There are frightened children who are convinced she is an evil witch. Her grandma might actually *be* a witch. This new world is very strange and exciting, and Isabelle can't wait to take it all in. But just what is Isabelle doing there—and will she ever get home?

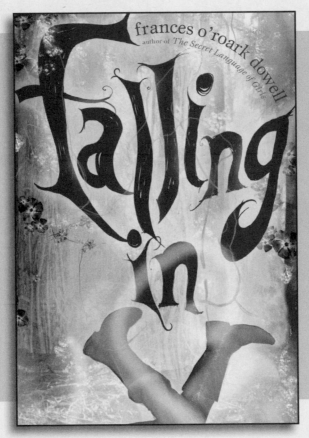

EBOOK EDITION ALSO AVAILABLE
From Atheneum Books for Young Readers
KIDS.SimonandSchuster.com

How far would you go
to make good on a promise?

EBOOK EDITION ALSO AVAILABLE
From Atheneum Books for Young Readers
KIDS.SimonandSchuster.com

If your destiny is to be a monster hunter,
it doesn't really matter if you
believe in them or not.

The first book in
THE HUNTER CHRONICLES
series is in stores fall 2011.

The Hunter Chronicles
Snare #1: Return to Exile

THE HUNTER CHRONICLES

Return
to Exile

E. J. PATTEN

EBOOK EDITION ALSO AVAILABLE

From SIMON & SCHUSTER BOOKS FOR YOUNG READERS
KIDS.SimonandSchuster.com

MIDDLE-GRADE ADVENTURES FROM
THREE-TIME NEWBERY HONOR–WINNING AUTHOR

Zilpha Keatley Snyder

The Egypt Game

The Headless Cupid

The Witches of Worm

The Bronze Pen

The Treasures of Weatherby

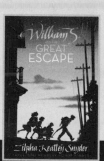

William S. and the Great Escape

William's Midsummer Dreams

From ATHENEUM BOOKS FOR YOUNG READERS
Published by SIMON & SCHUSTER